PRAISE FOR THE
BESTSELLING SCUMBLE

"Bounces along with gently wry humor and jaunty twists and turns. The quintessential amateur sleuth: bright, curious, and more than a little nervy."
—Earlene Fowler, Agatha Award–winning and national bestselling author

"Swanson serves up another romance-sweetened tale of murder in the endearingly zany town of Scumble River." —*Chicago Tribune*

"Smartly spins on a solid plot and likable characters."
—*South Florida Sun-Sentinel*

"An endearing and realistic character...[A] fast-paced, enjoyable read." —*The Herald (MA) News*

"Another great book by this master of the small-town mystery." —*Crimespree Magazine*

"Well-crafted... From normal to nutty, the folks of Scumble River will tickle the fancy of cozy fans."
—*Publishers Weekly*

"Humor continues to be the strongest aspect of this long-running series, although it runs neck and neck with the smoldering romantic relationship between Skye and Wally." —*Kings River Life Magazine*

"Swanson shows once again why she's one of my favorite cozy mystery authors... Another phenomenal hit."
—*Fresh Fiction*

"A well-plotted, intriguing mystery... Each book in the series is like a little gem." —*MyShelf.com*

Murder of a Cranky Catnapper

A Scumble River Mystery

Denise Swanson

BERKLEY PRIME CRIME
New York

BERKLEY PRIME CRIME
Published by Berkley
An imprint of Penguin Random House LLC
375 Hudson Street, New York, New York 10014

Copyright © 2016 by Denise Swanson Stybr
Excerpt from *Murder of a Small-Town Honey* © copyright 2000
by Denise Swanson Stybr
Penguin Random House supports copyright. Copyright fuels creativity, encourages
diverse voices, promotes free speech, and creates a vibrant culture. Thank you for buying
an authorized edition of this book and for complying with copyright laws by not
reproducing, scanning, or distributing any part of it in any form without permission.
You are supporting writers and allowing Penguin Random House to continue to
publish books for every reader.

BERKLEY is a registered trademark and BERKLEY PRIME CRIME and the B colophon
are trademarks of Penguin Random House LLC.

ISBN: 9780451472120

First Edition: September 2016

Printed in the United States of America
1   3   5   7   9   10   8   6   4   2

Cover art by Ben Perini
Cover design by Katie Anderson

To my sweet black cat,
Boomerang,
who strayed into my life fifteen years ago and
made himself at home.
Thanks for being my mews.

CHAPTER 1

The cat has too much spirit to have no heart.
—ERNEST MENAULT

May 2007

As school psychologist Skye Denison-Boyd hiked down the main hallway of Scumble River Elementary School, she juggled her purse, a bulging tote bag of files, an old shoe box containing reinforcement rewards, and a cup of heavily sweetened and creamed decaf coffee. Passing the front office, she glanced through the window of the closed door. There was still no sign of her visitor.

Not that she really expected to see him. Although he wasn't due for another fifteen minutes, she'd hoped he'd arrive early enough for her to greet him and explain a few things.

Skye hesitated, wanting to wait for her guest, but then walked on. The boys in her fourth grade counseling group would show up any second, and she couldn't risk not being in the room when they got there. Rule number one in any educational setting was never leave children unsupervised.

Hmm! She should start writing that type of information down for next year's school psych intern. Rule number two had to do with the secretary and custodian. The first day of Skye's own internship, her supervisor had sat her down and explained that those two individuals had the power to make her job a heck of a lot easier or nearly impossible. He had advised her to find out their preferences, then provide them with a steady stream of treats.

And although her internship had been almost a decade ago, Skye had always remembered his words of wisdom. She'd quickly discovered that as an itinerant school staff member, more often than not, she needed the custodian or secretary's assistance on a daily basis. And keeping on their good side was a matter of self-preservation.

Which was why Skye had made a mental note when she'd overheard Fern Otte, the grade school secretary, tell someone that she loved Chicago's famous Garrett popcorn. Fern had confided that the caramel and cheese combination was her one gustatory weakness.

So today, when Skye had stopped by to ask Fern a special favor, she'd dropped off a canister of the costly snack. It was a small price to pay for having her visitor escorted through the warren of corridors instead of left to wander through the labyrinth alone.

Speaking of which, Skye paused at the T-intersection leading to the building's oldest wing. This was where the real maze began. She sighed and turned the corner.

Instantly, the smell of mildew hit her full force and she sneezed, then sneezed again. *Great!* Now her eyes would water and all the effort she'd spent putting on mascara, shadow, and liner would be wasted.

Skye didn't generally bother with much makeup, usually settling for a quick dusting of bronzer—and if it had been a late night, a dab of concealer. However, this morning when it had taken her three tries to find a pair of slacks that zipped, and none of last spring's blouses would button over her baby bump, she'd decided that in order to face the day, she needed everything in her cosmetic case.

Intellectually, she knew that her clothes were tight because she was pregnant, and that she should buy some maternity outfits. But emotionally she just felt fat, so she'd needed the ego boost that only perfectly styled hair and full makeup could provide.

In her teens, Skye had struggled to fit into single-digit sizes. She'd starved herself, eating less than eight hundred calories a day, trying to look like the women she saw in the movies and in the magazines. Then when she finally exited the dieting roller coaster, it had taken her a long time to come to terms with being larger than was considered attractive. Now that those curves were expanding again, she was having trouble accepting her new silhouette.

Determined to stop fretting about her blossoming figure, she reminded herself that while she couldn't stop the bird of sorrow from flying over her head, she could prevent him from building a nest.

Smiling at her silly thoughts, she descended the final stairs into the original school building. Immediately, the humidity enveloped her like a spiderweb. Beads of sweat formed on her upper lip and she could feel her hair start to frizz. Any hope of saving her smooth curls or makeup melted away with her foundation. It was the first Monday in May, and Illinois was experiencing a preview of the coming summer.

Skye grimaced. She was not fond of heat, and the soaring temperatures would be even less fun while carrying around an extra twenty-five or thirty pounds. It was a good thing that school would be over in less than a month and she could ride out the most blistering part of June, July, and August planted in front of her home air conditioner.

As Skye continued down the corridor, she noted that evidence of the wing's previous occupants was still present. The space had been rented out to a church group, and although the religious objects had been removed, their outlines in the faded paint remained.

Anywhere but Scumble River, Illinois, a town with a population hovering around three thousand, an image of a cross in a school would cause a parent protest. Here, no one seemed to notice.

The church had found a better facility and moved, but four years later, the school board was still trying to figure out whether to bring the wing up to code for classroom use or to tear it down.

It wasn't the best location for a counseling session. Not only was it stifling in the warmer weather and freezing in the winter, but it was dreary and cut off from the rest of the school. However, Caroline Greer, the grade school principal, had assured Skye that other than the psych office, it was the only available area in the building for her to meet with her group.

With those being the only options, Skye wisely chose dilapidated over jam-packed. There was no way she could squeeze five lively nine- and ten-year-old boys into her refrigerator-carton-size office, and the kids wouldn't notice the annex's shabby decor.

Working in public education, conditions were rarely ideal. As always, she'd have to make do with what was available. Another pearl of wisdom Skye needed to write down for her future intern, because whining about the spaces they were assigned to use would only make things worse.

On the bright side, this wing's isolation was what had helped Skye convince Caroline to allow her to try a new type of therapy with her counseling group. Initially, the principal had been reluctant to grant permission for anything so unconventional, but Skye had provided her with data that persuaded Caroline to authorize six pilot sessions.

Skye was determined to give the innovative therapy every chance for success. Which was why today, instead of using her normal spot, the pastor's old office, she had moved the group to one of the larger rooms. She'd spent most of last Friday afternoon making sure the walls were bare and the blinds on the windows worked. Then, with the exception of seven chairs placed in a semicircle, she had removed all the other furniture and vacuumed the ancient gray carpeting.

A lesson Skye had learned early on was that when attempting a group counseling session, it was best to have an area free of visual or auditory distractions. And this afternoon's meeting would be stimulating enough without any extra diversions.

Skye was relieved to see she had made it to the room before the boys, and she quickly settled into the center chair. Taking a sip of her coffee, she waited for her group to arrive. After a couple of swallows, she became aware of the silence. Usually schools were full of noise, but in this unused annex, she was totally alone.

Before she could even enjoy the quiet, the boys burst into the room with the teacher's aide hurrying after them. The aide had a harried expression on her reddened face and was breathing in short gasps. Evidently the kids had had her running most of the way.

She wheezed hello, then waved, turned on her heels, and fled. While her charges were with Skye, the woman was able to take a much-needed and well-deserved break, and she clearly wasn't wasting a minute of that precious time on small talk.

Skye yelled her thanks at the aide's disappearing back, then studied the five boys exploring the unfamiliar room. Three of them had Individualized Education Plans that specified the counseling goals they were working to achieve. The other two were in the group mostly as role models. Their parents had noticed some mild attention issues and asked that they be included.

The boys with IEPs were among the most unusual with whom Skye had ever worked. Although Clifford

Jirousek had tested out of the stratosphere on every intelligence test he'd ever been given, he was so obsessed with books that he had isolated himself from all social interactions.

He carried a book with him at all times and his mother reported that he hyperventilated if she removed a single volume from his bedroom. Normally, liking to read would be considered a positive trait in a student, but Clifford refused to do anything else. Left on his own, he wouldn't listen to instruction, participate in class, or interact with his peers.

Each session, Skye worked on including Clifford in the rest of the boys' play, but today, as always, the moment he came into the room, Clifford separated himself from the others. He sat on the chair farthest from Skye, and opened an enormous all-in-one edition of *The Lord of the Rings.*

Christopher Hardy, another member of the group, walked over to him and asked, "What ya doing?" Clifford ignored him and the boy persisted. "It's really thick. I bet you're not going to read the whole thing."

Peering over the book, Clifford sneered, "I'm not saying that you're stupid." He glanced at Skye. "Because Mrs. Boyd told me that I can't call kids that. But you sure have bad luck when it comes to thinking."

Christopher's hands fisted and he snapped, "Well, my imaginary friend thinks you have some serious problems." He opened his mouth to continue, but when he looked over at Skye, she made a motion for him to walk away.

Once he complied, she got up and gave him a token. Then she went over to Clifford, and tapped the front of his novel. Glaring at her, he closed the cover and clutched it to his chest. She held out her hand, and after a long moment, he placed the book in her palm. She deposited it in her tote bag and gave Clifford a token. When he earned fifty, he could cash them in for lunch with the librarian.

Skye then went to check on the others. While she had been busy with Clifford, Alvin Hinich, the second boy with an IEP, had gotten down on all fours and was crawling around the room's perimeter. He sniffed the corners and made excited yipping noises. When he raised his leg, Skye hurried over to him and touched his nose with her finger, then pointed to the circle of chairs. He growled, but scuttled over and took a seat.

Alvin insisted he was a dog by the name of Spot, and when Skye had begun working with him, he'd refused to speak. After a year of counseling, he would now talk, but he still preferred barking to communicate, and he had to be constantly reminded to use his words.

When Skye continued to stare at him, Alvin mumbled, "Hello, Mrs. Boyd."

"Hello, Alvin." Skye reached into her pocket and gave him a sticker for his behavior chart. When he filled all the squares, he earned playtime with the PE teacher. Skye frowned. She needed to check to make sure Mrs. Lake wasn't allowing Alvin to turn their activity into a game of fetch or retrieving Frisbees with his mouth.

The third boy with an IEP in place was Duncan Canetti—or as the kids called him, Mr. Clean. Duncan liked everything to be perfectly orderly and hygienic. When Skye had first met him, his head had been shaved. His mother had explained it was because her son couldn't stand to have even a hair out of place. He'd also insisted on wearing disposable gloves to school. Skye still couldn't believe Mrs. Canetti had gone along with either of those notions.

After some intense negotiation, Skye had convinced Duncan to forgo his bald-headed look for an extremely short buzz cut. She had also asked the teachers and other staff to intervene if they heard any of the children using his nickname. She was pleased with Duncan's progress. He no longer sprayed a can of Lysol in front of him as he walked into a room and he had stopped wearing the plastic gloves out on the playground. Now she had to work on getting the hand sanitizer away from him.

During the first year of counseling, Clifford, Alvin, and Duncan hadn't been able to make any friends outside of the group. This had concerned their parents, as well as the school personnel. And while each had made some headway on their more unusual issues, they still had difficulty joining the rest of the children's play during recess.

Last spring, at their IEP conferences, after much discussion about their lack of social skills, Skye had suggested including a few regular education students in their group. Which was how Gavin Girot and Christopher Hardy became members. Both of the boys' parents had given their permission, with the understanding that Skye would concentrate on improving Gavin's and Christopher's attention span and on-task behavior.

Skye looked over the assemblage and said, "Okay, boys. Everyone take a seat so we can get started. I have a surprise for you."

Gavin immediately obeyed and Skye gave him a coupon for five extra minutes of art time, but Christopher seemed mesmerized by the black cord hanging from the projector screen. He flicked it, watching it swing back and forth. Duncan stood frozen by a shelf, staring at a dust bunny the size of a Chihuahua. He whimpered and reached into his pocket for his Purell.

Skye exhaled noisily. Obviously, she still had her work cut out for her.

Walking over to Duncan, she closed the lid on the sanitizer bottle and pointed to an empty chair. Then in a mild tone she said to Christopher, "Please take your seat so we can be ready for our surprise."

Once the boys were all sitting, Skye joined them and said, "Today we're going to have a visitor. His name is Dr. Quillen and he's—"

"No doctors!" Duncan screamed, jumping to his feet and backing against a wall. "They touch you and poke you with dirty needles."

"Please return to your seat, Duncan," Skye said. "Dr. Quillen isn't a people doctor. He's a veterinarian. He's going to help us—"

"No!" Alvin dropped to his knees, then tilted his head toward the ceiling and howled.

"Alvin, use your words." Skye checked her watch. The vet would be here any second. She had to get control of the session. With one boy cowering in a corner and the other baying at the moon, she wasn't sure which to address first.

As she considered her options, the door swung open and Dr. Linc Quillen strode inside. He had a beautiful Maine coon cat in a Pet Taxi and a Siberian husky on a leash.

"Wolf! It's a wolf!" Clifford screamed. "He's going to eat us."

"It's only a dog." Skye jumped to her feet, trying to calm the boys and herd them back into their chairs. "He's a nice doggy. Really."

But it was too late for reassurances. Group hysteria took over and the boys scattered. Alvin, Duncan, Gavin, and Christopher huddled against the far wall, but Clifford skirted around Dr. Quillen and the animals and ran out the door.

"Sorry!" Skye yelled, dashing after the escapee, adding, "Keep an eye on the boys. I'll be right back."

Skye sprinted down the hallway, then realized the

others might try to follow her. Just as she twisted her neck to look, she heard footsteps in front of her. Before she could swing her head toward the sound, she slammed into what felt like a brick wall. Flailing her arms for balance, she lost her footing. But before she could fall, hands gripped her arms and steadied her.

Skye's gaze shot to her rescuer's face. *Shit!* The man holding her upright was Palmer Lynch, the school board member who was running against her godfather, Charlie Patukas, for the presidency. She was so screwed.

CHAPTER 2

Time spent with a cat is never wasted.
—COLETTE

Half an hour later, Skye sat in the principal's office trying not to cringe as Palmer Lynch paced back and forth yelling at her. He was an attractive man in his late forties, with blond hair and gray-blue eyes. However, despite his handsome face, at over six feet tall and with a muscular build, he was a bit intimidating.

"What in God's green earth were you doing with animals in a school?" Palmer demanded.

"Pet therapy." Skye kept her voice unruffled, but she was clenching her hands so tightly her fingernails were digging into her palms.

"You mean snake oil," Palmer jeered, then whirled around and pointed toward Caroline Greer. "How could you approve of exposing our precious children to those vicious creatures?"

Skye looked at the grade school principal, who sat calmly behind her desk. Caroline reminded her of a partridge—short, round, and with a considerable mono-bosom. She had poufy white hair, black-framed glasses, and a beaky red nose. But that was where the resemblance ended. Caroline was anything but fussy. Although nurturing toward the students in her charge, the woman had a no-nonsense attitude toward adults, a trait that Skye admired.

When Caroline remained silent, Palmer continued, "As the principal, I would expect better judgment of you. Do you have any kind of excuse?"

"Many of the students in the group Skye is working with have proven exceptionally difficult to help and the parents requested additional services," Caroline answered, seeming unaffected by the board member's outrage.

"Right," Palmer sneered. "If your kid can't hack it, blame someone else and seek counseling."

"In attempting to support them," Caroline continued as if Palmer hadn't spoken, "Skye suggested animal-assisted therapy and provided me with studies that show this therapy has been successfully utilized to improve social, emotional, and cognitive functioning." The principal raised an eyebrow. "And I hardly call a dog and cat wild beasts."

"Obviously some of the children felt differently since one boy was running down the hall as if the hounds of hell were on his tail." Palmer's face was the color of a freshly boiled lobster.

"I'm afraid the introduction of the new treatment didn't go as smoothly as I would have liked," Skye admitted. "But once Dr. Quillen had a chance to properly introduce the boys to his therapy animals, they enjoyed the sessions. And after they've had a few more meetings, I'm sure they will gain some new coping strategies."

"There will be no future sessions!" Palmer hit his hand on Caroline's desk so hard, the pencil holder fell over, spilling the contents across the blotter. "The liability for animals in the building alone—"

"Skye obtained written permission from all the children's parents and I've cleared things with the school attorney, as well as the insurance carrier. Therapy animals are no different from having a Seeing Eye Dog in the classroom. We are totally covered." Caroline rose from her seat, marched to the door, and opened it. "Now, if you'll excuse me, I have another appointment."

"What?" Palmer stuttered. "We aren't through discussing this."

"I've noted your concerns." Caroline stood firm. "And if the board votes with you on this matter, I will, of course, follow their instructions. But as an individual member, you do not have the authority to stipulate the day-to-day running of this school."

"You girls haven't heard the last of this. You'd better obey me," Palmer threatened as he snatched his cell phone from his jacket pocket. When Caroline didn't respond, he snarled, "Are you deaf?"

"I am not hard of hearing, Mr. Lynch," Caroline said coolly. "But I have heard enough."

"Are you sassing me?" Palmer's eyes bulged.

"No." Caroline's tone was icy. "I'm saying that you do not have the right to come into my school and play God."

"The position was vacant," Palmer snapped.

"It's time for you to leave." Caroline gestured to the open door.

"Little lady, you're making a big mistake." Palmer's eyes narrowed and he fumbled with his phone. "You'll see just how much power I already have." As he dialed, he skewered Skye with a cold stare. "And your precious Uncle Charlie won't be able to help you."

Once Palmer was out of sight, Caroline folded her arms and said, "That man reminds me of a cloud."

"Huh?"

"When he finally goes away, it's a beautiful day."

"Right." Skye chuckled.

She was stunned by Caroline's reaction to Palmer. Usually, the principal would have been much more deferential toward a board member. What had gotten into her?

Caroline leaned against the wall. "Lynch had better not be elected board president or I'm retiring."

"Do you think Charlie has anything to worry about?" Skye asked.

"It's hard to say." Caroline frowned. "There were several new members from the last election and no one knows which way they're leaning." She paused. "And unfortunately, nowadays good judgment is so rare, it could almost be thought of as a superpower."

"Too true," Skye agreed. "Maybe we should have Captain Common Sense T-shirts printed up."

"But who would we give them to?"

"Point taken." Skye smiled, then said, "I think I'll call Uncle Charlie and fill him in about today." Skye glanced at the principal, who nodded her agreement. "I'll let you know what he has to say about Palmer's chances."

"You do that." Caroline nodded. "You said that the rest of the pet therapy session went well once the boys settled down and Dr. Quillen got started."

"Yes." Skye smiled. "The animals were amazingly obedient and the kids really responded positively to the exercises."

"Thank goodness for small favors." Caroline stepped back inside her office and said, "Stop by Wednesday after the next pet therapy group and give me an update."

"Will do." Skye waved and hurried away.

She was glad she'd decided to have twice weekly sessions with the animals. With so little time left in the school year, any fewer meetings wouldn't have been productive.

When Skye walked past the school secretary, Fern looked up from her computer screen and handed Skye a phone message on a pink slip of paper. Before she could read it, the woman grabbed her arm.

Clutching Skye's wrist, Fern said, "I'm so sorry I couldn't let you know that Mr. Lynch was heading your way. I'd just got back from showing Dr. Quillen where your group was meeting when that awful man barged into the office. He was quite rude when I told him that Mrs. Greer was on the phone. He said he didn't have time to wait for a babysitter, demanded the keys for the old wing, and took off on his own."

"That's okay." Skye pried the secretary's hand from the death grip the woman had on her arm. "I doubt a warning would have helped."

"Mr. Lynch wasn't on my schedule." Fern blinked rapidly, pecking at her fingernails with her teeth.

"How inconsiderate of him, Twe—" Skye cut herself off just in time.

Fern was a small-boned woman who dressed in shades of brown and tan. When she was upset, she flapped her arms as if she was about to take flight. That, along with her tendency to sound as if she were cheeping when she spoke, had earned her the nickname *Tweets*. Not that anyone in the school was unkind enough to call the fragile woman that to her face, but sometimes it was hard not to slip up.

Skye smiled at Fern, then quickly said, "I'm sure you did your best to accommodate him."

As the secretary continued to apologize, Skye glanced at the while-you-were-out memo. It was from Homer Knapik, the high school principal. He was rescheduling the next day's Pupil Personnel Services meeting from the afternoon to the morning.

PPS meetings were held in each school to assist students exhibiting academic, social, or physical needs. Skye, along with the principal, special education teacher, speech therapist, and nurse met to discuss children experiencing difficulties in those areas.

Skye grimaced. Homer's note meant she'd have to

contact Neva Llewellyn, the junior high principal, and tell her she needed to flip around her hours there. Skye didn't have to cancel any appointments at the junior high, but the principal would still be unhappy.

Neva felt that Homer monopolized Skye's time, and unfortunately, her complaints to the superintendent had been ignored. Scumble River was still very much a typical male-controlled small town. Although the vast majority of teachers were women, the head honcho was a man, who treated his female employees more like chattel than valued professionals.

Skye checked her watch. She'd better get to her office and call Neva right now while she had a chance. The elementary school's day would be ending in half an hour and she needed to talk to a couple of faculty members after the kids were dismissed, but before the staff was officially allowed to leave. Although a lot of the teachers remained late, Skye tried not to be the reason they had to put in overtime. Especially since there was no additional pay for any of the extra hours the faculty worked.

Twenty minutes later, after apologizing and repeatedly promising that the junior high would get its fair share of her services, Skye finally hung up the telephone and gazed unhappily around the room. Caroline might be the nicest of the three principals, but the space she provided for the psych office was the worst. It had started out as a storage room for the dairy refrigerator and other cafeteria supplies, and it still smelled like spoiled milk.

For some reason, no matter what type of tape, putty, or hangers Skye attempted to use to fasten posters to the drab gray walls, they refused to stay up. And with no windows, the only illumination came from the fluorescent fixture attached to the ceiling and the sickly light cast a nauseating chartreuse glow over everything.

When Skye worked with kids in there, it was disconcerting that their faces looked greener than Kermit the Frog.

Thank goodness her morning sickness had finally gone away or the revolting color would be too much for Skye's unsettled stomach to handle. Unfortunately, her increasing girth was another matter. It made navigating the small office even trickier than before.

The pair of visitor chairs occupying two thirds of the floor left little room to maneuver. There was no room for a file cabinet, and the desk had only one locking drawer, forcing Skye to carry most of the confidential folders with her. There were just too many people who had a key to the office to make it secure enough to leave restricted information unsecured.

Skye spent as little time as possible in the depressing spot, and when she heard the dismissal bell ring, she was more than ready to get out of there. To avoid having to return to it before heading home, she'd already loaded her tote with files and tucked her calendar into the side pocket of the bag. Now she settled her purse strap over her shoulder, switched off the light, and locked the door behind her.

The first person on her to-see list was Virginia Elders. Virginia was Clifford, Alvin, and Duncan's fourth grade teacher and Skye wanted to touch base with her about that afternoon's counseling session. Since Gavin and Christopher hadn't experienced the same degree of problems with the introduction of the pet therapy, she'd talk to their teacher afterward, or if he'd already left, just send him an e-mail to make sure they hadn't demonstrated any ill effects from the session.

When Skye entered the classroom, Virginia was grading papers at her desk. She was an attractive divorcée in her mid-forties. She'd been born and raised in Scumble River, taught at the elementary school ever since she graduated from college, and in ten years or so she would probably retire from that same position.

After losing her nineteen-year-old son to a drug overdose, Virginia had sought out Skye's advice. Because of this, Skye felt more comfortable with her than some of the other teachers she didn't know as well.

"Hi, Virginia," Skye said as she crossed the room. "How's it going?"

"Good." Virginia looked up and smiled. "The grief counselor and I have decided that I'm ready to stop going to the weekly meetings."

"That's great." Skye looked around for a place to sit down. She was pretty sure she no longer fit in the pint-size student chairs with the attached desks. Unable to spot another option, she remained standing. "I'm glad that the Laurel Hospital group I suggested worked for you."

"Me, too." Virginia put down her red pen and wrinkled her brow. "A year ago, I would have sworn that I'd never get over the depression. Now, although I still think of Jameson every day and I'm sad a lot, I've admitted that he's truly gone."

"That's really good progress." Skye mentally checked off the four stages of recovering from losing a loved one—accepting the loss, getting through the pain, adjusting to life without the person, and moving on.

"I feel like I'm going to make it. Like I can start to have a life again."

"I'm so glad for you."

"Palmer has been a big help." Virginia's brown eyes sparkled. "I think having someone—other than a counselor or member of the grief support group—to be with and to take my mind off the past was that final piece of the puzzle that I needed to heal."

"Palmer Lynch?" Skye asked, her heart sinking. Her recent encounter with the overbearing man had not made her a fan of the district's newest board member.

"Yes." Virginia looked at her quizzically. "Do you know him?"

"Of course I know *of* him, but we actually just met for the first time this afternoon."

"Here at school?" Virginia asked, then answered herself. "Oh. That's right. Last night at dinner, he mentioned that he was going to drop by today to inspect the old wing. He feels strongly that it should be demolished."

"Unfortunately, he showed up just as Clifford ran out of the room." Skye wrinkled her nose. "I was chasing him and bumped into Palmer."

"Oh, my." Virginia's lips quirked. "And Palmer was not amused?"

"No." Skye exhaled loudly. "He was especially upset when he found out about the pet therapy. He called it snake oil and practically accused me of selling cureall elixirs from my traveling medicine show."

"Palmer is sort of old-fashioned about stuff like that," Virginia said slowly, then added, "But I think the real problem is that he's not an animal lover." She frowned. "His mom bred prize-winning German shepherds. One day he and his mother were having some sort of argument and a couple of her dogs attacked him."

"Ah. That explains a lot." Skye nodded. "And I do have to admit, he didn't get a very good introduction to the whole concept." She smiled wryly. "I mean one kid running down the hall and the rest screaming about wolves."

"That's a real shame." Virginia tented her fingers and rested her chin on them.

"It is." Skye blew out a frustrated breath. "Because once Dr. Quillen properly introduced the animals to the boys, they really seemed to enjoy the therapy session."

"They loved it." Virginia nodded. "When they got back to class, Alvin and Duncan voluntarily talked to the other kids. They told them all about the dog and cat they got to pet. Then Clifford joined in the discussion, and he didn't even try to read his book for the rest of the afternoon."

"That's amazing." Skye beamed. "Way better results than I had hoped for."

"Did Palmer make you discontinue the pet therapy?" Virginia asked.

"He tried," Skye said. "But Caroline told him he didn't have the power to dictate her decision on that matter."

"Oh, my! That's not good." Virginia's voice held a note of alarm. "Palmer gets very angry when people question his authority."

"What do you think he'll do about it?"

"I'm not sure, but you and Caroline need to watch your backs." Red crept into the teacher's cheeks and she murmured, "Palmer demands complete control."

CHAPTER 3

*Cats seem to go on the principle that it never does any
harm to ask for what you want.*
—JOSEPH WOOD KRUTCH

After Virginia's warning about Palmer, Skye headed
straight out to her car. Talking to Charlie had become more of a priority than checking in with Christopher and Gavin's teacher. She'd send the man an e-mail
when she got home. And just for good measure, she would
e-mail all five of the boys' parents with an update from
the afternoon session. She'd found that keeping everyone overinformed often prevented frantic phone calls
and lengthy explanations.

When Skye slid inside her 1957 aqua Chevy Bel Air,
she frowned. Her husband of a little over four months,
Wally Boyd, wanted to buy her a new car. The moment
that they'd found out she was pregnant, he'd started
lobbying for a safer and more baby-friendly vehicle.

Skye understood that Wally, as the chief of the Scumble River Police Department, had seen too many fatal
accidents to be comfortable with his expectant wife
driving a fifty-year-old automobile with retrofitted seat-
belts and less than terrific safety ratings. However, lately
he'd been muttering about moderate front overlap, side
and roof strength, and head restraints, which made her
wonder if she'd end up riding around in a tank.

And while Skye wasn't fond of her Chevy Bel Air, the aqua behemoth had been a gift from her father and Uncle Charlie. The two men had lovingly restored the vintage car and presented it to her when she was in dire need of transportation. If she traded it in for a new model, she was afraid her dad and her godfather would be hurt.

Still, Wally was tempting her with offers of a Mercedes-Benz M-Class SUV. She'd always wanted a Mercedes, but had never dreamed she could ever afford one.

Although no one knew it, Wally was the heir to a Texas oil dynasty. And while he didn't work in the family business and lived on his salary as a police chief, his mother had left him a hefty trust fund. Up until his marriage to Skye, he'd seldom touched the money he'd inherited, but lately he'd been more willing to dip into that account.

When she'd told him that he didn't need to buy her expensive presents, he'd gotten a tender look on his face, then he'd taken her hand and said, "You are the love of my life. I waited nearly twenty years for you. It's because you never ask for anything that it makes me happy to give you the occasional treat."

Skye had blinked back tears and said, "I don't want you using those funds just because you think it will please me. I know how much you value your independence from your family."

"A lot of the reason I never spent that money was because I knew that if I did, Darleen would see it as the first step toward me quitting my job and moving back to Texas."

Darleen was Wally's ex-wife. He had been divorced for five years, but had never talked much about his previous spouse. One of the few things about her that Wally *had* shared with Skye was that Darleen had found it extremely frustrating to be married to a rich man, but living a middle-class life.

Thrilled that her new husband was finally revealing

that part of his past, Skye had let the subject of his lavish gifts to her drop. Now as she put the Bel Air into gear and headed out of the parking lot, she considered his offer of a new car. Perhaps it was time for a fresh start for the two of them.

Both she and Wally had come into the marriage with a lot of emotional baggage. He had his ex and his secret fortune, while Skye had arrived back in Scumble River after being jilted and fired from her position as a school psychologist in New Orleans. Maybe they needed to get rid of all those past issues. To concentrate on the future. And what better way to do that than in a brand-new luxury SUV?

Grinning at the idea of owning a car like that, Skye turned onto Maryland Street, which was part of historic Route 66. Charlie's motel, the Up a Lazy River Motor Court, was just across the bridge.

It was located on the banks of the Scumble River and adjacent to the town park. Most of its guests were fishermen or hunters, with the occasional tourist traveling down the Mother Road thrown in for variety.

Skye drove into the motor court's parking lot and pulled the Bel Air into one of several empty slots. Exiting the vehicle, she crossed the asphalt and pushed open the old-fashioned screen door. Charlie, dressed in his standard uniform of gray twill pants, limp white shirt, and red suspenders, was busy barking orders into the phone.

He waved a hand at her, then said into the receiver, "You are about to exceed the limits of my medication." He listened briefly, ground his teeth, and warned, "There's a thin border between brave and stupid. Make sure you're in the right county when you make your choice."

Skye rested her hip against the registration counter while she waited for Charlie to finish his conversation, and ignoring his shouts, she scanned the small office.

Little had changed since her first memory of the place when as a child she'd visited her godfather while her mother ran errands around town.

The walls were still painted a drab brown, the desktop was scarred and in need of refinishing, and the only chair was occupied by the owner. It had been specially designed for Charlie's six-foot-tall, three-hundred-pound physique, and no one sat in it without his express permission, which he rarely gave.

Charlie taunted, "You obviously went to school to become a wit. Too bad you only made it halfway."

Skye's gaze shot to Charlie's face and she frowned. His complexion was ashen, and his rapid breathing scared her. He was seventy-seven, after all, with high blood pressure and a fondness for beer and heavy meals, and she worried about his health. Especially when he lost his temper, which happened at least once or twice a day. Sometimes more.

While she watched, Charlie's cheeks reddened and his lips drew back in a snarl. Suddenly, he roared into the phone, "You tell that asshole that I've been running things in Scumble River for forty years, and I'll be running them long after no one can remember his name!"

Skye murmured, "Uncle Charlie, you need to calm down or you're going to have a heart attack."

He covered the receiver and said, "When it's your time, it's your time."

"Possibly," Skye conceded. "However, there's no need to oil the locomotive's wheels." She glared at him. "We certainly don't want you getting into Heaven's train station early."

Charlie flipped his hand back and forth as if getting rid of a pesky mosquito, then went back to his conversation.

Before Skye could respond, the window air conditioner made a high-pitched squeal. Its laboring attempt to keep the tiny room cool reminded her that when she'd driven past the Scumble River First National Bank, the thermometer had read eighty-three degrees. Not a good sign for this early in May. If this kept up, summer would be a scorcher.

Skye dug into her pants pocket until she found the hair elastic she'd stashed there that morning. Gathering her now frizzy chestnut curls into a thick ponytail, she narrowed her emerald green eyes against the smoke from Charlie's cigar. Rapping her knuckles on the counter until she got his attention, she pointed to her baby bump and stared until he grudgingly extinguished his White Owl in the overflowing ashtray at his elbow.

Swiveling away from Skye, Charlie pounded on the desk and bellowed, "Tell him to check the goddamn bylaws! He demanded a copy when he took office so why in the hell didn't he do that in the first place?"

Charlie banged down the phone, ran sausage-like fingers through his thick white hair, and muttered, "I gotta stop asking people, 'How dumb can you be?'" He shook his head. "Some folks seem to take it as a challenge."

Sighing, he heaved himself out of the battered wooden swivel chair and swooped Skye into a bear hug. Intense blue eyes under bushy white brows scrutinized her face and he demanded, "Are you okay? Everything all right with the baby?"

Skye was breathless from his tight embrace, but returned his hug. "I'm fine and my obstetrician says Juniorette's progress is on track."

A month ago, after Skye and Wally had announced the blessed event, everyone had driven her crazy asking about her health. While most people had finally relaxed, her mother, May, and Uncle Charlie were not most people. They still demanded daily updates.

Releasing her, he settled back down into the creaking chair and his expression turned cunning. "Juniorette? So is it a girl?"

"I call it Juniorette and Wally calls it Junior." Skye wagged her finger in front of Charlie's nose. "You know darned well that we asked the doctor not to tell us the baby's sex."

"Hey." Charlie held up his hands as if in surrender. "I just thought maybe you changed your mind and May forgot to tell me."

"As if." Skye scoffed. Charlie may not be May's real father, but they were as close as if it were his blood flowing through her veins.

"So what's this I hear about your run-in with Palmer Lynch?"

"I don't know. What did you hear?" Skye answered evasively. *Shoot!* She'd been hoping to get to Charlie before the gossip mill did.

"Lynch has been burning up the phone lines accusing you and Caroline of turning the grade school into a wildlife park. He's telling everyone that you had wolves running up and down the hallways."

"Son of a—" Skye stopped herself when Charlie shot her an outraged look. Clearly, he could swear like a drunken sailor, but she couldn't. "The boys in my fourth grade group haven't been making much progress with their issues, so when I read about Dr. Quillen's animal assistance therapy in the *Scumble River Star*, I wanted to give it a try."

"You got all your ducks in a row, right?" Charlie puckered his brow. "Caroline and the school lawyer signed off and so did the parents?"

"Yes. And the insurance agent said we were covered, as well."

"Good. You make sure you document everything." Charlie tapped the side of his nose with his finger. "And from now on, copy me on your reports."

"Got it. More paperwork, just what the job of school psych needs." Groaning, Skye leaned her forearms against the counter. "Does anyone believe Lynch about the wolves? You know it was just a dog, right?"

"I told the idiots Lynch was exaggerating, but some of them are too stupid to think for themselves." Charlie rolled his eyes and folded his hands over his enormous stomach. "Which is why I gotta think for them. Otherwise this town would go to hell in a handbasket."

"And that brings me to why I'm here." Skye lowered her voice. "Is there any chance that Mr. Lynch will beat you out for board president?"

"Hell, no!" Charlie boomed. "What would make you ask a question like that? He's got a few members stirred up, that's all."

"Stirred up how?" Skye's gaze followed Charlie's hand as he nonchalantly slid a stack of papers into his desk drawer and locked it.

"The thing is, Lynch is a tricky bastard." Charlie picked up the cigar from the ashtray and ran it longingly between his fingers. "He's real good at innuendo and poking at folks' weak spots."

"And he's doing that with you. Making insinuations?" Skye said. When Charlie nodded, she asked, "Did he bring up your gambling problem?"

Seven or eight years ago, Charlie had gotten in a little over his head with the riverboat casinos in the area. Luckily, he'd been able to pay off his debts with an unexpected inheritance and now he was supposed to be going to Gamblers Anonymous, but Skye knew that he still played poker with friends. Had his participation in his weekly game caused him to spin out of control again?

"Skye, honey, if you think there isn't a person in Scumble River who doesn't know every last detail of my past problem with the casinos, then your pregnancy hormones are taking over. There are no secrets here."

"True." Skye frowned. Charlie wasn't telling her something. "So what *is* Mr. Lynch doing?"

"Nothing that you need to worry about." Charlie's expression was stubborn. "Your only job right now is having a healthy baby."

"Hogwash." Skye tapped her fingernails on the counter. "Spill."

Charlie remained silent.

"I'll just ask someone else." Skye leaned across the counter and prodded Charlie's shoulder. "As you just reminded me, there are no secrets in this town."

"Sometimes when you open your mouth, your mother comes out." Charlie glowered.

"You sure know how to hurt a girl," Skye teased, putting her hand on her chest. "That was an arrow right through my heart."

"May's a good woman," Charlie protested. "She tries to take care of everyone."

"And drives us all nuts doing it," Skye shot back. Was she getting too much like her mom? Was the baby already changing her?

"Your point?" Charlie raised an eyebrow. "Sounds a lot like you, right?"

"Don't try to distract me." Skye ignored her godfather's disturbing suggestion and said, "For the love of God, just tell me what Mr. Lynch is doing."

"I'm so old my birth certificate expired, so I sure as hell can handle Lynch without you getting involved," Charlie retorted. Then, seeming to realize that Skye wouldn't give up, he said, "Fine. He's got the booster club believing he'll back their request for a bigger budget for sports. And he's convinced the religious nuts that he'll make sure their values are the ones that are taught in the curriculum."

"So he's playing everyone?"

"Exactly." Charlie smiled meanly. "And all I have to do is make sure the various groups know it. Once they're aware that he's promising everyone everything, none of the board members will dare vote for him because they would piss off their constituency."

"But there's nothing he's doing that you can't neutralize." Skye noticed a flicker of something in her godfather's eyes. "Right?"

"Right." Charlie got up, lumbered over to her, and gave her a one-armed hug. "But you could do me a little favor."

"What?" Skye tried to back away, but Charlie held on to her.

"Let me know what you hear in the teachers' lounge about Lynch."

"You want me to be your mole?"

"Don't think of it as spying. Think of it as being a good listener and observer. Kind of like the job description of a psychologist." Charlie walked her to the door.

"I guess that I can do that." Skye was willing to be Charlie's secret agent if it meant that Palmer Lynch wasn't elected president of the school board.

"But don't let Lynch know that you're involved," Charlie cautioned. "He's a vengeful son of a b."

"Okay." Skye bit her lip.

Charlie's words reminded her of Virginia's warning. Maybe she should mind her own business. *Nah!* Charlie had always been protective of Skye and her brother, Vince, and since Skye had gotten pregnant, his concern was edging into the realm of paranoia. He wouldn't ask her to do anything that put her at risk.

Palmer Lynch was just another small-town politician. He might threaten her job, but it wasn't as if he would physically harm her.

CHAPTER 4

Dogs believe they are human. Cats believe they are God.
—ANONYMOUS

The rest of the week passed uneventfully. Skye had texted Caroline that Charlie wasn't worried about Palmer winning the election for board president and the principal had been relieved. The e-mails Skye had received in response to her message to the parents of the boys in her group had all been positive. The second pet therapy meeting on Wednesday had gone extremely well. And when Skye described the session to the principal, she was pleased with the students' progress.

Dr. Quillen was a sweetheart and Skye wondered why the handsome veterinarian was unmarried. Even though Virginia Elders was a bit older than Dr. Q, Skye would have been tempted to try to arrange a blind date between the teacher and the animal doctor if she wasn't already involved with the odious Mr. Lynch.

Heck! She might still fix up those two. Virginia deserved a nice guy, not a control freak like Palmer.

Skye and her best friend, Trixie Frayne, the high school librarian, had spent Saturday afternoon at Eastland Mall in Bloomington. While Trixie tried on cute little size 4 shorts and T-shirts, Skye looked for maternity clothes to take her through to the end of this school year and the first couple of weeks of the next one.

There hadn't been anything that made her feel remotely pretty, but Sunday morning as she got ready for church, Skye was thankful she didn't have to go through her entire wardrobe to find an outfit that wasn't too tight. Even if it felt as if she were putting on a tent.

Sighing, she slipped the navy and white knit dress over her head, tied the belt, and smoothed down the striped knee-length skirt. After weaving her hair into a French braid, she applied some bronzer and mascara, then slid her feet into a pair of sandals.

Hurrying down the stairs, she paused to grab her purse from the foyer table and yelled toward the sunroom, "I'm leaving for Mass."

Her husband's voice floated down the hallway. "Say a prayer for me."

Wally had jumped through all the hoops in order to obtain an annulment so that he and Skye could get married in the Catholic Church, and they'd talked about him converting to Catholicism, but he hadn't made a decision yet. Although he usually attended services with her, yesterday he'd wrenched his back helping one of his officers subdue an unruly suspect and had decided to skip the agony of sitting for over an hour on the hard wooden benches.

As Skye drove to town, she worried about his injury, but was distracted when she turned into the church parking lot. Although Mass didn't start until nine, and it was only eight forty-five, there wasn't one empty space.

Skye was angry at herself for arriving so late. It wasn't as if she didn't know that in Scumble River, people showed up early to stake their claim for the prime spots. Fuming at her tardiness, she squeezed the Bel Air into an opening on the street and hiked the two blocks to the church.

She was already sweating by the time she pushed through the frosted glass doors and climbed the stairs. When she dipped her fingers into the cool holy water to bless herself, she was tempted to splash her face. But the thought of having to confess that particular transgression helped stifle her impulse.

She reminded herself that the water was there for purification before approaching the presence of God, not to take a sponge bath, and she dutifully made the sign of the cross before scanning the pews for an open seat. Seeing that all the good places were taken and the only ones left were in the front, Skye groaned.

If she'd made it at her usual time, she could have nabbed a spot in the rear. But in order to do that, she would have had to get there at least twenty minutes earlier, and making Wally breakfast had put her behind schedule.

He'd been so upset about his injury she'd wanted to cheer him up. It bothered her that he was so down. He'd mentioned more than once his concern about being an "older" father. Hurting his back seemed to heighten his anxiety, and nothing Skye had said had helped.

At forty-four, Wally was eight years her senior. While the age difference had been a sore point with Skye's mother, it had never been a concern for her or Wally. At least until Skye had gotten pregnant. Now Wally was intent on staying strong and fit. She only hoped it didn't turn into an obsession. And if it did, she prayed he wouldn't expect her to join his strenuous workout routine.

Resolving to take her husband's mind off his perceived weakness once she got home, Skye marched down the entire length of the aisle searching for an open seat. She could feel the congregation's eyes following her every step, like her cat Bingo watching her open his can of Fancy Feast and scoop it into his dish.

Skye preferred to be one of the observers rather than

one of the observed, and for some reason this felt a lot like a walk of shame. In Scumble River, folks attended Mass for several reasons—many to worship God, but others to exchange the latest gossip. Skye was afraid that today the latter group's focus was on her. Especially now that she had officially begun to wear maternity clothes.

It was bad enough that she was somehow related to half the people in town, but both her jobs put her in the public eye. Not only was she the local school psychologist, but she also consulted for the police department. And as the psych consultant, she was often involved in high-profile crimes.

Add to that her ex-boyfriend's outlandish attempt to change her mind about marrying Wally, as well as her pregnancy coming so soon after her marriage, and Skye was Scumble River's version of one of *The Real Housewives of Orange County*. Not a role she enjoyed.

Skye breathed a sigh of relief when she finally found an empty spot and was able to slide into a pew, but her reprieve was short-lived when she saw that her seatmate was Palmer Lynch. She had never seen the school board member at Mass before. Was he even Catholic?

Keeping her expression neutral, Skye nodded at Lynch, who ignored her. When they stood for the processional, he whispered something to the man beside him and they traded places. What was that all about? Did he think she had cooties? Or maybe he was afraid she had a dog or a cat hidden in her purse.

As usual, Mass was both soothing and uplifting, and Skye felt herself unwind. Father Burns achieved a perfect balance between showing concern for the community and radiating confidence that good would triumph over evil. He didn't shy away from controversial world matters, but he always managed to present both sides of the issues, offering hope and forgiveness for all parties.

When the Mass ended, the priest said, "Let us all be

vigilant. Following the path of least resistance is fine for rivers and streams, but it makes many people and organizations crooked."

Father Burns generally ended the service with a veiled message related to whatever was currently the community's hot topic of conversation. Most of the time, Skye could guess where his words were aimed, but not today. Who or what was he talking about? Could it be Palmer's campaign for the school board's presidency?

As the recessional played, Skye watched Palmer Lynch make his way down the aisle. Time after time, he stopped to shake someone's hand and whisper in their ear. She noticed that while most nodded and smiled, some shook their heads and turned away from him.

Skye waited until Palmer walked out the door before leaving her pew. She didn't want to be forced to exchange any kind of pleasantries with the obnoxious man. A few minutes with him, and she was afraid that all the serenity that she'd gained from the service would evaporate.

When she finally reached the rear of the church, she overheard a group of men discussing the upcoming school board meeting. She recognized Tony Zello, a local doctor, and Nate Turner, the owner of a successful landscaping company, but while she knew the other guy was one of the deacons who often assisted at Mass, she couldn't recall his name.

While listening to the men's conversation, Skye pretended to be fascinated by a notice tacked to the bulletin board that read, A BEAN SUPPER WILL BE HELD ON FRIDAY IN THE CHURCH HALL. MUSIC WILL FOLLOW. Skye stifled a giggle and glanced at the trio behind her.

Nate folded his arms across his enormous stomach and said, "Lynch guaranteed the athletic department's budget would be restored."

Dr. Zello frowned. "He told me they were going to

hire another science and math teacher to strengthen the college prep track."

Skye's lips twitched. Clearly, Lynch had underestimated the Scumble River grapevine. Did he really think he could promise everything to everybody and no one would notice the discrepancies?

The third man patted his hair, which was teased and sprayed into the shape of a helmet, and said, "As long as Lynch brings the district back to good Christian values, I don't care which group he funds. I'm not as judgmental as you two self-righteous, holier-than-thou jerks."

"Don't be an idiot, Joel." Nate lowered his head, causing his double chin to have a double chin and emphasizing his resemblance to Jabba the Hut. "In towns like ours, sports *are* the most important thing. Do you want Brooklyn's teams to beat us?"

Skye blinked. Seriously? A football or basketball victory was the community's greatest concern? After her recent involvement with a fanatical volleyball coach, she should be surprised, but she wasn't.

"The tasks ahead of us are nothing without the power behind us." Joel aka Helmet Head poked Dr. Zello's side with his elbow. "You think morals are more important than home runs, right, Doc?"

"Well." Dr. Zello ran his fingers through his thin mouse-colored hair. "I see your point, Joel, but our tax dollars should be spent to produce students prepared to enter top universities. The U.S. is way behind other nations in science and math. Do you want your only choice to be a foreign doctor?"

"As long as they can speak English, I don't give a rat's ass where they were born." Nate shot Dr. Zello a dirty look. "You afraid of the competition?"

"Right," Dr. Zello drawled. "Because you're so accepting of other cultures and diversity." He shot Nate a malicious glare of his own. "Or maybe you are, since

you depend on folks coming across the Mexican border to work cheap cutting grass and shoveling snow for
your business."

"Now, brothers." Joel spread his arms as if to embrace
the two men and they flinched. "We're losing sight of the
real issue here."

"Which is?" Nate dug a white hanky from the pocket
of his shiny polyester pants.

Sweat was pouring off the large man and Skye wondered if he was okay. With the church now nearly
empty, the air-conditioning had lowered the building's
temperature to an almost uncomfortable coolness.

"The fact that Palmer seems to have guaranteed
each of us something different," Dr. Zello chimed in.
"And I doubt the school board has the resources to
provide all of them."

Voices rose as the three men offered opinions on the
feasibility of Lynch's promises and Skye strolled away.
The dialogue about Lynch had been enlightening, but
she was fairly sure she had heard everything that three-
some had to offer. Maybe some of the others chatting
in front of the church would have more information
she could share with Uncle Charlie.

As Skye walked down the steps and out the double
doors, she spotted Pru Cormorant and Shamus Wraige
chatting on the lawn. The high school English teacher
and the school superintendent appeared way too chummy
for Skye's peace of mind. Neither individual was much of
a fan of hers or Charlie's, and the feeling was mutual.

Skye stopped near them, hidden by a large ever-
green. In case anyone spotted her and wondered why
she was standing there, she pulled her cell phone from
her purse and made believe that she was texting.

From Skye's very first encounter with Pru Cormorant, the woman had been a pain in her posterior. The
teacher's voice was as irritating as the whine of an

electric pencil sharpener and the words that came out of her thin-lipped mouth were usually pointier than the lead tip.

Pru regularly sent parents insulting notes—a recent one had included the unforgettable line: *You might want to consider spending your money on plastic surgery for your daughter rather than tutoring because there is no way she's making it into college. Her only hope is to snag a rich husband.*

The English teacher had also flat out refused to have children with special needs in her classes. She was the speech and debate team sponsor and preferred to deal with only the intellectually gifted and extremely motivated pupils. At the first sign of a behavior issue, she complained until the principal removed the student.

As Skye listened, Pru said, "Did I tell you what one of my little darlings said?" When the superintendent raised a questioning brow, she continued, "We were getting ready for a debate on different religions and the boy you insisted I allow on the team stated that a Muslim wears a turban on his head because he wants to make a profit."

"Did you correct him?" Dr. Wraige asked, chuckling.

"No." Pru giggled. "I figured he deserved the tongue-lashing he was going to get during the event."

"Didn't you feel the least bit guilty?"

"Not even an iota." Pru lifted her chin. "I've accepted my inner sociopath."

"Good for you."

"Speaking of lunatics, I certainly hope you've taken care of the problem we were discussing earlier." Pru narrowed her watery blue eyes. "Lynch is a loose cannon and we can't trust him."

"Palmer has assured me that he has everything under control."

Shamus Wraige had been the superintendent of schools for the past decade. He'd made it clear that he was unhappy that he'd been forced to hire Skye, and she couldn't totally blame him. Her employment had been heavily influenced by Charlie's position as school board president.

Then again, it wasn't entirely nepotism on the part of her godfather. There hadn't been, and still weren't, any other applicants for the psychologist job. And in Skye's seven years working for the Scumble River school district, there hadn't been anyone interested in the social worker contract either. At least no one sane.

"Lynch has been *assuring* a lot of people a lot of things." Pru folded her stick-like arms. "How do we know he'd follow through on his promises?"

"It's one of those handshake deals," Wraige stated. "Men understand."

"Nonsense."

For once, Skye agreed with Pru. A large part of the reason Skye and the superintendent hadn't hit it off was his good-old-boy attitude. The way he treated women, especially his wife, got on her last nerve. In Skye's view, cheaters were among the worst villains.

"I'll keep an eye on him until the election." Wraige patted the teacher's shoulder. "Let me worry about Palmer, Prudence. You'll just give yourself one of your migraines if you don't relax."

Skye was shocked to hear the genuine caring in Wraige's tone. Surely, he wasn't having an affair with the unappealing woman? He was already sleeping with his much more attractive secretary.

Unless Karolyn had finally wised up. Or maybe her husband had caught on and put a stop to her extracurricular activities. Or, Skye wrinkled her brow, what had Charlie said a while back? Hadn't he mentioned that he had to take Karolyn out because of a favor?

"You're right, Shamus." Pru squeezed the superintendent's hand. "With all the end-of-the-year activities, I can't afford to be sick."

Skye decided it was time to leave. If she stuck around much longer, someone was sure to notice and say something. Besides, it seemed that she'd missed whatever problem Pru and Shamus were discussing about Lynch. It was a shame that the important part of the conversation had taken place before Skye had started to eavesdrop.

When Skye arrived home, she found her husband snoozing in the sunroom on his recliner with Bingo on his lap. Although the cat swished his tail, when Skye greeted them, Wally didn't stir, so she went into the kitchen, grabbed the gallon of milk from the fridge and a package of cookies from the cupboard, and called Charlie.

She really wanted coffee or tea, but her obstetrician had instructed her to drink twenty-four ounces of nonfat milk a day and she tried to get it down as soon as possible so she could enjoy her preferred beverages without guilt. At least the Oreos helped. Although, according to her OB-GYN, she really shouldn't be eating the added calories. She cringed at the thought of stepping on the scale at her upcoming appointment.

When Charlie picked up the phone, between sips and bites, Skye quickly brought him up-to-date on what she'd heard about Lynch at church, then asked, "So any idea what kind of problem Dr. Wraige and Pru could have with Palmer?"

"Not a clue." Charlie's voice rumbled out of the receiver. "But I'll get my spies working on it and I'll probably have the answer by this afternoon. Tomorrow at the absolute latest." His voice didn't sound as confident as usual and Skye could hear him blowing smoke from his cigar before he said, "You did real good, kid. Anything from the teachers' lounges to report?"

"Nothing." Skye swallowed the final bite of her cookie. "It's only been six days since you told me to keep my ears open at school, and everyone is too preoccupied with the end-of-the-year stuff to worry much about the school board right now." She chugged the last of her milk and rinsed the glass in the sink. "Either that, or they don't talk around me because they know I'm your goddaughter."

"Maybe we should recruit Trixie." Charlie grunted. "If they're secretive around her, she's small enough to hide in one of the cabinets."

"Are you calling me fat?" Skye teased. Then before he could answer, she said, "Gotta go. The veterinarian clinic is on the other line and I need to see why they're phoning me on a Sunday. Bye."

Wrinkling her brow, Skye clicked, holding her breath and hoping she didn't cut off the other call. She was still getting used to the call waiting and caller identification features that Wally had insisted on adding after they were married.

Tentatively, she said, "This is Skye." And blew out a relieved breath when she heard someone respond.

A clearly distraught Dr. Quillen said, "I wanted to let you know as soon as possible that I won't be able to conduct the pet therapy session tomorrow."

"That's fine," Skye assured him then asked, "Are you or the animals ill?"

Instead of answering her, the veterinarian said, "Hold on a minute."

As she waited for him to get back on the line, Skye fingered her dress. She and Wally had plans to go to brunch at Café des Architectes, but with his bad back, she wasn't sure if he'd be up to the long drive to Chicago. Should she cancel the reservations, change clothes, and start thinking about what she could cook?

Finally after several long minutes, Dr. Quillen returned

to the line and said, "Sorry, the police just got here and I have to go. Someone broke into my clinic and stole Princess Honey Bluebell."

"Your therapy cat?" Skye confirmed. The vet had introduced the feline to the boys in the group as Belle, but she recalled the cat's full name from the article she'd read in the local paper.

"Yes," Dr. Quillen said hurriedly. "That's why I have to cancel. Her partner is distraught, and at present, I don't have any other trained animals."

Before she could respond, the vet said good-bye and hung up. As Skye walked out of the kitchen, she wondered, *Who in the world would steal a cat?*

CHAPTER 5

*Those who'll play with cats must expect
to be scratched.*
—MIGUEL DE CERVANTES

Monday morning, Skye was running a little later than she'd planned when she drove into the high school's parking lot. She'd somehow managed to turn off her alarm—several times. Which, considering the fact that she had trouble locating her keys in her pocket, her wallet in her purse, and had never been good at pin the tail on the donkey, how in the heck had she succeeded in pushing the snooze button with her eyes closed from several feet away on her first try?

But maybe her luck was changing. There was a prime parking spot open by the front door. Quickly easing the Bel Air into the space, she cut the car's engine, then settled her purse strap on her shoulder and slipped the handles of her tote bag over her arm. Exiting, she hurried toward the building's entrance.

She hadn't had time for anything but an energy bar for breakfast so she savored the memory of yesterday's fabulous brunch. When Wally had woken up from his nap, his back had felt better and he'd insisted they keep their reservation at Café des Architectes.

Evidently, Wally had gotten over his latest bout of older-father-insecurity, and they had enjoyed the restaurant's famous Harney and Son's tea selection, lingonberry waffle with honey-whipped ricotta, and shaved foie gras torchon. The foie gras had a texture like the creamiest butter Skye had ever tasted and melted on her tongue. The distinct cured sweetness, sliced on a toast triangle with mint chiffonade, had been one of the most amazing bites she'd ever eaten

Skye frowned. How many calories had that meal-contained? Her obstetrician weighed her at every appointment and wasn't happy when the numbers on the digital scale increased by more than a pound or two.

When her cell started to play Hilary Duff's 2003 hit "Come Clean," she abandoned all worries about her doctor's impending wrath. Why was Dorothy Snyder calling her?

The last time Skye's former student, and now techie genius friend, Justin Boward, had visited her, he'd programmed her new smart phone with different ring tones for different callers. And this particular song was her part-time housekeeper's.

Curious, and a bit concerned, Skye stopped in midstride. She dug out the phone from her purse, swept the screen with her thumb, and said, "Hi, Dorothy. What's up?"

"Where are you?" Dorothy's voice cracked. "Can anyone hear you?"

"I'm on the sidewalk heading into the high school." Skye glanced around. "And I'm alone. Why?"

"I need you to come to Palmer Lynch's house right now," Dorothy wheezed.

"What's wrong?" Skye's pulse raced.

Was Dorothy having a heart attack? But why would she call Skye and not 911? Maybe Lynch had attacked her and she was hiding. But in that situation, the police would still have been a better choice.

"I . . . I can't." Dorothy started to sob. "Just come right away."

"But I'll be late for school." As soon as the words left her mouth, Skye could have kicked herself for being so stupid. It was obvious whatever was happening with Dorothy took precedence over having to explain her lack of punctuality to the principal. "Never mind. But tell me what's wrong so I can be more helpful."

"No!" Dorothy inhaled noisily. "Just get here as fast as you can."

"Wait!" Skye yelled into the phone, afraid that Dorothy was about to hang up. "Where does Palmer Lynch live? I don't know his address."

Dorothy named a road a block over from the school, and ironically also just a few blocks from the police station, then said, "It would be better if you walked so no one sees your car."

Before Skye could ask her housekeeper any more questions, Dorothy disconnected. Skye dashed to her Bel Air, unlocked the door, and threw her tote bag on the seat. As she half jogged out of the parking lot toward Center Street, she put her purse strap across her chest and then repeatedly hit redial on her cell.

The call kept going to voice mail, and by the time Skye approached the house number that Dorothy had given her, she was panting. Part of her respiratory distress was from running, but more was from anxiety. Would she arrive to find the housekeeper dead or dying?

Dorothy was one of May's oldest friends. She and Skye's mother had been classmates, and her deceased husband had been in the Navy with Skye's father, Jed. The two couples had been close, and as a child, Skye had spent a lot of time with the Snyder family.

As Skye turned into Lynch's driveway, she thought she saw something zip across the window of the pedestrian door of the huge detached garage looming in front of her. Before she could decide if she was imagining things, Dorothy moved out of the shadows at the side of the large house and motioned her over. Puzzled by the woman's behavior, but relieved that she appeared to be otherwise healthy, Skye stepped off the pavement and onto the grass.

When Dorothy grabbed Skye's hand and started walking toward the backyard, Skye asked, "Where are we going?"

"You'll see."

Dorothy was a tall, solidly built woman in her early sixties. She was usually quick to smile and crack a joke, but today her mood was somber.

Silently, she led Skye through a sliding glass door. Once they were in the kitchen, she opened her mouth to speak, then shaking her head, she started crying. Her shoulders shuddered from her sobs as she dug a tissue from the pocket of her jeans.

Unsure what to say or do, Skye patted Dorothy's arm and murmured soothing nonsense words. As far as Skye could see, everything looked normal. The granite countertops were spotless and the expensive stainless steel appliances shined as if they'd been polished for a photo shoot in *House Beautiful*. But clearly, since she'd just been snuck in the back by a woman who was now bawling her eyes out, something was wrong.

Finally, Dorothy sniffed, blew her nose, and said, "I think I'm in trouble."

"Why is that?" Skye asked, not sure she really wanted to know.

In her heart, she was well aware she should have called Wally the minute she got off the phone with Dorothy. But even though Dorothy had originally been Wally's cleaning lady and became Skye's only after they were married, for decades before that, she'd been a close family friend so it was hard to turn down a plea for help from her.

"Well, you know, I usually do clean for you and Wally on Mondays," Dorothy started.

"Right." Skye wrinkled her brow. Surely Dorothy didn't think Skye would be upset because she was cleaning Lynch's house instead of hers?

"But Palmer called me Sunday afternoon and asked if I could do a quick tidying up here this morning." She looked at Skye as if to gauge her reaction. "I was still going to get the work done at your place."

"Of course." Skye nodded. "Even if you had to postpone us, it wouldn't be a problem." She smiled reassuringly. "I'm not a neat freak like Mom."

"You can't tell May about this!" Dorothy's pupils dilated at the thought.

Ignoring the older woman's panicky expression, Skye infused her voice with a soothing calm and said, "So you came here this morning to clean for Mr. Lynch." She was afraid that keeping whatever "this" was a secret from her mom might be the least of Dorothy's worries, but crossing her fingers, she asked, "Did you break something?"

"I wish that was it." Dorothy cleared her throat. "I had told Palmer that I needed to start here at seven and he said that was fine."

"So you arrived at seven, and . . ." Skye trailed off encouragingly.

"And he didn't answer the doorbell." Dorothy twisted the tissue in her hand until pieces littered the floor at her feet. "I knocked and rang and even telephoned, but nothing."

"But you didn't want to leave because you'd promised," Skye guessed.

"Exactly." Dorothy rushed to explain. "I didn't have time to come back, and Palmer could get real nasty if he didn't get his way."

"If he's a regular, don't you have a key to let yourself in?" Skye asked.

"No." Dorothy shook her head. "Palmer always insists on being here when I clean."

"So . . ." Skye said slowly, realizing where this was going. "You broke in?"

"Technically, I didn't break in, but I entered." Dorothy stared at the floor, a dull crimson staining her cheeks. "When I peeked inside and saw that the security bar that Palmer usually keeps in the tracks of the sliding glass door was leaning against the cupboard, I wiggled the handle and it slid right open."

"Okay." Skye grimaced. "And now you're afraid Mr. Lynch will be upset?" She doubted that was what had Dorothy so distraught, but it seemed like the least bad scenario.

"Not anymore." Dorothy winced. "His days of getting mad at folks are over."

"Because?" Skye was pretty darn sure she knew the answer, but clung to a small shred of hope that she was wrong.

"He's dead." Dorothy's gaze searched Skye's face, then added, "As a doornail."

"Are you positive?" She fought to keep her expression neutral.

"No. I just called you here to chew the fat." Dorothy wasn't one to pull her punches. "There's a bullet hole in the middle of his chest, so unless he's a zombie or something, he's dead."

"Are you sure whoever killed Mr. Lynch isn't still in the house?" Skye asked, looking over her shoulder as if she expected someone to spring out of a cupboard and start snacking on her brains.

"I grabbed a butcher knife and checked the house before I called you." Dorothy shrugged at Skye's gasp. "I know that wasn't smart, but I wasn't thinking too straight."

Skye nodded her understanding, then asked, "Where's Mr. Lynch?"

"In the master bedroom." Dorothy jerked her thumb upward toward the second floor. "I found him when I went to get the sheets to wash."

"Why didn't you call 911?" Skye pressed, then asked, "Because you were here illegally?"

"That, and because Palmer is . . . uh . . . not himself." Dorothy blushed.

Skye barely kept from rolling her eyes. "In what way is he different?" If the man was dead, he certainly wasn't his normal self.

"He's naked." Dorothy crossed her arms. "But that ain't the half of it."

"Naked and dead isn't enough." Skye snorted. "This just keeps getting better and better." She narrowed her eyes. "What else?"

"I . . ." Dorothy's face turned a deeper shade of red and she grabbed Skye's wrist, towing her down the hall, up the stairs, and into the shadowy bedroom.

Before Skye's eyes could adjust to the darkness, Dorothy flipped on the overhead light fixture—an elaborate chandelier. Squinting, Skye turned toward the massive four-poster bed and gulped. Palmer Lynch was indeed naked. He definitely had a bullet hole in the center of his chest, but strangely even more disturbing, he was blindfolded and tied spread eagle across the mattress.

Skye was beginning to feel like maybe she had never woken up, and this was one of those stress dreams— the kind that no matter how hard she tried, she couldn't make sense out of what was happening. After all, nudity was often an element in those nightmares. Although most of the time she was the one without clothes, not someone else.

Blinking, Skye tried to erase the image from her

retinas, but it was there to stay. In an effort to remain calm, she scanned the rest of the room. The furniture was dark cherry and reminded her of a picture she'd seen of a Victorian brothel. The burgundy walls and heavy red velvet drapes only reinforced this impression.

Skye glanced at Dorothy, who was resolutely staring at a gilt-framed painting on the far wall. Taking a deep breath, Skye looked back at Lynch. Except for being dead, he was in good shape. He had a muscular chest, broad shoulders, and a trim waist.

Taking a closer look at the man on the bed, Skye saw that his skin had a waxy appearance and was almost blue-gray in color. She fought the urge to take Lynch's pulse or listen for breathing. It was clear he was dead, and that he had been for some time.

"I'm calling Wally."

Skye fished her cell from her purse, but before she could dial, Dorothy plucked the phone from her fingers and said, "Wait."

"For what?" Skye asked. Did Dorothy think that Lynch might reanimate?

"Couldn't we untie him and put some pajamas on him?" Dorothy took a step toward the bed, but this time it was Skye's turn to grab her.

"You can't disturb a crime scene." Skye's nails dug into the older woman's biceps as she struggled. "Heaven knows what has already been lost."

"You're right." Dorothy hung her head. "It's just that Palmer's mother is a friend of mine from church. She's a sweet lady, a widow, and she'll be mortified if word gets out that her son was into this kinky stuff."

"I'm sorry for Mrs. Lynch." Skye's voice softened. "Truly, I understand. I'll ask Wally if I can be there when he informs her about Mr. Lynch's death and I'll try to soften the blow as best I can. But you and I both know there's no way around this getting out. In Scumble River a secret is just something that is told to one person at a time."

Something flickered behind Dorothy's eyes. She wrenched herself free, ran toward a wastebasket near the dresser, and vomited.

"Are you okay?" Skye found a packet of tissues in her purse, walked over, and offered it to the distraught woman.

Dorothy nodded and wiped her mouth. "I just realized what a freaking mess this is." She dabbed her lips again. "Why didn't I just leave when no one answered the door? Everyone will be talking about this, and my name is going to be linked with this sick shit."

"No one would think that you were a part of Mr. Lynch's unusual sex life," Skye said.

However, even as the words left her mouth, she knew no matter what the facts, some people would always believe that Dorothy was involved. The housekeeper's complexion took on a greenish cast and Skye was afraid she would be sick again.

But Dorothy only swallowed loudly and said, "Oh, my God. What if my other clients drop me?"

"They won't," Skye assured her, stepping away from the trashcan.

Although she wasn't experiencing morning sickness anymore, strong odors made her stomach roil. Certain smells seemed more pronounced now that she was pregnant and it didn't take much to make her gag. She forced down the bile rising in the back of her throat.

"This sucks!" Dorothy tossed Skye her cell and headed for the door.

Skye followed, and when they were both outside, she said with a straight face, "If the world didn't suck, we'd all fall off." It was a retort she often made to teenagers who expressed that sentiment.

There was a moment of silence, then Dorothy snickered, breaking the tension. The two women walked around the house and Skye suggested they sit in Dorothy's car, an old Cadillac Catera, while she called the police.

Wally's cell went directly to voice mail, as did their home phone and his private number at the station. Sighing, Skye dialed the nonemergency police number. As she listened to the phone ring, she checked her watch. It was after eight, which meant her mother should be finished with her shift and on her way home.

May worked part-time as a police, fire, and emergency dispatcher. Normally she worked afternoons, but Thea, the daytime dispatcher, was on vacation this week. If May was working a double shift to fill in for her, the situation would take twice as long to explain.

By the sixth ring, Skye was beginning to worry that she'd stumbled into the *Twilight Zone*, where everyone had disappeared except Dorothy and her, and of course, the naked body upstairs in the bedroom. She was about to hang up and try 911 when her call was finally answered.

"This is Skye." She identified herself. "I need to talk to Wally."

"He's busy." A sultry feminine voice that Skye didn't recognize as belonging to any of the regular dispatchers said, "Call back later."

"No! I'm—" There was the distinct click of a disconnection and Skye frowned at her cell. What in the hell was going on?

CHAPTER 6

A cat bitten once by a snake dreads even rope.
—ARAB PROVERB

"You can't hang up on me," Skye muttered at her cell. "I'm his wife."

"What's wrong?" Dorothy asked, her brow wrinkling. "Who hung up on you?"

"I have no idea." Skye shrugged, trying to appear unconcerned. "Guess I'll have to call 911 after all and hope someone else answers."

Skye dialed and for once was relieved to hear her mother's voice. Her previous thoughts about having to deal with May as the on-duty dispatcher aside, she was happy to reach someone at the police station who knew her.

"Mom, it's me," Skye said, immediately adding, "I'm fine. The baby's fine. Everyone you care about is fine. But I need to talk to Wally ASAP."

"Why?" May's single word oozed with suspicion. "Are you positive you're okay?"

Skye repeated her assurances and her request to speak to Wally.

"If everything is okay, why are you calling 911 to talk to him?"

"There is a problem," Skye said carefully. "But it doesn't involve me."

"What kind of problem and who does it involve?" May demanded.

Skye ignored her mother's interrogation. "I really need to speak to Wally."

"He's kind of occupied at the moment," May said. "Tell me and I'll tell him."

"What's going on there?" Skye gave up trying to get Wally on the phone and decided to get some information instead. "Who was that who answered the nonemergency number a few minutes ago?"

"Hold on a second while I transfer your call to another line." There was silence, then a click, and finally May said, "Chantal from the American Legion picked up the phone before I could stop her." May's disapproval of the woman's actions was evident. "Around two in the morning, someone smashed the Legion's front door and tried to get into their safe."

"Is that what Wally is working on?" Skye asked, realizing the only way she was going to talk to her husband was to tell May about Lynch. "Because, I can trump a break-in with a dead body."

Immediately, the Fifth Dimension singing "Going out of My Head" blared in Skye's ear. Before the song's chorus repeated, Wally got on the line.

Sounding out of breath, he asked in a rush, "Are you okay? Is the baby okay? Did something happen at school? Who's the deceased?"

Skye assured him that she and the baby were fine, then rushed to explain. "I'm with Dorothy Snyder at Palmer Lynch's house." Skye rattled off the address. "Dorothy cleans for him, too. We're sitting in her Cadillac, but we were previously inside and he's dead."

"I take it you don't believe it was natural causes," Wally stated.

"There's a bullet hole in his chest," Skye answered. "So no."

"Son of a b!" Wally bellowed. "Are you sure the killer's not still around?"

"Dorothy claims to have searched the house and didn't find anyone." Interrupting Wally's cursing, she added, "I wasn't here. She knows it was stupid, but it's done and we're now in her car."

"I'll be right there," Wally said. "Sit tight and keep the doors locked."

"Will do," Skye agreed, then added, "You'll want to keep the particulars of this case quiet so you might want to stay off the radio."

"What—" Wally cut himself off and said, "Never mind. I'll be there in five. You can explain then. Call my cell if anything happens."

"Come alone," Skye warned just before he hung up. She turned to Dorothy and said, "On a positive note, everyone will be so caught up in the attempted burglary at the American Legion, maybe the more salacious details of Mr. Lynch's murder might not get out."

Dorothy grunted, then leaned against the back of the seat and closed her eyes. While the older woman rested, Skye called the high school and left a message that she wouldn't be coming into work and asked that all her appointments and meetings be canceled.

She indicated that her absence be marked as a personal day. There was nothing in her current contract that allowed for time off because of involvement in a murder investigation. Although considering Skye's past record, she should try to add a dead body clause next time she signed a new agreement.

Seconds later, Wally's cruiser, without lights flashing or sirens wailing, raced down the street. He pulled the squad across the driveway, effectively blocking anyone from entering or leaving, and leaped from the vehicle.

Skye popped the lock, scrambled out of Dorothy's Catera, and threw herself in her husband's arms. He ran his hands over her as if to check for injuries and rained kisses on her face.

Once he was convinced she was okay, he said, "Why all the secrecy?"

Summing up the housekeeper's call, what happened once Skye arrived, and the condition of the corpse, she concluded, "One way or another, if bondage is truly Lynch's sexual preference or the killer did this to him to humiliate him, as soon as the details get out, we both know the case becomes that much harder to solve."

"Of course." Wally gave her one last squeeze, then released her and said, "Let me go look things over, then I'll decide how to proceed."

"Shouldn't you have backup?" Skye asked. "I know I said to come alone, but—"

"How long were the two of you in the house?" Wally raised a brow, but didn't wait for her answer before adding, "And Dorothy was there awhile before that, so unless the murderer is dumber than a box of rocks, they were already long gone before either of you arrived. Or at least he or she escaped when you two came out and sat in the car waiting for me to get here."

"Right." Skye knew she was being silly. Surely the killer would have attacked Dorothy or her rather than wait for an armed police officer.

When Wally returned a few minutes later, he was tucking his cell phone into his shirt pocket. His expression was grim and he rubbed the back of his neck.

Approaching Skye, he said, "The county crime techs will be here in about forty minutes. Reid is on his way. He was preparing for a memorial service so I caught him at the funeral home. And Quirk will be here as soon as he drops off a witness at her car."

Sergeant Roy Quirk was Wally's right hand at the PD. Simon Reid was the coroner and owned the local funeral parlor and the bowling alley—which his mother,

Bunny, managed. Unfortunately, Simon was also Skye's ex-boyfriend.

They had dated on and off for over two years, until Skye thought she caught Simon cheating on her. He'd been too stubborn to explain his actions, and shortly afterward, Wally and Skye became an item. To say that the three of them working together presented an awkward situation was way beyond an understatement.

Skye nodded her understanding, then leaned against the car. Dorothy was still inside and had either dozed off or was now in a catatonic state. Skye hoped it was the former because she wasn't ready to deal with the latter.

"While we wait, are you up to giving me some more details about what transpired thus far?" Wally asked.

"Of course." Skye took a deep breath. "I was walking into the high school when Dorothy called me on my cell. She wouldn't tell me what was wrong, just begged me to come to Palmer Lynch's house."

"Where's your car?" Wally asked, looking both ways down the block.

"Dorothy asked me to walk over, then she hung up and stopped answering her phone." Skye shoved her hair behind her ear. "She was waiting for me when I arrived. She led me into the house via the patio doors and explained that Lynch had asked her to do an unscheduled cleaning job, but when she got here, he didn't answer the door."

"But she didn't go away?" Wally crossed his arms. "Why in God's name would she break into a house to clean it?" Skye opened her mouth, but he answered his own question. "Because she was on a tight schedule and didn't want to disappoint either him or us."

"Uh-huh." Skye nodded. "But she didn't really have to break in. According to Dorothy, she saw that the bar that Lynch normally kept in the sliding door tracks was leaning against the cupboard. She just wiggled the handle and was able to slide it open."

"So it might not have been locked?" Wally ran his fingers through his short black hair, ruffling the silver strands at his temples.

"That was my thought." Skye nodded. "When Dorothy led me down the hallway to the stairs, I saw that the front door's chain guard was in place and figured the killer left through the sliders."

"Did she show you the body right away?" Wally had taken out a small pad from his uniform shirt pocket and was jotting down notes.

"No." Skye's teeth caught her lower lip and worked it for a moment. "Actually, it took what seemed like quite a few minutes to get to the point before Dorothy finally showed me Lynch. That was when I tried to call you, but she grabbed my cell." Skye shook her head. "Dorothy wanted to put some clothes on him first."

"Since he was still buck-naked when I saw him, I take it you stopped her." Wally's dark brown eyes were warm.

"Yes." Skye nodded again. "Lynch's mother is a widow and is a friend of Dorothy's from church. She didn't want the poor woman to be subject to gossip. When Dorothy realized there was no avoiding the rumor mill, and that she would probably be tainted by the innuendos, too, she vomited in the trashcan. After she stopped being sick, I was finally able to get her out of the house, into her car, and I called you." Skye puckered her brow. "Or at least, I tried to call you."

"Yeah." Wally rolled his eyes. "The mess at the station." He pinched the bridge of his nose. "Shortly after you left for school, May phoned for me to come into the PD. The American Legion break-in has had me tied up ever since. Chantal was working late last night, and when the would-be thieves broke into the building, she locked herself in a utility closet. By the time she came out this morning, she was nearly hysterical."

"She sounded pretty calm when I talked to her." Skye smoothed her black shirt over her baby bump. "I don't think I know Chantal."

"She's new in town. She just started managing the Legion a few months ago." Wally didn't meet Skye's gaze. "She's a friend of Emmy Jones. They both belonged to the same dance studio in Chicago."

"I thought Emmy came here from Nevada." Skye wasn't sure how she felt about the gorgeous performer.

"Who knows all the places Emmy has probably lived." Wally shrugged.

Emerald Jones had arrived in Scumble River after getting into some kind of trouble in Las Vegas. She had promptly flirted with Wally at his gun club, then ended up dating Skye's ex. Not exactly BFF material. Skye and Chantal didn't seem to be starting out any better.

Oh, please! What was wrong with her? So Chantal had hung up on Skye, had a sexy voice, and was a friend of Emmy's. None of those facts meant the woman was trying to seduce Wally. For all Skye knew, Chantal resembled Peppermint Patty more than she did Jessica Rabbit.

Skye frowned. She had never been a jealous person, but some combination of her recent marriage, pregnancy hormones, and Wally being so handsome was setting her off. She needed to stop imagining every woman was trying to steal her man before she turned into a shrew.

Swallowing hard, Skye realized that maybe she wasn't really jealous. Maybe she was just trying to avoid thinking about the real issues. Palmer Lynch was dead. He apparently enjoyed an alternative lifestyle that would set Scumble River on its ear once the news got out. And Uncle Charlie would be a prime suspect.

Skye blanched. *No!* Charlie would never do something like this. He might want to remain school board president, even be willing to fight a little dirty for it, but he'd never kill to retain the position. Still, Skye prayed that he'd have an airtight alibi.

Uh-oh. She must have been quiet for too long because Wally stroked her arms and said, "Do you feel all right? I can drive you home."

"I'm fine," Skye reassured him. "Just considering what I know about Lynch."

"Right." Wally tapped his chin. "I'd forgotten about that business with the pet therapy and that he was on the school board. Tonight, you'll have to give me the whole rundown on who might have had it in for him."

"Sure." Skye's smile was halfhearted. "It's a date. Suspects and supper."

Wally looked at her quizzically, but before he could respond, Simon pulled his Lexus behind the squad car. He jogged up the driveway carrying a black doctor's case, containing a camera, stethoscope, flashlight, rubber gloves, and liver thermometer. The body bag would arrive with his assistant in the hearse.

As soon as Simon got near them, Wally put his arm around Skye's shoulder.

At the same instant, Simon took her free hand and asked, "What happened?"

Simon was the antithesis of Wally. Where Skye's husband was muscular, her ex was lean. Wally's hair was cut close to his head while Simon's auburn tresses were professionally styled. But the biggest difference was Simon's golden-hazel eyes. Even in the heat of passion they were cool and appraising, while Wally's were always warm when Skye looked into them.

"The vic's in the master bedroom," Wally said, stepping back and bringing Skye with him, which caused

her hand to slip from Simon's. "We'll have to wait for
the crime techs to get here before you can move the
body, but in the meantime, try to get a time of death."

Clearly unhappy with Wally's dictatorial tone, Simon didn't budge. The two men glowered at each
other, and Skye held her breath.

Relieved, she spotted a patrol car driving down the
block and said to Wally, "Oh. Look. Sergeant Quirk is
here already."

"Good." Wally glanced over his shoulder. "He can
set up the perimeter."

"Do you want me to wait in the car with Dorothy?"
Skye asked. She rubbed her belly and added, "I'd like
to get off my feet for a bit."

"That's right." Simon looked between Skye and
Wally. "I understand that congratulations are in order." His lips thinned. "I see you two didn't waste any
time creating Baby Boyd." He stared at Wally. "I guess
that's one way to win over your new mother-in-law."

In addition to Wally's divorced status and the fact
he wasn't Catholic, his age had been a huge issue with
Skye's mother. May had been afraid that he'd have difficulty producing a grandchild for her.

Wally's expression hardened, but he ignored Simon's comment and said to Skye, "Why don't you just
let me drive you home, sweetheart?"

"I'll wait until you're through with Dorothy," Skye
said, chewing on her thumbnail. "She pretends to be a
tough old broad, but this really knocked her for a loop
and I think she needs my support."

"Okay, darlin'." Wally led Skye a couple of steps
over to the Cadillac, where the older woman still appeared to be napping, and opened the door. "I'll get
Quirk and Reid situated, then talk to Dorothy."

Skye slid inside the car, but as Wally turned to go, she
said, "Wait. Before I forget, Lynch was in church yesterday

and afterwards he was making a lot of campaign promises. Once he left, I overheard some of those conversations and people weren't happy."

"Another thing for us to discuss tonight." Wally kissed her cheek.

Simon had followed them and tsked. "May said you promised to attend Mass with Skye. That didn't last long. Did it, Chief?"

Skye had had enough of her ex and she glared at him. He had moved on. He was dating Emmy Jones. What was his problem?

CHAPTER 7

Beware of people who dislike cats.
—IRISH PROVERB

Dorothy opened her eyes when Skye got into the car.
However, as soon Skye started to tell her what was
happening, she quickly closed her lids and turned away.
Understanding that the distraught woman wasn't ready
to face the situation, Skye swiveled her head and gazed
out of the Caddy's back window.

Because it was a weekday morning, most of Lynch's
neighbors were at work. But the few who were present
were intent on finding out what had happened.

Less than a minute after the arrival of the second
squad car, an older couple had taken seats on their
porch to watch the show. Next, a woman and toddler
came outside and sat on their front steps. That two-
some was quickly joined by another mother and child.

Wally had assigned Sergeant Quirk the task of cor-
doning off the property. He had draped yellow ribbon
around the yard's perimeter and placed a pair of sawhorses blocking the driveway.

With the crime scene tape up, the onlookers moved
closer, gathering behind the barricade. The small
group was now asking Quirk questions.

Rolling down the car's window, Skye tried to hear

what was being said, but she caught only an occasional word or phrase. It sounded as if the sergeant was claiming ignorance, which wasn't far from the truth. Wally hadn't given him any details beyond the fact that there was a suspicious death.

Skye studied Quirk. Roy was in his mid-thirties, and, except for his lack of hair, he still looked like the football player he'd been in high school. She could tell the sergeant was starting to lose his patience with the nosy neighbors because he was making shooing motions with his hands and his face had turned an ugly shade of red.

Even from where she sat, Skye could see that Quirk was having trouble remaining civil. She knew that in the past the sergeant had issues with his temper—she'd been on the receiving end of his short fuse a few times herself—but Wally had insisted Quirk see a therapist and he'd been doing better.

Hoping to avoid a relapse, she quickly hopped out of the Caddy. She hurried to where the irate officer stood glowering at an elderly man waving a cane.

Pushing against the wooden barricade, the man shouted, "We have a right to know what's happening in our own neighborhood!"

"Sir," Quirk said between clenched teeth, "please step back."

A young woman holding a toddler who was chewing the end of her blond ponytail asked, "Did something happen to Palmer?"

"Ma'am." Quirk heaved a sigh. "As I've said repeatedly, I have no information."

"Why should we believe that? On television, cops lie all the time." She wagged her index finger under Quirk's nose. "What are you hiding, Roy?"

"Nothing!" Quirk bellowed, swatting away both the cane that the man was poking at his chest and the hand waving in his face. "Return to your homes. Once the situation has been fully assessed, the chief will make an announcement."

Skye stepped closer to the sergeant and in a low voice suggested, "Maybe you need to take some deep breaths."

"I'm okay," Quirk muttered, then surprised Skye by winking as he said, "You know if folks would control their effing stupidity, I wouldn't have to manage my anger."

Before Skye could respond, the elderly woman grabbed her hand and asked, "Are we in danger?"

"That is highly unlikely," Skye assured the group, then had an inspiration. "But just in case, it probably would be best to lock yourself inside your house until the police have completely secured the area."

The blonde shrieked, clutched her child to her bosom, and ran. The other mom, dragging her toddler by the hand, was right behind her friend, but the older couple hesitated, glancing at their screen door.

Skye's gaze followed theirs and she asked, "Did you leave your place unlocked?"

The couple nodded.

"Sergeant." Skye gave Quirk's arm a meaningful squeeze. "Perhaps you could walk through Mr. and Mrs. . . ."

"Cooperson," the woman supplied.

"Mr. and Mrs. Cooperson's house to make sure no one entered it while they've been distracted," Skye finished, smiling at the couple.

"The chief told me to stay here." Quirk's lips formed a stubborn line.

"I guess I could go with the Coopersons and check." Skye raised a brow. "If you think Wally would be happier with that alternative."

"No." The sergeant frowned, clearly envisioning the

chief's reaction to his pregnant wife walking into an even remotely dangerous situation because Quirk refused to go.

"Look." Skye gestured to the deserted street. "I'll stop anyone from entering the crime scene while you ensure the Coopersons' safety."

"Fine," Quirk growled. "Get your cell out and ready to call for help. If there's a problem, lock yourself in the car."

Once the sergeant disappeared into the Coopersons' bungalow, Skye returned to the Caddy and sat sideways with her feet on the pavement. She'd wanted Quirk to help out the elderly couple so that they would see him as a man who had come to their rescue instead of one who had refused to answer their questions and barked orders at them.

Roy needed to learn the value of positive public relations. He was an excellent cop, but his reputation wasn't as good as his abilities warranted. People saw him as a brusque control freak, and in today's world, that image of a police officer didn't cut it anymore.

Skye was toying with the idea of suggesting that she run a social skills group for Scumble River's police officers when suddenly Dorothy screamed and clawed at the door handle, trying to get out of the car. Instinctively, Skye grabbed her and wrapped her arms around the woman. Her attempt to comfort Dorothy was futile. The woman continued to shriek and struggle to break free.

Scanning the area, Skye didn't see anything or anyone that should have frightened Dorothy. After several seconds, the woman blinked, then collapsed, breathing heavily and clutching Skye's biceps.

"What happened?" Skye asked, stroking Dorothy's hair out of her eyes.

"I must have fallen asleep." Dorothy straightened. "I dreamed that a man with a whip was chasing me around my bedroom telling me to beg for it."

As Skye struggled to contain an inappropriate giggle, Wally came running around the house and rushed up to her. "Are you okay? What the hell happened?"

"Dorothy had a nightmare," Skye said. "Did Simon figure out the time of death?"

"We'll talk later," Wally answered, glancing at Dorothy, then looked around and asked, "Where's Quirk? I didn't see him in the back."

Skye explained the sergeant's absence, then pointed over her husband's shoulder. "There he is now." When Wally turned to look, Skye gestured in the other direction. "And isn't that the county's crime tech van?"

"It's about time." Wally patted Skye's cheek. "I'll get the techs started, then come out and talk to Dorothy so you both can get out of here."

After what seemed like another interminable wait, Wally reemerged from Lynch's house and headed to the car. Skye got in the backseat of the Cadillac and Wally slid into the front next to Dorothy. As he took the woman through her arrival and discovery of the body again and again, Skye mentally composed a to-do list.

Missing a day of school meant rearranging all of her appointments and squeezing them into the rest of the week's schedule. She still had a couple of re-evaluations to complete before the end of the year, and most of the rest of her hours were filled with annual reviews.

All children receiving special education had to have a mandated re-eval every three years. The purpose of the assessment was to determine whether there was a continuing need for special education and related services, as well as to figure out if any changes had to be made in the student's Individualized Education Plan.

Annual reviews were formal meetings conducted by the school at least once a year to assess special education students' progress and determine future requirements.

Both took up the majority of Skye's time in April

and May. And this year, she also needed to get things arranged for the intern who would be joining her after summer break. She would only have a couple of weeks in the fall before the baby was born and then she'd be on maternity leave.

Theoretically, during Skye's absence a school psychologist from the county special education cooperative would supervise the intern. In reality, Skye knew that even if she had to guide the intern via telephone, she would end up with the brunt of the responsibility.

Lost in thought, Skye didn't see the crime tech approach the car, and she let out a startled yelp when he tapped on the window.

Wally scowled at the man in the blue coveralls, opened the car door, and said, "What?"

"Do you want us to process the garage?"

"Hmm." Wally pursed his lips then, plainly coming to a decision, nodded. "Probably better include it. Considering how the vic met his maker, God only knows what he might have stashed in his garage."

The tech's shrug conveyed that the crime scene hadn't made the same impression on him that it had on Wally. Even though the tech's unit covered the entire county, Skye wondered if the guy was just pretending to be so blasé or if he'd seen other criminal situations involving naked men or women tied to their beds.

She opened her mouth to ask, but before she could form the question, Wally said, "If the garage is locked, there's a bunch of keys hanging from a hook in the kitchen. Otherwise, break a window."

"Okay, Chief. When we're done inside, we'll get right on it." The tech sketched a mock salute and hurried away.

Wally turned back to Dorothy and said, "I'll get your statement typed up this afternoon, and you can come by the station tomorrow to sign it."

"Can I leave?" Dorothy asked, slumped in her seat and clutching her purse.

"Yes." As Wally exited the car, he added, "But stay in town."

Dorothy paled and cringed at his words. She had aged ten years since Skye had seen her a few days ago. Leaning forward, she patted the woman's shoulder and the housekeeper gripped Skye's fingers.

"Do you want me to drive you home and stay with you?" Skye asked, easing her hand free.

"No." Dorothy got out of the Catera's passenger seat, walked around the hood, and slid behind the wheel. "I'll call Tammy to come over."

Tammy was Dorothy's daughter. She was a year older than Skye, and because their parents had been friends, as children they'd been forced to hang out with each other. But when they hit adolescence, they'd gone their separate ways. And when Skye left for college, rarely returning to town for the next decade, she'd lost touch with Tammy.

Now that Skye had been back in Scumble River for seven years, she'd run into Dorothy's daughter a few times. But other than a shared past and their mothers' friendship, they didn't have much in common.

"Terrific. Tammy will keep you company and she'll make sure you don't get into any more trouble."

Skye scooted out of the Cadillac's backseat and winked at Dorothy. She and May were a lot wilder than Skye and Tammy. When they were growing up, it had been a big joke that the girls had to keep their moms in line rather than the usual vice versa.

Dorothy smiled at Skye and waved good-bye to her. Dorothy waited while Quirk removed the squad car and barricade from her path, then backed down the driveway and sped off. Once the red Cadillac disappeared from sight, the sergeant replaced the barrier and returned to his discussion with Wally.

Curious, Skye joined the men. Wally absentmindedly slid his arm around her waist and she rested her head against his shoulder. It wasn't even noon yet and she was exhausted. She should go to the grade school, do the observation she'd scheduled, and finish writing a report, but she could barely keep her eyes open.

Quirk spoke quickly, informing Wally that the two mothers and the older couple hadn't seen anything unusual at Lynch's last night or this morning. He added that the other residents weren't home.

"Call in Martinez to do a door-to-door along the road behind this one," Wally ordered. "And when she is done with that, the folks around here should be back from work so she can do Center Street, too."

Zelda Martinez was Scumble River's newest police officer and the only woman on the force. Zelda had joined the department a little over a year and a half ago. She'd been hired fresh out of college and was still inexperienced in dealing with everyday issues not covered in the curriculum so Wally often assigned her the routine stuff.

"Should I call Anthony in to work with her?" Quirk asked. "He could use the practice and Martinez will have backup if things go south."

"Good idea." Wally nodded.

Anthony was a part-timer. He was also employed by his father, who owned an appliance repair business. Lucky for Wally, the young officer's dad was willing to let his son off at a moment's notice.

"I'm on it, Chief." Quirk grabbed the radio on his shoulder.

"Use your cell," Wally instructed. "Let's keep this under wraps as long as possible. I need to get ahold of

Lynch's mother before someone tells her the cops are at her son's house."

"I think it might be too late." Quirk pointed to a shiny silver Lincoln MKZ pulling to a stop in front of them.

A tall, thin woman in her early seventies exited the car and marched up to Wally. "What's going on, Chief? The Coopersons called to tell me that the police had Palmer's house surrounded. I'm his mother. Where is my son? Does he know you're here? Has there been a burglary?"

"Ma'am," Wally said. "How about if we sit in the squad car and I'll explain."

"I'd rather talk to Palmer." Mrs. Lynch pulled her beige cardigan closed. "I called his home phone and his cell several times this morning, but he didn't answer."

"Mrs. Lynch." Skye glanced at Wally and he nodded his permission. "I'm the police department psych consultant, Skye Denison-Boyd."

"May's daughter?"

"Yes." Skye moved around the barricade and took the woman's arm. "I really think it's best if we sit down so we can tell you everything."

Mrs. Lynch frowned and said, "I may be old, but you don't have to coddle me."

"Did Mom tell you that I'm expecting my first baby?" Skye asked stroking her stomach with her free hand. When Mrs. Lynch nodded, Skye said, "I've been on my feet all morning and could really use a rest."

"Of course." Mrs. Lynch glared at Wally and Quirk. "Men have no idea what it's like to be pregnant. When I was carrying Palmer, my ankles used to swell up to the size of cantaloupes and Palmer Senior, may he rest in peace, would tell me walking would help."

"Wally's been trying to get me to go home and take it

easy," Skye defended her husband. "But I promised your friend Dorothy Snyder that I'd stick around until I was able to speak to you." Skye patted the older woman's shoulder. "Dorothy wanted to make sure you were okay."

"Something bad has happened to Palmer." Mrs. Lynch's face paled.

"I'm afraid so." Skye tugged on the older woman's hand. "Let's sit down in your car and I'll tell you what I can."

Mrs. Lynch nodded, tears already seeping down her wrinkled cheeks.

Skye assisted the older woman onto the passenger seat of the Lincoln, but before she could close the door to walk around the car, the crime scene tech came running out of the detached garage. Blood was dripping from scratches on his face and arms and he yelled, "Someone needs to catch that damn cat or I'm going to shoot it."

CHAPTER 8

*You will be lucky if you know how to make
friends with strange cats.*
—COLONIAL PROVERB

Skye was torn. She couldn't very well leave Mrs. Lynch crying in her car to see what was going on with the cat in Palmer's garage. And since crime scene techs didn't carry guns, she wasn't too worried that the kitty was in any real danger from the guy. Then again, she was anxious to make sure the animal was captured safely.

As Skye vacillated, Wally sent Quirk off to stand guard in the backyard and motioned for her to return to his side of the barricade. She patted the older woman's hand, promised to be right back, then walked over to her husband.

When she reached him, he said in a low voice, "Don't share any details with the vic's mother before I get back from dealing with the cat."

"Not even that he's dead?" Skye whispered. "I already inferred that."

"Nothing." Wally turned toward the detached garage, then paused and added, "On second thought, maybe you should come with me."

"Why?" Skye's chest heaved in indignation. "You don't trust me?"

"That's not it." Wally wrapped an arm around her and smiled. "You have a way with cats. Maybe you can get him to come to you on his own. We can't afford to let him get away. The murderer could have locked him in the garage after killing Lynch. The animal could have evidence caught in its claws or teeth or even clinging to its fur."

"Since you put it that way, okay," Skye conceded. She did seem to attract kids and animals. "What about Mrs. Lynch?" She glanced over her shoulder at the poor woman, who had risen and was standing at the barricade again. "I need to say something to her. I can't just leave."

"Give us a minute," Wally called to the woman, then tried to lead Skye away, but she dug in her heels until he sighed, turned toward Mrs. Lynch, raised his voice, and said, "Skye and I will return shortly. I apologize for the delay, but this needs to be handled immediately."

"Sorry," Skye hollered as Wally tugged her toward the garage. "Hang in there."

The tech was standing with his back to the pedestrian door holding on to the handle as if he thought the cat had grown opposable thumbs and could turn the knob. His skin was dead white and the red scratches stood out like a scene from a horror movie.

As Skye and Wally approached, he blurted out, "I found the key ring in the kitchen just like the chief said. It took me a few minutes to figure out the right one for this door, and when I opened it, some giant demon cat from hell jumped me from above. It was all I could do to get it off me and close it inside the garage."

Skye and Wally glanced at each other. Wally's gaze flitted to her stomach and he frowned, obviously having misgivings about involving his pregnant wife. He opened his mouth, but Skye scowled at him.

Evidently reconsidering what he'd been about to say to her, Wally exhaled and straightened his shoulders. Nodding as if accepting her silent reprimand, he motioned for the tech to move out of the way.

When the guy hesitated, Wally ordered, "Go into the house and see if you can find a can of cat food."

"I didn't notice any food or bowls or litter box," the tech said. "There wasn't any sign of a pet inside that residence."

"I just remembered that Palmer's girlfriend told me he didn't like animals so I doubt this is his cat." Skye exchanged another glance with Wally, then turned to the tech and said, "Look for a can of tuna or salmon."

Once the tech took off toward the house, Wally said, "I'll open the door a crack and you start talking to the cat like you do with Bingo."

"Bingo only listens to me about a tenth of the time," Skye warned.

"Which is ten times more than he listens to anyone else," Wally said as he eased the door open a couple of inches. "Especially me."

"True." Skye sank to her knees and, softening her voice, said, "Mr. Kitty, we're here to help you. If you come out, I'll get you something yummy to eat. I bet you'd like some tuna fish."

Nothing happened. Skye groaned, moved closer to the opening, and sat cross-legged—she was too off balance because of the baby to kneel or squat for long. She continued to speak in a soothing tone, offering food. When there was no response, she promised a variety of toys.

Just as she was about to give up, a gray and white face appeared. Skye reached out and rubbed under the kitty's chin. He purred, half closing his blue eyes, and leaned into her fingers, revving his engine.

Wally opened the door wider and the cat strolled through, climbed on Skye's lap, and wrapped his fluffy tail around her arm. She continued to pet and scratch the kitty as she inspected it.

"Is he okay?" Wally asked, leaning down and stroking the cat's back.

Before answering, Skye examined the tag on the collar. After reading it, she said, "*She* seems fine. And as I suspected, the reason that there's no animal stuff in the house is that this isn't Palmer's pet."

"Then who does she belong to?" Wally asked, wrinkling his brow.

"Princess Honey Bluebell is Dr. Quillen's therapy cat." Skye bit her lip. "I thought I recognized her."

"What's she doing in Lynch's garage?" Wally asked, continuing to pet the cat. "Do you think she got locked in by mistake?"

"I seriously doubt it." Skye passed the kitty to Wally, then held out her hand for him to help her to her feet. "Dr. Quillen called me after I got home from church to tell me he had to cancel the session with my grade school group because Belle had been stolen."

"Shit!" Wally gave the cat back to Skye. "Why didn't I know about that?"

"If I recall correctly, you told me that shortly after I left for school, Mom called you into the PD because of the American Legion break-in." Skye walked back toward the house. "I'm guessing you didn't have time to do anything but handle that situation. Certainly not sit around and read about yesterday's cases."

"Oh. Yeah. Right." Wally ran his fingers through his hair. "Which means, we now have what seems to be three really weird crimes."

"I can't figure out how the Legion break-in fits in, but the fact that a stolen cat was locked in Palmer's garage has to mean something." She smiled as Belle climbed up her chest and draped herself around Skye's neck. "What I can't understand is why Miss Kitty here attacked the crime scene guy. Dr. Quillen would never use her for therapy if she wasn't trained and as gentle as a lamb."

"So she seems." Wally tapped his chin. "Maybe once the tech processes the garage, we'll have more of an idea what set Belle off."

"In the meantime"—Skye gestured toward the woman standing at the barricade—"we really need to talk to Mrs. Lynch. It's cruel making her wait any longer. She looks like she's ready to faint."

"What are we going to do with Belle?" Wally asked. "It's too warm to lock her in the squad car and I don't want to bring her inside the house because any trace she leaves might contaminate forensic evidence of her previous presence in Lynch's place."

"I'll just hold her." Skye shrugged. "Palmer's girlfriend told me that his mother bred prize-winning German shepherds, so she must be an animal lover."

"Who's this girlfriend?" Wally asked as he moved the sawhorses so Skye could walk between them. "And how do you know her so well?"

"Virginia Elders," Skye said. "She's a teacher."

Wally took out a pad and pen from his shirt pocket and made a note.

"Mrs. Lynch," Skye said to the woman when they reached her. "I'm so sorry for keeping you waiting."

"I see you tamed the cat." Mrs. Lynch's tears had disappeared, and she reached out to stroke Belle's fur. "I'm shocked it was in Palmer's garage. He doesn't like animals. He . . . he . . ." She stuttered to a stop, took a deep breath, and asked, "What's happened to him?"

"I'm sorry to inform you that your son is dead," Wally said.

"How?" Mrs. Lynch swayed and Wally reached out to steady her. "Was it a heart attack? I warned him he was working too hard."

"When is the last time you saw him?" Wally ignored the woman's question.

"We spoke on the phone late Saturday afternoon, just before I went to five o'clock Mass."

"Did he tell you what his plans were for the rest of the night?" Wally asked.

"Just the usual." Mrs. Lynch sniffled. "He said he was going to order a pizza, watch the Cubs on television, and go to bed early."

"How about Sunday?"

"Go to church, make some campaign calls about his run for school board president, and work on some bookkeeping for his stores."

Skye was impressed that the older woman was holding up so well, but from the way her hands were shaking and her lips quivering, she would break down any minute. Elbowing Wally, Skye directed his attention to the signs that they were about to lose Mrs. Lynch. He nodded his understanding, opened the Lincoln's passenger door, and eased Palmer's mother onto the seat.

"Skye saw your son at Mass on Sunday." Wally squatted down so that he was eye level with the woman. "Was he planning to go out for brunch with anyone or have them over to this house after that?"

"Not that he told me." Mrs. Lynch's voice trembled and she blinked away the moisture filling her eyes. "He'd recently had a tiff with his lady friend and he hadn't mentioned seeing anyone else."

"I work with Virginia Elders and she told me they were dating just last Monday," Skye said, then glanced at Wally to see if it was okay if she continued. He smiled and Skye asked, "What happened?"

"I don't have the details." Mrs. Lynch frowned. "Palmer said she took offense at something he said, but he was sure that she'd get over it."

"Virginia is pretty easygoing," Skye said. "I wonder what upset her."

"Who knows?" Mrs. Lynch shrugged. "Young people are so politically correct nowadays it could be anything. Palmer had strong opinions and he wasn't shy about sharing them with people."

"So I understand," Skye murmured, stroking Belle's soft fur.

"Mrs. Lynch, where were you last night between eleven and one?" Wally asked.

"I went on a senior trip to Franklin Barn Theatre. The bus left from the bank at three. Dinner was from six thirty to seven thirty and the show started at eight. Afterwards, once everyone used the restroom and such, we left for Scumble River about ten. We arrived back around one. I drove my friend Glory to her place and I walked into my house at one fifteen." Mrs. Lynch frowned, then comprehension dawned in her eyes and she gasped, "Are you asking me if I have an alibi? Oh. My. God! Palmer was murdered?"

With that, Mrs. Lynch burst into hysterical sobs and collapsed against the seat. Skye thrust Belle into Wally's arms, knelt beside the open car door, and took the older woman's hand. She let her cry, handing her the last of the tissues from her purse, which thankfully was still strapped across her chest.

Once Mrs. Lynch's weeping subsided, Skye said, "I can't imagine how awful it is to lose a child, especially to violence, but we really need your help." The older woman sniffled and nodded. "Do you have any idea who would want to harm your son? A business deal gone bad maybe?"

"He didn't talk about that kind of thing with me," Mrs. Lynch said. "He always tried to protect me from the harsher truths."

"What about his personal life?" Wally asked, and

Skye knew he was thinking about the sexual implications of how Palmer's body was found.

"Virginia seemed like a lovely girl." Mrs. Lynch shrugged hopelessly. "And as I said, I'm not aware of anyone else he might have been dating." She paused. "Although that doesn't mean he wasn't seeing another woman. Maybe that's what they fought about."

There was an uneasy expression on Mrs. Lynch's face, and Skye wondered if the woman knew more than she was sharing about her son's love life. Even if that were true, this wasn't the time to push her to reveal it.

After several more questions, Skye could tell that Wally was wrapping up the interview. She tugged him aside and whispered, "Can I tell Mrs. Lynch about Palmer being tied up, et cetera? I think she'll react better with it coming from me and maybe be more open regarding what she knows about her son's sex life."

"I want to keep that quiet as long as possible." Wally rubbed his cheek. "Although I'm not sure how long Dorothy will last before blabbing."

"From what she said to me, Dorothy is afraid of somehow being tarnished from the same brush of this scandal. I sincerely doubt she'll tell anyone," Skye reassured him. "And there is no way in heaven that Mrs. Lynch is going to share the information."

"Okay." Wally squinted at the broken woman sitting with her head in her hands. "But first let me confirm her alibi with the bank's Senior Club director, then warn Mrs. Lynch not to say a word about the murder."

"How about if I drive her home?" Skye suggested. "She's in no shape to be behind the wheel of a car. I can tell her about Palmer then."

"Good idea." Wally gave Skye a one-armed hug, then gestured to the cat he was holding. "What about Princess Honey Bluebell here?"

"Want me to call Dr. Quillen?" Skye offered. "I'm

sure he'll be relieved she's okay and will come right over here and get her."

"You do that, but don't give him any information other than that his cat has been located. While you telephone him, I'll go round up the crime scene tech to process her for evidence. Then I'll contact the bank's activity director." Wally started toward the garage, but paused and said, "I better get the guy in the house to handle Belle. The one in the garage might still be bleeding and holding a grudge."

Skye dug out her cell and made the call to the vet. Ten minutes later, Dr. Quillen's Ford E-450 pulled up behind Mrs. Lynch's Lincoln. The white cutaway van had STANLEY COUNTY MOBILE VETERINARY CLINIC painted in blue on the side along with yellow and brown paw prints climbing up and over the roof.

The vet burst from the vehicle and raced toward Skye. He skidded to a stop in front of her and demanded, "Where's Belle?"

"The tech is processing her." Reading the worry in the vet's face, Skye added, "She seems to be fine, but this is a crime scene."

"Wow." Dr. Quillen seemed to look around for the first time and said, "I'm impressed. I had the impression that the officer that took my report about Belle's catnapping wasn't going to do much to find her."

"I'm not aware of what was put into place regarding that search," Skye hedged, thinking that the vet's assessment was probably correct. Missing animals didn't get much attention. "Belle was discovered during another investigation."

Wally joined them before the vet could respond and introduced himself, then said, "The tech is almost through. We'll bring her to you as soon as he's finished scraping under her claws."

"Great."

Wally steered Dr. Quillen toward his van, with Skye trailing behind. "Belle has been a perfect lady since she came to Skye, but she attacked the first crime scene tech when he entered the garage. Do you have any idea why she'd act that way?"

"She's the most docile cat that I've ever worked with." Dr. Quillen looked at Skye. "You've seen her with the boys in your group."

"Exactly." Skye patted the vet's arm. "That's why her behavior seems so odd. All the guy did was walk into the garage. He didn't threaten her in any way. He said she leaped on his head from above."

"The only explanation that I can think of is that she was drugged," Dr. Quillen said. "I received a call Sunday night from a guy who claimed to have Belle and wanted me to supply him with ketamine to get her back."

"Did you recognize the number or the voice?" Wally demanded.

"The ID was blocked and the voice was mechanically altered."

"Did you agree?" Skye asked gently. "Did you set up the exchange?"

"I told him I needed time to get the pharmaceutical as I don't keep much in the clinic." Dr. Quillen winced. "I didn't want to give him the drugs."

"Of course not," Skye said sympathetically.

The vet wiped the sweat from his brow with the back of his hand. "The catnapper told me I had until Tuesday. If I didn't give him the ketamine by then, he'd send me one of Belle's paws. And every day after that, I'd get another piece of her."

CHAPTER 9

No matter how much cats fight, there always
seem to be plenty of kittens.
—ABRAHAM LINCOLN

Skye watched Dr. Quillen drive away with Princess Honey Bluebell. Wally had questioned him about the catnapping and the ransom call, but he had had nothing meaningful to add. After advising him that the police would want to talk to him further, Wally allowed the vet to leave.

Since the animal clinic had been closed Sunday and Monday, Wally had expressed hope there still might be some usable evidence present and had ordered the crime scene techs to process the break-in as soon as they finished with the murder scene. Dr. Quillen had been cautioned not to touch anything until after they were finished. The vet had promised full cooperation and stated that he'd make himself available anytime that Wally needed him.

As Dr. Quillen's van disappeared from sight, Skye turned to Wally and asked, "So was Palmer the catnapper? Or do you think maybe the catnapper killed him and for some unknown reason put Belle in his garage to frame him for the crime?"

"Your guess is as good as mine." Wally shrugged, then pointed to Mrs. Lynch. "You better drive her home.

She looks as if she's fading fast. Maybe on the ride you can ask her if she knows anything about her son taking ketamine."

"Yeah." Skye rolled her eyes. "Right after I tell her about the kinky sex stuff."

Wally's expression was sheepish as he said, "Reid and the crime techs are just about done here, and I'll leave Quirk to watch over the scene." He kissed Skye on the cheek. "I'll pick you up at Mrs. Lynch's in twenty minutes or so. We can grab some lunch somewhere nice while you fill me in on her reactions."

"Sounds good." Skye started toward the Lincoln. "I'm starving."

Wally grabbed her arm. "Do you need to eat something right now?"

"No." Skye waved her hand. "Juniorette and I can wait a little longer."

Before Wally could answer, the tech that Belle had attacked came up to him and announced, "We're finished here and the coroner is ready to remove the body. Want to take one last look to make sure we processed all the areas you're interested in before we go?"

"Sure." Wally squeezed Skye's fingers and said, "See you in a few."

It had taken a bit of persuasion, and all of Skye's counseling skills, but Mrs. Lynch had ultimately agreed that it was best if Skye drove her home. The older woman told Skye that her house was by the north bend in the river and had been built by her grandfather over a hundred and fifty years ago—before Scumble River had even officially existed.

While Skye slowly navigated the narrow street, she examined Palmer's mother and decided this was as good a time as any to tell her how her son had died. She wanted to have the conversation in the car so that she could control the environment, and depending on traffic, which was generally nonexistent, the ride would take less than ten minutes.

"Mrs. Lynch," Skye said hesitantly, "we told you that Palmer was murdered. But we didn't explain the circumstances of his death."

"What do you mean?" Mrs. Lynch asked, a puzzled expression on her pale face. "I assumed he'd been killed during a home invasion."

"That's certainly still a possibility." Skye braked at the stop sign on the corner of Kinsman and Maryland Streets. "But there may be more to it than that."

"What do you mean?" Mrs. Lynch's voice was heavy with dread.

"I'm so sorry to have to tell you this"—Skye looked both ways, then eased the Lincoln across the intersection—"but your son was found nude. He was bound to his bed and wearing a blindfold."

"Oh." Mrs. Lynch stared out the windshield for several seconds, then said, "Will those details be released to the public?"

"My husband is going to try to keep them quiet." Skye wondered why Mrs. Lynch didn't seem more shocked. "Presently only Wally, the county crime scene techs, the coroner, Dorothy, and I saw him like that."

"But there's a good chance it will get out." Mrs. Lynch's mouth thinned. "I should have confronted Palmer when I found those magazines."

"What kind of magazines?" Skye asked, although she had a darn good idea.

"Smut." Mrs. Lynch scowled. "Naked people being tied up and . . ."

"I get the picture," Skye said quietly. "When did you discover them?"

"A year or so ago." Mrs. Lynch sighed. "He didn't hire Dorothy until he'd been divorced awhile and I

used to do his laundry and grocery shopping for him."
She quirked a brow. "He's my only child, so I suppose
I spoiled him a little bit."

Skye smiled her understanding, thinking of how much
her own mother tried to do for her and her brother. Thinking of May's obsessive need to be acquainted with every
detail of her children's lives, Skye figured Mrs. Lynch
knew more about her son's habits than the man thought.

"Palmer had someone do the heavy cleaning, but
while the clothes were washing, I'd tidy up." She slid a
glance at Skye then continued, "When I was dusting
his bedroom, I noticed that the mattress was sitting
funny on the box spring, so I shoved it over."

"And the magazines were there," Skye guessed. "It's
perfectly understandable that you didn't speak to your
son about them. He was a grown man and what he did
in the privacy of his own home was no one's business but
his and his partner's." She paused then added, "That is,
as long as the relationship was consensual."

"Maybe that was what he and Virginia fought about,"
Mrs. Lynch murmured.

"It's certainly something to consider," Skye agreed,
knowing Wally was undoubtedly intending to investi-
gate that possibility.

"Virginia was the first woman since my son and Felicia
split up whom he dated seriously," Mrs. Lynch offered.
"And he's been single for over a year."

"Why did he and his wife separate?" Skye asked.
She hadn't realized that Palmer was divorced, but at
his age it made sense. It was rare to find an unattached
man in his late forties who didn't have an ex or hadn't
been widowed.

"Irreconcilable differences was the official reason."
Mrs. Lynch shrugged. "But I suspect it was because Felicia had been diagnosed with multiple sclerosis. My son
saw her illness as a weakness."

"I see." Skye kept the disgust she felt for Palmer's actions from her voice, then forced herself to ask, "I hate to bring this up and I can't tell you why I'm asking, but are you aware of any reason Palmer might want to secure a large amount of ketamine?"

"Palmer did not use drugs if that's what you want to know." Mrs. Lynch folded her arms and glared at Skye. "My son might have had unusual sexual preferences, but he was too much of a control freak to take any form of recreational pharmaceuticals."

After making that statement, Mrs. Lynch was silent except to tell Skye when to turn. Following the older woman's directions, Skye realized that Palmer's mother lived just to the west of Red Raggers' territory.

Two groups of people dwelled in an uneasy alliance along the river. There were the upstanding citizens, like Mrs. Lynch, who either had inherited the land or bought it for their retirement homes, and the others who the locals disparagingly called the Red Raggers.

The Red Raggers was a group that consisted mostly of loosely related individuals who lived near one another on a two-mile stretch of land beside the Scumble River. Skye likened the group to a pack of wild hyenas. They were extremely loyal to their own kinfolk, but lacked the ability or desire to care about anyone else. They weren't known for being the brightest gems in Scumble River's crown, but they did have a talent for stumbling on, and taking advantage of, those who were even lesser jewels.

As the car approached the river, Skye's heart raced—and not from concern that she was entering the Red Ragger zone. It was the darn bridge. She knew it was silly, she'd crossed the one-lane structure that would take them to Cattail Path many times, but lately she'd been avoiding it.

The first time that she'd driven several miles out of

her way rather than drive across the shaky surface, she'd told herself that her fear was due to the fact that a lunatic had tried to kill her there.

But she knew she was lying to herself. Although she'd been forced to crash her car over the side in order to save herself, that had happened several years ago, and she'd never been afraid to drive over it before. So what had caused her sudden paranoia?

Maybe it was the narrow planks of wood that vehicles were supposed to position their tires on in order to cross safely that scared her. Wally had been telling the mayor that the city needed to widen that bridge or at least pave it, but his recommendation had fallen on deaf ears.

Still, the structure was in no worse shape than a few months ago when she'd crossed it several times a week. What was different now?

The only reason she could come up with was that she was pregnant. As a psychologist, she knew that it wasn't uncommon for people on the threshold of an enormous life-changing event to develop phobias. Even good changes—and lately she'd had a lot of those—could cause anxiety.

After being jilted a few months before her thirtieth birthday, Skye had prepared herself for the reality that she might never find her soul mate. Never have a baby. Never have a family. Then suddenly the man she had always loved was free to love her back.

In what seemed like the blink of an eye, she was married and pregnant. There were times she still couldn't believe it was true and she half expected to wake up alone, broke, and unemployed. The same way she arrived in Scumble River seven years ago.

It occurred to Skye that she was terrified that it all would be taken away. That Wally and the baby might vanish into thin air if she made one poor decision. Like choosing to cross a wobbly old bridge.

Glancing at Mrs. Lynch, a woman who had just lost her only child, Skye felt panic clawing at her throat. What if something happened to her baby? Or to Wally? He was a police officer. That was a dangerous profession. He could be shot. Or held hostage. Or—

Taking a deep breath, Skye forced herself to calm down. She clenched her jaw and slowly started the Lincoln over the rickety structure. A frisson of fear burned down her spine when she heard the hollow thumping sounds that the car's tires made on the wooden boards.

Clutching the steering wheel, she silently chanted, "The bridge is safe. I'm safe. The baby's safe. We will all live happily ever after."

A few seconds later, pulse still racing and perspiration dripping down the back of her neck, she turned the Lincoln onto Cattail Path. A mile after that, she pulled the car into Mrs. Lynch's driveway, turned off the engine, and placed the keys in the woman's outstretched hand. They both exited the vehicle and walked up the steps to the porch of a large, well-maintained Victorian.

Mrs. Lynch unlocked the door, then reluctantly said, "Would you like to come inside?"

"Is there someone you can call?" Skye asked. "A relative who could stay with you?"

"My sister lives in Laurel." Mrs. Lynch sighed. "She'll come over. But first, I need a few minutes by myself. Then I'll telephone her."

Understanding the woman's desire to be alone with her grief, Skye said, "You go ahead. I'll sit on the swing here and enjoy your beautiful yard while I wait for my husband to pick me up."

It was a little before two when Wally's squad car pulled into Mrs. Lynch's driveway and Skye hurried down the steps to meet him. Skye had developed an awful hunger headache and she really hoped he didn't have to be somewhere before he fed her. To make it worse, the baby must be pressing on her bladder because she had to pee.

As soon as the cruiser rolled to a stop, Skye hopped in and said, "I need a bathroom sooner than later."

"Wouldn't Mrs. Lynch let you use hers?" Wally shot an angry glance at the old Victorian's closed front door.

"She wanted some time alone to process her son's death," Skye explained, warmed by his concern. "I certainly wasn't going to bother her with my little problem."

"You need to stop being so damn nice."

Skye ignored his comment and asked, "Where are we going for lunch?"

"I was thinking we'd try that new restaurant in Clay Center," Wally said. "But it'll take fifteen minutes to get there."

Skye's mouth watered. Everyone had been talking about Pesto's food. Crossing her legs, she said, "I think I can make it."

"I can always use the sirens," Wally teased with a lopsided grin.

"It might come to that, but I'm okay for now." Skye gripped her purse as he reversed onto the road and peeled rubber. "Not that I'm not thrilled with your company, but I'm surprised you're willing to leave town with a fresh murder case."

"Quirk's holding down the fort at the scene and co-ordinating Martinez's and Anthony's house-to-house canvass for possible witnesses." Wally sped up to pass a slow-moving tractor. "The crime techs are working at Dr. Quillen's clinic and Reid's on his way to Laurel to drop off the vic at the ME's."

"How long do you think it will take the medical examiner to give an official cause and time of death?" Skye squirmed in her seat.

"Depends if there's any bodies ahead of us." Wally shrugged.

Remembering his question to Mrs. Lynch, Skye said, "I take it that eleven p.m. to one a.m. is Simon's estimate for the TOD."

"Yep." Wally lifted a brow. "I'm hoping the ME can narrow it down some."

"So you don't need to be at the PD?" Skye asked, still surprised he was willing to take the time to have lunch with her.

"Nope." Wally turned the car onto the road leading to Clay Center. "Next of kin is notified and I want to get my ducks in a row before doing interviews."

"Makes sense." Skye recrossed her legs. She really had to go.

"Besides, nothing is more important than you." Wally traced a finger down her cheek. "You seemed a little shaken up after everything this morning and I wanted to make sure you had a decent meal."

"That is so sweet, but I'm fine—starving and in dire need of a ladies' room—but otherwise fine." Skye grabbed his hand and kissed his palm. "Although I am glad we can have an uninterrupted conversation because it seems like there are so many pieces to this puzzle and I don't want to forget to tell you anything."

"Hold on to that thought." Wally turned into the restaurant lot, parked the car, and got out to open Skye's door. "Let's find you the bathroom first."

After the pause that refreshes, Skye located Wally in a corner booth. He was sipping a glass of iced tea, and there was a Diet Coke with a lime wedge waiting for her. She slid onto the bench and took a long drink, then, her stomach growling, she grabbed the menu sitting on the tabletop and scanned the selections.

Once they'd placed their orders, Skye finally looked around the restaurant. It was bright and cheerful with a wall of windows facing the street. The décor was modern, but welcoming, and the air smelled of oregano, garlic, and melting cheese.

Skye sighed in contentment. A yummy lunch with her handsome husband was a real luxury. If she were at school, she'd be lucky to grab a sandwich between meetings. She felt a twinge of remorse, knowing she wouldn't be enjoying this treat if Palmer Lynch were still alive.

To assuage her guilt, Skye was determined to work on finding his killer. She might not have liked the man, but she'd do her best to get him justice.

With that in mind, she asked, "Did the crime scene techs find anything interesting?"

"Lynch had a concealed closet full of fetish gear." Wally tilted his head and quirked his lips. "You know what that is, right?"

"Of course I do. I'm not that naïve. I had a very enlightening class on human sexuality in graduate school." Skye's cheeks turned pink. "One of our assigned readings was *The Story of O*."

"My criminal justice courses didn't include that book." Wally winked. "Should I pick up a copy?"

"Absolutely not!" Skye choked on the sip of water she'd just taken.

"Just checking." Still chuckling, Wally asked, "Was Lynch's mother aware of his tastes?"

"To a certain extent." Skye paused as the server put a basket of warm bread on the table. "She found some magazines when she was cleaning his house."

"Did they discuss it?" Wally asked, tearing off a piece of the loaf.

"No. In fact, she regrets not confronting him." Skye broke off her own slice.

"Between the kinky sex, the drugs, the catnapping, and everything he was promising for the school board president election, Lynch was a man with a lot of secrets."

Wally dragged the bread through the dish of olive oil and popped it into his mouth.

"I wonder which one got him killed?" Skye asked, then frowned and added, "And with all of Palmer's secrets about to become public, let's hope no one else is in danger."

CHAPTER 10

*Women and cats will do as they please, and men and
dogs should relax and get used to the idea.*
— ROBERT A. HEINLEIN

"Good point. Any time secrets get revealed, people get hurt." Wally licked the oil off his fingers. "Any guess which one of Lynch's secrets caused his murder?"

"Well, since he was naked, I'd go with sex as a motive first." She hesitated, then said, "Which means Virginia is the . . ."

Noticing that their server was approaching, Skye paused as the woman placed their lunches in front of them. After asking if they needed anything else and acknowledging their refusal, she left them to their meal.

Immediately, Skye bit into her veggie panini and moaned. The roasted peppers, mushrooms, red onions, lettuce, tomato, and provolone cheese tasted heavenly. Either the chef was really good or she was really hungry. Probably both.

Wally watched her in amusement, then sampled his rib-eye steak sandwich. A Texas native, he was a carnivore, and he often told Skye that he liked vegetables— in their place on the side of his plate.

"I was thinking along those lines too," Wally said

after he swallowed. "So tell me about the girlfriend. You mentioned that you work with her."

"Virginia teaches fourth grade. She has three of the boys in my counseling group in her class. So after the initial pet therapy session started out so badly, I talked to her to make sure the kids were okay. That's when she mentioned dating Palmer."

"Is she divorced, widowed, or never married?" Wally asked.

"Divorced." Skye sampled her French fries and nearly swooned at the salty goodness.

"How long had she and Lynch been seeing each other?" Wally asked.

"I'm not sure." Skye wrinkled her brow, thinking. "Mrs. Lynch said that her son divorced his wife a little over a year ago, and Virginia was his first serious relationship after he and his ex went their separate ways."

"If Virginia told you last Monday they were going out, their breakup was less than a week ago." Wally ate half of his baked potato before he said, "We need to know what caused her to end things."

"Definitely." Skye finished her Panini. "I really like her, but sadly, Virginia is our most likely suspect." Skye brightened. "Unless, after she dumped him, Palmer hooked up with someone else."

"At the very least, Virginia should be able to tell us about his alternative lifestyle." Wally polished off the last of his sandwich.

"Speaking of that, was there anything odd in the garage?" Skye pushed her empty plate away. "Anything to explain why Belle attacked the tech?"

"Not really." Wally signaled the server and asked for the dessert menus. Once they were delivered and the waitress walked to another table, he said, "The usual. His car, a lawn mower, a snowmobile, a motorcycle, a boat—"

"Wow. Palmer really liked his toys. He must have been pretty well off." Skye scanned the list of tempting treats. "Or in a lot of debt."

"Good point." Wally took out his note pad and jotted something down. "We need to get a warrant to look at his financial situation."

"But nothing in the garage to give us an idea about the cat's behavior?" Skye asked.

Before Wally could answer, the server returned. Skye had intended to skip dessert, but she caved in and asked for the fudge cake. She'd do a few extra laps at the pool the next morning. After all, chocolate was plainly God's way of saying he liked her a little curvy. And she didn't want Juniorette to feel deprived.

Once the waitress left, Wally said, "We found a cage. It had food and water, but no litter box. Judging from Bingo's fastidiousness, my guess is that Belle refused to pee where she slept—it was a fairly small pen—so she managed to somehow open the latch."

"I wonder if she thought that the crime tech was the person who locked her up and she was defending herself," Skye mused. "From what I've seen during the therapy sessions, Belle seems pretty darn smart."

"Beats me." Wally smiled at the server as she brought his tiramisu. He waited until she poured coffee for each of them—decaf for Skye—and left, then said, "Probably a mystery we'll never solve."

"Too bad cats can't talk," Skye mumbled around a mouthful of fudgy bliss.

"If they could, Bell might be our prime witness." Wally grinned at her obvious pleasure in the cake. "But since she's refusing to cooperate, let's figure out who else we need to interrogate."

"Besides Virginia"—Skye put down her fork and held up a finger—"Dr. Wraige and Pru Cormorant." Skye summarized the conversation she'd heard after church between the school superintendent and the English teacher, concluding with the statement that Dr. Wraige had promised to keep an eye on Palmer and handle him if he became a problem. "We need to know what the issue was and why Pru thought they couldn't trust him."

"Absolutely." Wally sipped his coffee. "You mentioned overhearing others that were beginning to catch on that Lynch might be making a lot of promises he wouldn't be able to keep. Any names?"

"Tony Zello and Nate Turner." Skye stirred sweetener and cream into her decaf. "And a deacon named Joel. I can't recall his last name."

Wally made a note, then took Skye's hand and said, "You know that I'll have to talk to Charlie." She winced and he stroked her palm. "He and Lynch were in a very public battle for control of the school board. There's no way I can avoid questioning him."

"I understand." Skye blew out a breath. "Let's just pray he has an alibi."

"That late at night, most people won't," Wally warned gently.

"Our only hope is that he had one of his many girlfriends sleep over."

"That'll be awkward." Wally's lips twitched. "Probably not an interview you want to sit in on." Sobering, he added, "Anyone else we need to consider as a suspect? You said Lynch and the grade school principal had words over the pet therapy."

"If you think Caroline Greer might be a suspect due to that incident, you'd have to add me to that list." Skye raised a brow as she sipped her coffee.

"Don't worry, darlin'. You have the best alibi of anyone." Wally leered playfully. "You were in bed with the chief of police."

"Lucky me." Skye smiled widely. "Still, Caroline

should be at the bottom of our list. She didn't seem very threatened by Palmer."

"I trust your instincts." Wally nodded, then asked, "Anyone else?"

"I hate to say it, but Dr. Quillen." Skye bit her lip. "If he figured out that Palmer was the catnapper, he might have done something rash. Dr. Q loves his animals and would be incensed if one was mistreated." She perked up. "But he wouldn't have left Belle in the garage."

"If he knew she was there." Wally ate the last bite of tiramisu and crossed his arms. "I'm definitely having a conversation with him."

"Hmm." Skye pressed her fork into the chocolate crumbs on her plate and licked the tines. "How about Palmer's ex-wife? According to his own mother, he dumped Felicia because she was diagnosed with multiple sclerosis. I'd sure as hell be furious if you divorced me because of an illness that I had no control over."

"Which I would never do," Wally assured her, leaning across the table to press a soft kiss to her lips. "Until death do us part."

"I know." Skye kissed him back. "How about his employees? He owned a string of shops in several of the surrounding small towns."

"The Dollar or Three stores," Wally confirmed, signaling the server for their check. "There are four or five of them, right?"

"Let's see." Skye closed her eyes. "They're in Scumble River, Clay Center, Brooklyn, and . . . I think there's one more location."

"I'll have Martinez check it out." Wally dug his wallet out of his back pocket. "Do you need to use the bathroom again before we go?"

Although Skye wanted to snap at Wally for treating her like a child, she forced herself to smile sweetly at him. "Probably a good idea." Because, in fact, she really should empty her bladder in case something came up on the way home.

The fifteen-minute ride could easily turn into something a lot longer. It would be so embarrassing to have an accident while in hot pursuit of a possible murderer.

After availing herself to the facilities, Skye found Wally waiting for her at the restaurant's entrance. He escorted her to the cruiser, opened her door, and helped her inside. They were both silent, lost in their own thoughts, as he drove her to the school to pick up her car.

It was only after he kissed her good-bye and she headed the Bel Air toward home that she realized that they hadn't discussed the ketamine. If Palmer was indeed the catnapper, what was his interest in the drug?

Skye was still contemplating why a man like Lynch would want to secure a large amount of ketamine, when she turned into her driveway and swore. A large white car was parked in front of the sidewalk leading up to her porch. The only one in town who drove an Oldsmobile Eighty-Eight was Skye's mother. What was May doing there?

Instead of following her first impulse, which was to throw the Bel Air into reverse, Skye blew out a breath and pulled into the garage. Gathering up her belongings, Skye trudged toward the house. She slowly climbed the stairs and tried the knob, not surprised that it turned without having to use her key. May wasn't a fan of locked doors.

As she stepped inside, Skye's nose twitched at the distinctive odor wafting down the hallway. Her mother loved to clean so much that Skye and her brother joked that if May had Windex in her hand, it was best to keep a safe distance or you might find yourself covered in the blue liquid.

Dropping her purse and tote on the hall bench, Skye followed the smell into the sunroom. May was concentrating so hard on the window she was polishing, she didn't see Skye at first, but when she did, she put down the bottle and rags and hurried toward her.

"Are you okay? Is my grandchild okay? Where have you been?" May demanded, grabbing her daughter's arms and gently shaking her. "Roy said that you drove Mrs. Lynch home a couple of hours ago."

"I'm fine. The baby's fine. We're all fine." Skye was getting tired of reassuring everyone about her and Juniorette's well-being. She eased out of her mother's grasp. "When Wally picked me up, he suggested we go to the new restaurant in Clay Center."

"You went to lunch during a murder investigation?" May's tone was doubtful.

"Yes." Skye shrugged. "I hadn't had anything since breakfast and I needed to eat."

"What's wrong with the Feed Bag here in town? Or McDonald's?"

Suspicion glimmered in May's emerald green eyes. She patted her short salt-and-pepper hair and tilted her head, examining Skye.

"I'm trying to cut back on fast food and we've been to the Feed Bag so many times I have the menu memorized." Skye shrugged. "Wally just wanted to treat me to a nice meal after I spent my morning with a dead body."

"Wally doesn't generally go off to have a leisurely lunch a few hours after a murder has been committed." May fingered the crease in her perfectly ironed tan capris. "Did you two have a fight?"

"No! Why the heck would you assume that?" Skye was tired, and between the day's events and May's hovering, her temper flared. "I'm married to a wonderful guy that I love more than life itself. I'm pregnant with our first child. We both are gainfully employed with little or no debt. What do I need to do to prove to you

that I'm a successful adult? What more do you want
from me, Mom?"

"How can you talk to me like that?" May sniffed,
then clutched her chest. "It just seemed odd that you
two would leave town."

"We wanted a few minutes of peace." Skye ignored
her mother's nonverbal threat of a heart attack. During Skye's teenage years, May had often claimed she
couldn't breathe and was having a coronary whenever
Skye or her brother did something that displeased her.
"Is that too much to ask?"

Skye patted her baby bump and pasted a sad look
on her face. Now that she was carrying May's grandchild, two could play the guilt game.

"No. Of course not." May nudged her daughter toward the sofa. "Why don't you sit down and I'll go get
you a glass of water."

"Milk would be better." Skye hid her smile at May's
about-face.

"I brought some of the lemon bars that I baked yesterday." May hurried away. "I know they're your favorite. I'll put a couple of those on a plate for you, too."

"No, thank you. I already had dessert," Skye called
after her mother.

But either May didn't hear her or chose to ignore
Skye's words because, a few minutes later, May returned
with Skye's snack. She placed it on the coffee table and
took a seat next to her daughter.

"When I got off of work, I went to see Dorothy."
May reached for a cookie. "She told me all about finding Palmer Lynch dead."

"What did she say?" Skye asked carefully, unsure of
how much Dorothy had revealed and not wanting to
add to what May already knew.

"That she arrived early so that she'd have time to
clean for you." May shot Skye an accusing glance and

muttered, "I don't know why you don't just let me do your house instead of hiring someone."

"What else did Dorothy tell you?" Skye ignored her mother, who had been repeating that same sentiment since Wally announced that he was bringing his cleaning lady with him into the marriage.

"The back door was open, and when she went to get the sheets to wash, she found Palmer in bed dead so she called you," May reported.

"Is that all?" Skye crossed her fingers that Dorothy had kept to herself the fact that Palmer was nude and tied up.

"That's all Dorothy said." May's eyes narrowed. "What else is there?"

"Uh." Skye thought fast. "We found Dr. Quillen's cat in Palmer's garage."

"What was Palmer doing with that animal?" May asked, a look of distaste on her face. She was not fond of indoor pets. "Had it run away?"

"No." Skye took a sip of milk, but resisted the lemon bars. "Belle was Dr. Quillen's therapy cat. She was stolen from the veterinary clinic sometime between Saturday night and Sunday morning."

She opened her mouth to mention the ransom call, but stopped herself. That might be something Wally wanted kept quiet.

"How odd. A stolen animal, a break-in at the American Legion, and a murder all within the same twenty-four to forty-eight hours." May scrunched up her face. "What's going on around here?"

"My thoughts exactly," Skye agreed. "I can sort of see how the cat and the murder might end up being related, but not the break-in."

"Why would the animal have anything to do with Palmer's death?"

"I don't know." Skye shrugged, then gave in to

temptation and picked up a cookie. "But at least they are geographically connected."

"Yeah." May ate the last bite of her lemon square and dusted the powdered sugar from her fingers. "The Legion is all the way across town."

"Why would anyone decide to burglarize the American Legion Hall?" Skye allowed the buttery cookie to melt in her mouth, then asked, "How much could they possibly hope to get?"

"Well." May stood, retrieved her cleaning supplies, and went back to washing the sunroom's windows. "The King of Diamonds raffle currently has a prize worth thirty-two thousand dollars." May scrubbed at a stubborn streak. "That would certainly be enough for folks to consider stealing."

Skye inhaled sharply. "That's for sure. A lot of people have killed for less."

CHAPTER 11

In a cat's eye, all things belong to cats.
—ENGLISH PROVERB

Relieved that her mother's attention had been diverted from the murder, Skye said, "Tell me about this King of Diamonds raffle."

"It started as a little fund-raiser for the Legion, but it just got bigger and bigger," May said while continuing her pursuit of sparkling windows. "They have it every Sunday night at seven o'clock."

"What exactly is it?" Skye mumbled around the second lemon bar she'd shoved into her mouth.

She really had to stop eating like this. Either that or quit worrying about it. She so didn't want to regress to that person she'd been in high school. The one who obsessed about calories and her dress size.

"The object of the game is to find the king of diamonds," May explained, moving on to the next window. "They take a deck of cards, including the two jokers, and number them from one to fifty-four on the back. Then the cards are taped facedown on a huge whiteboard."

"Uh-huh." Skye nodded her understanding, gesturing for May to continue. "Do the people playing buy a certain number?"

"Not exactly." May closed her eyes, clearly trying to visualize the process. "For five bucks they get a raffle ticket and write their choice of number on it. At seven o'clock a name is pulled from the entries, and if that person has picked the right card, they win."

"And if they don't, the money rolls into the next week's pot," Skye guessed, then did a little mental math. "If there's thirty-two thousand dollars, I assume no one has won in a while."

"Almost three months," May confirmed. "This is the longest it's been between winners, and that means it's the biggest prize."

"Wow." Skye shook her head. "If no one wins, does the number they picked come off the board?" Then she answered herself. "Of course it does, because it's been revealed as a loser."

"Right." May sprayed Windex on the next pane. "So every time someone picks the wrong number, there are fewer and fewer cards left."

"When someone finally does win . . ." Skye stopped to take a sip of milk, swallowed, then continued, "Do they get the entire amount?"

"If the person is there, they get seventy percent of the pot," May answered distractedly as she used her fingernail to scrape something from the window. "If not, they only get forty-five percent."

"So the Legion gets thirty to fifty-five percent of the proceeds and sells a lot of booze and snacks while people wait for the drawing."

"Exactly." May frowned. "It's actually turning into a bit of a problem."

"Why?" Skye glanced down at the last cookie on the plate and sighed.

"Because while folks can buy their tickets at any time throughout the week, they all want to be there when the drawing happens so they can win the big money." May put her hands on her hips. "People are coming in from all over the county to play."

"Ah." Skye rested her hands on her stomach in an effort not to grab the final lemon bar. "That means heavy traffic clogging the streets leading to the American Legion and parking issues for the businesses and houses nearby. I bet the Legion's neighbors are thrilled."

"When I've dispatched on those nights, we get a lot of complaints."

"I can imagine," Skye said, envisioning the average Scumble Riverite's reaction. "Anything besides traffic jams and cars blocking driveways?"

"Some guy claimed that the Legion's parking lot was a hotbed of drug deals and prostitution." May snorted. "But it's the same man who's always writing letters in that gripe column in the *Star*."

The local newspaper had added a section that encouraged its readers to voice their opinions. Occasionally there was something positive, but more often than not, the content was negative.

"I've been saying attempted burglary, but did the thieves actually get the money?" Skye asked. "Would the Legion keep that amount in cash?"

"No and yes," May answered, finishing with the windows and tucking the bottle of Windex and used rags into her large purse. "The safe wasn't opened and evidently it was too heavy for them to carry out of the building because it wasn't moved." May shrugged. "But the cash *was* inside. One of the big draws of the raffle is seeing the pile of dough in this clear box they keep next to the whiteboard with the cards."

"Well, I'm glad they didn't get the money." Skye drank the last of her milk, still resisting the lemon bar staring at her from the coffee table. "Was the woman who locked herself in the closet okay?"

"Chantal was fine when she was with me or Zelda.

Heck, she even was answering the nonemergency police line although I told her only employees were allowed to touch the phones and she sure as shooting doesn't work for the PD. But the minute any of the male officers were around, she was suddenly overcome with hysteria over her ordeal of being at the Legion during the break-in." May looped her purse straps over her arm, then picked up Skye's empty glass and the cookie plate. "She's a dead ringer for Miranda Lambert, even down to that Texas twang. And the skirt and top she was wearing weren't much bigger than two washcloths."

"Really?" Skye chewed her thumbnail. Maybe she hadn't been as paranoid as she thought when Chantal hung up on her earlier. Skye forced a casual tone into her voice and asked, "Any guy in particular?"

"Chantal appeared to be an equal opportunity flirt." May headed toward the kitchen with Skye at her heels. "Although she seemed like the type of gal who would start at the top and work her way down."

"Oh." Skye caught a glimpse of herself reflected in the microwave door and bit her lip. She'd gotten used to being curvy, but . . .

May returned the sole remaining lemon bar to the Tupperware container holding the rest of the batch and placed the empty plate in the sink. Turning from the counter, she stared at Skye's face, wrinkled her brow, then walked over to hug her.

"Wally loves you like mad," May whispered into her daughter's hair. "You can see it in his eyes every time he looks at you."

"I know." Skye leaned into her mother's embrace and absorbed her unexpected reassurance. "But I'm having a harder time than I thought I would with looking"— she pointed to her middle—"like this."

With a final squeeze, May let go of Skye and stepped back. "Then I guess," she said as she moved toward the kitchen counter, "I should take the rest of these cookies home. Not to mention the chicken parmesan and garlic bread I put in the refrigerator for your supper."

"Let's not get crazy." Skye stood in front of the fridge to protect her dinner.

She'd been wondering what she could cook, since on Mondays, Dorothy usually did the grocery shopping and prepared their evening meal after she cleaned. *Hmm.* It looked as if a visit to the supermarket was in Skye's immediate future. Their cupboards were nearly bare.

May's teasing voice refocused Skye's attention to the present. "Only if you promise to stop worrying about your husband not finding you attractive now that you're pregnant."

"I know it's silly." Skye hated it when her mother was the voice of reason in their discussions. "And I know women will always flirt with him."

"He's a good-looking man." May marched down the hall to the foyer. "You have to come to terms with the fact that gals will come on to him."

"You're right." Skye's head was spinning. This was not like any other conversation she'd had with her mom. "Wally would never cheat on me, but since I started showing, it feels as if all the other women look so beautiful and perfect next to my beach ball belly." She sniffed. "I can't even find clothes that I like."

"Oh, honey." May tsked. "Every woman who has ever had a baby goes through this." Cupping Skye's chin, she said, "Just try real hard not to say anything to Wally about it. It's not fair to him. Even if it's always in the back of your mind, keep it to yourself." She lightly slapped her daughter's cheek. "Believe me, no matter how big you get, Wally will still feel like you're the most beautiful woman in the world because you're carrying his child."

"Did you go through this with Vince and me?" Skye

asked, still dazed to see this side of her mother. "Were you jealous of Dad?"

"Sure." May moved back, opened the front door, and chuckled, "Once I even poured a pitcher of lemonade over one of my friends when I thought she was getting a might too friendly with Jed."

"Who was that?" Skye asked, intrigued. "Let me guess. Hester?"

"Nope." May stepped outside. "It was Dorothy. You know how she likes to play up to guys. She never means it and usually it's funny, but . . ."

"But not when you were feeling ugly," Skye said, following her mother onto the porch. "What did she do after you doused her?"

"She dumped a full plate of spaghetti on me." May waved and walked down the steps. "I never did get that stain out of my white blouse. It looked as if I'd been beheaded."

Skye giggled.

Getting into her car, May said, "Just remember, this, too, shall pass." She paused before closing the door. "It might be as excruciating as a kidney stone, but it'll pass."

Skye stood watching the white Oldsmobile disappear down the road. What had happened to May? Had she been kidnapped and replaced by a Stepford Mom? Or was it because Skye had stood up to her?

It had felt good to say exactly what she was thinking. To tell May that it seemed that no matter what Skye did, it would never be enough to please her mother. She'd have to do that again sometime. Especially concerning the baby.

Walking back into the foyer, Skye almost stepped on Bingo. When she'd first arrived home, she wondered why he didn't greet her at the door. He normally demanded a hug and a chin scratch before allowing her past the foyer.

The cat and May didn't get along, but instead of hiding, Bingo usually stalked her. Had Skye's mother somehow managed to lock Bingo up somewhere and only now he was able to get loose? Skye squinted. *Yep.* Her ferocious feline seemed ticked off. His routine greeting was to rub against her ankles, but instead, he was sitting in the middle of the throw rug glaring at her.

Once Bingo was sure he had her attention, he got up and strolled toward the stairs. Aligning himself with the oak newel post, he extended his claws, then glanced back at Skye and smirked.

Uh-oh. Major cat snit.

Skye hurried to appease the fuming feline before he ruined the woodwork. She rushed into the kitchen, flung open the cupboard door, and grabbed the bright yellow bag.

Dr. Quillen had warned her about Bingo's weight and told her not to give him treats, but this was an emergency. Her fingers were clumsy as she tried to tear the top strip off the package and it made a loud crinkling sound. She glanced down at Bingo.

He paced back and forth in front of her, his green eyes mere slits, as he stared at the crackling bag as if to say, "Feed me now or I'll have you arrested for rustling."

"Give me a second," Skye muttered, sighing in relief as the bag finally opened. She poured a handful out onto the floor and bargained. "These are in exchange for whatever Grandma did to you."

Bingo half growled, half meowed, then demolished the treats and licked his chops. He strolled to his water dish, sniffed it, then deliberately put out a paw and flipped over the half-full bowl.

"I take it you'd like your beverage freshened?" Skye asked, mopping up the mess with a wad of paper towels. "Perhaps some Dasani?"

Wally had been the one to fill the dish this morning

and he refused to give the cat bottled water. He claimed there was no way Bingo could tell the difference between what came from the faucet and the expensive stuff.

"Why don't you ever do this when Daddy's around?" Skye asked. "He's the one that deprives you of your Dasani fix, not me."

Bingo ignored her, his tail thumping impatiently as he waited for his drink to be served. Once she put down the refilled bowl, he touched the liquid with his nose, then drank.

The sound of the cat's lapping was soothing and Skye idly glanced at her watch. She was surprised that it was only four thirty. It seemed a lot later. Wally had said that unless something came up, he'd be home at his usual time between six and six thirty.

She should use the time to write a report, but she felt too distracted to do a good job. Maybe she'd take a ride and see if Vince and Loretta were home. Her brother and his wife had just had a baby girl a few months ago, and it had been a while since Skye had seen the three of them.

If it were anyone else in Scumble River, Skye would be afraid of interrupting supper preparations, since most folks ate at five. But Loretta considered dining before seven o'clock uncivilized.

Vince owned a hair salon in town and it was closed on Mondays so he should be home. And although Loretta was a successful criminal defense lawyer who commuted to Chicago, she was on maternity leave for five more weeks.

After leaving Wally a note, just in case he came home early, Skye picked up her purse and walked out to the garage. As she slid into the Bel Air, she smiled. It would be nice to have a chance to talk to Loretta.

She hoped she could get her alone for a frank discussion of pregnancy and motherhood. In addition to being Skye's sister-in-law, Loretta was also her sorority sister. They both were members of Alpha Sigma Alpha and had known each other in college.

Since Loretta was a few years older than Skye, they'd only been in the sorority house together for a couple of semesters, but sisterhood was a lifetime commitment. And when Skye had called Loretta for help to defend Vince from an erroneous murder charge, she'd come running.

After successfully defending Skye's brother, Loretta and Vince had fallen in love. Then, much to Skye's amazement, since her sister-in-law was a born-and-bred Chicago girl, Loretta agreed to live in Scumble River.

Lucky for everyone, a lot of Loretta's job as an attorney could be done electronically and she only had to go into the city for client meetings and trials. Now that she'd been off work for almost five months, Skye wondered if her sister-in-law would have trouble returning to her demanding job.

Then again, Loretta did thrive on stress. She'd been immersed in designing and building a new house almost until she gave birth. Prior to deciding to build, she and Vince had made an exhaustive search for the ideal home, but nothing had been quite right.

Skye hadn't been shocked by their decision. Loretta wasn't the type to be satisfied with anything less than perfection, and Vince had already proven that he'd move heaven and earth to fulfill his new wife's every wish. For a man who had an Olympic gold medal in dating, he was an astonishingly devoted husband.

When Vince and Loretta decided to build, his and Skye's parents had deeded a couple of acres from the land they farmed to their son and new daughter-in-law. The only drawback was the property's location. Because it was so close to May and Jed's place, May found numerous excuses to drop by and Loretta was not amused.

As Skye turned down the long lane leading to the house, she tried to visualize what the oaks, pecans, and hickories interspersed with redbuds, hawthorns, pawpaws, yellowwoods, and crab apples that had been planted a few months ago would look like once they matured. When they were grown to their full size, the tree allée would make an elegant entrance to the spectacular home.

Skye parked along the circular driveway—praying her car didn't leave an oil stain or any other kind of mark on the still pristine concrete pavers. She strolled up the cobblestone walkway leading to the double mahogany doors, rang the bell, and smiled when she heard the percussion solo from Iron Butterfly's "In-A-Gadda-Da-Vida."

Vince had won the argument for the programmable doorbell's musical selection. In order to be home on weekends, he might have stopped performing with his band, the Plastic Santas, but he would always be a drummer at heart.

Several seconds went by, and Skye was considering pushing the button again when Loretta flung open the door and said, "I suppose you'll take his side."

"His side being Vince's?" Skye asked cautiously. What had she interrupted?

Loretta nodded, yanked Skye over the threshold, and said, "That SOB got me pregnant again and he's thrilled."

CHAPTER 12

Cats don't like change without their consent.
—ROGER CARAS

Skye heard Vince's victory shouts coming from up-stairs. She hid a smile at his obvious excitement. It was hard to believe a guy who rarely dated the same woman twice was so ecstatic at the news that he was going to be a father a second time.

Keeping her expression neutral, Skye took her sister-in-law's hand and gave it a comforting squeeze, then questioned, "You're not pleased?"

"No. Yes. Hell, I don't know." Loretta jerked her fingers from Skye. "I finally lost all the baby weight and April is just starting to sleep through the night and I have to go back to work and . . ."

"And your perfectly scheduled life is messed up?" Skye suggested. "Believe me"—she glanced down at her stomach—"I understand."

"But no one expects you to fit into a size 6 designer suit," Loretta snapped, then put her hand over her mouth and said, "Sorry." Her shoulders slumped. "You know what I meant."

Skye nodded. Her sister-in-law was always perfectly put together. Loretta was six feet tall with a lean-muscled body, gorgeous creamy dark brown skin, and impeccably coiffed shiny black hair that never had a strand out of place. Skye had rarely seen her friend look anything but ready to walk a runway during fashion week in New York.

"I take it you just found out? Like only a few seconds ago?" Skye asked warily. When Loretta nodded, Skye offered, "Maybe I should leave, so you and Vince can discuss this in private."

"No!" Loretta yelped, grabbing Skye's arm and tugging her through the foyer and the family room and into the kitchen, complaining as they walked, "I'm not ready to talk to Mr. We-Don't-Need-to-Use-a-Rubber."

"Too much information." Skye clapped her hands over her ears. Then seconds later, she negated her statement and said, "I thought the doctor let you go back on the pill a few months ago."

"It decreased my milk and made April fussy so I had to stop."

"And you still let Vince talk you into doing it without protection?" Skye figured she already knew way too much about their sex life, so what the heck? "You do realize that condoms should be used on every conceivable occasion?" Skye punned.

Loretta snickered, then said, "Vince is very persuasive." She refused to meet Skye's gaze.

"But you're a lawy—"

"I don't want to discuss it right now." Loretta stalked over to the gleaming stainless steel refrigerator, yanked open the double doors, and peered at the glass shelves. "Yes!" She pumped her fist in the air twice, reached inside, and emerged with a Boston cream pie.

"What are you going to do with that?" Skye asked, eyeing the confection as if it were about to leap off the serving plate and into her mouth.

"Eat it." Loretta plunked the dish in front of Skye,

opened a drawer, and pulled out a fork. Just before she dug in, she asked, "You want some?"

"No, thanks." Skye licked her lips. Between her cake at lunch and the lemon bars with her milk, her dessert account was already overdrawn.

As Loretta shoved a huge bite into her mouth, Skye gazed around the mammoth room, counting three sinks, two dishwashers, and a refrigerated wine rack. The kitchen was probably better equipped than a lot of restaurants. You could feed the entire Leofanti and Denison clans combined in it.

Taking a breather from stuffing her face, Loretta eased onto the stool across from Skye and ordered, "Tell me how you're doing."

"Well . . ." Skye had wanted to discuss her pregnancy concerns with Loretta, but now didn't seem like the best time to bring up that subject.

"How's school going?" Loretta used her fingers to dig out a scoop of custard.

"Busy." Skye folded her hands over her stomach. "The end of the year is hectic."

"How much longer do you have?" Loretta sucked the cream from her thumb.

"The kids have a little over three weeks left." Skye shrugged. "I'll probably be working awhile after that."

"Why?" Loretta got up and tossed the decimated pastry into the trash, then opened the freezer and started rummaging inside it.

"I need to have everything ready for the intern." Skye wondered what was next on her sister-in-law's menu. "I might not be in too good a shape in September."

"Right." Loretta plopped back on the stool holding a carton of Blue Bunny and a serving spoon. "You'll be close to popping out the kid."

"Don't tell anyone, especially Mom, but that may be nearer than we first thought." Skye watched her friend devour the birthday cake–flavored ice cream. "At my last checkup my obstetrician said that I might be further than along than the first calculations indicated. When I see the doctor later this week, I should know for sure."

"Is May driving you crazy?" Loretta selected a confetti-shaped candy from the container and popped it into her mouth.

"No more than usual." Skye leaned her elbows on the granite counter. "Although today she dropped over and washed all the sunroom windows."

"Well, she nearly drove me insane, both when we were building the house and when she found out about the baby." Loretta worked the edge of her spoon under a ribbon of blue frosting. "I thought I would have to get an unlisted number and a guard dog to have any privacy."

"Mom actually had a sort of good reason for being at the house today," Skye confessed. "Her friend Dorothy Snyder, you know the woman who cleans for us"— when Loretta nodded, Skye continued—"found a dead guy and called me to come help her with him."

"What in the hell did Dorothy want you to do?" Loretta seemed so shocked she actually put down her spoon and pushed away the carton of ice cream. "Help her dig a grave and bury the body?"

Before Skye could come up with an acceptable answer that didn't involve the words *bondage* or *stark naked*, Vince strolled into the kitchen and opened the fridge. His butterscotch blond hair brushed the collar of his bright blue polo shirt as he bopped his head to the beat of whatever he was listening to through his earbuds.

Loretta's mouth tightened as she glared at her husband's back. Unaware of his wife's ire, Vince selected an apple, bit into it, and turned around. He seemed somewhat startled to see the two women watching him. Although how he had missed them, even in such a gargantuan kitchen, was beyond Skye. Then again, her brother didn't just march to a different drummer, he composed the music.

Yanking out his earbuds, he smiled and said, "Skye, when did you get here?"

"During your happy dance." Skye glanced uneasily at Loretta, but stood up and hugged Vince, then bravely said, "Congratulations. I hear April is going to have a little brother or sister."

"Thanks, sis." Vince squeezed her so hard Skye gasped for breath and pushed out of his embrace. Proving he wasn't totally oblivious, he snuck a peek at his wife, then beamed. "We didn't exactly plan this, but I couldn't be happier. I'd love a houseful of kids."

Skye would have sworn she heard Loretta growl, but when she turned toward her sister-in-law, Loretta's expression was Madonna-like. Vince moved over to his wife and wrapped his arms around her. Fascinated, Skye watched Loretta melt into her husband's chest.

But a split second later, Loretta pushed Vince away and said, "We are not having a houseful of kids." She pointed to her stomach. "This is it. Two and done."

"Now, honey," Vince massaged Loretta's shoulders, "don't be silly."

"Silly!" Loretta roared, whirling to face him. "Don't tell me not to be"—she used her fingers to make quotation marks in the air—"silly. You aren't the one that blows up like a balloon in the Macy's Thanksgiving Day Parade." She pushed up her considerable cleavage. "You aren't the one who feels like Elsie the Cow every time you pump breast milk." She poked him in his washboard abs. "And you aren't the one that's going to be trying to juggle a cutthroat career with less sleep than I got in law school."

"Sweetheart, you know you don't have to do all that by yourself." Vince took his wife's hand, but she wrenched it from his grasp.

"Really, Vincent?" Loretta's voice was deceptively

mild and Skye cringed. "Are you going to carry the baby? Are you going to breastfeed?"

"I can't do that, sweetie, but I will get up during the night with the baby." He once again put his arms around his wife.

Loretta started to lean against Vince, then stiffened and went very still. "No." She narrowed her eyes and said, "What you will do is practice safe sex. Go screw yourself."

"Now, baby—"

Loretta interrupted her husband. "Or you can have a vasectomy."

Skye watched as Vince jumped back and instinctively covered his crotch. He gazed at his wife as if she might grab a butcher knife and perform the operation right there on their gleaming granite counter.

Slowly backing away, he held up his hands and said, "Let's not do anything rash."

"You mean like have sex without a rubber?" Loretta arched a brow.

"Hey." Vince lifted a shoulder, a grin quirking up his lips. "You forgot to pick up a new box of Trojans when you were in Kankakee shopping and we were a little too far along to stop and run to the drugstore."

"Seriously?" Loretta advanced on her husband. "This is my fault?"

"It's no one's fault." Vince waited until his wife was in reach, pressed her against him, and murmured into her ear, "It's a blessing."

After a long and intense kiss, which seemed to take the fight right out of Loretta, Vince lifted his face and winked at Skye over his wife's head, then asked, "What are you two talking about?"

Loretta straightened. Her anger appeared to have been temporarily vanquished by her husband's attentions and she said, "Skye was telling me about the—"

Skye quickly said, "Just girl talk." She patted her baby bump to emphasize her answer. "Nothing you need or want to hear."

"Sure." Vince's green eyes held a degree of calculation that Skye hadn't often seen in them. "Then I'll leave you ladies alone."

After Vince disappeared down the hall, Loretta cleaned up the debris of her food orgy and, her mood lightened, said, "Come look at all the new stuff I got for the house since the last time you were here."

"Okay." Skye stood and followed her sister-in-law into the family room.

"What do you think?" Loretta swept her arm around the enormous room featuring a wet bar at one end and a fireplace at the other.

"Nice." Skye wasn't sure what exactly had been added, but wasn't about to say so.

"Wait until you see the bedspread in the master suite," Loretta announced, seeming not to notice Skye's lack of specific praise.

They made their way to the opposite end of the house, where the master suite took up the entire west side. In addition to a gorgeous bedroom with French doors leading to a patio and an in-ground pool, there was a huge bathroom and double walk-in closets that shared a dressing area. Each time she saw it, Skye was stunned by the lavishness of the suite.

Loretta may be a partner in a prestigious law firm, but just how much money did attorneys make? Vince certainly couldn't afford anything half as luxurious as this on the income from his salon. Even with the free land and all the family connections for cheap labor, the house had to have cost them close to a million, maybe twice that amount.

Granted, they probably had an enormous mortgage, but how had they qualified for such a big loan? Loretta's salary had to be gargantuan. No wonder she was worried about being pregnant again. Even if her interests had strayed from her high-powered career, there was probably no way she could cut back on her billable hours and keep up this lifestyle.

Would she ever consider opening a much less glamorous practice in Scumble River? Could she and Vince afford for her to do so?

Once Loretta had shown Skye the new oriental rugs and curtains in the three upstairs bedrooms, one of which was Vince's music studio, they ended up back on the main floor near the master bedroom, admiring the nursery.

The subtle mushroom-and-ecru color scheme, the soft fawn carpet, the draperies tied back with heavy tassels to give the curtains a scalloped look, and the one-of-a-kind cherub chandelier were striking. Skye felt a twinge of guilt. She hadn't even thought of how she would decorate her baby's room yet.

Gazing at April, who was sleeping like an angel in the elegant iron scrollwork crib, Skye tried to picture her child. It wasn't surprising that Vince and Loretta had produced a beautiful baby. April had a flawless caramel complexion, her mother's dark ringlets, and her father's emerald eyes surrounded by lush dark lashes.

Wally was handsome, but Skye knew that she was only passably pretty. How would her son or daughter compete with his or her dazzling cousin? Would he or she feel cheated?

No! Skye would make sure that her child had the self-confidence to understand that no one should allow themselves to be judged by their appearance.

Skye forced a smile, complimented Loretta on the baby's exquisiteness, and said, "I ought to get going." She glanced at her watch. "Wally will be home any minute, and you probably want to start supper."

"It's Vince's turn to microwave our dinner tonight."

Loretta led Skye into the foyer, but didn't open the door. "Before you leave, tell me why Dorothy called you when she found the dead guy."

"Well . . ." Skye knew she shouldn't, but she looked her friend in the eye and said, "You have to swear not to tell a soul."

"I swear."

"No. I can't." Skye shook her head. "Wally would kill me, and rightly so, if I was the reason this information leaked out."

"Give me a dollar." Loretta held out her palm. "Once I'm your attorney, I can't break confidentiality. Everything you say is privileged."

Fumbling in her purse, Skye produced a crumpled bill. "All I have is a five."

"Hand it over." Loretta pocketed the money and demanded, "Spill."

After Skye summarized the events of the day, she said, "What do you think?"

"I think that the Scumble River Police Department is in for a bad time. People are going to freak out at the idea of a killer going around and tying their victims up bare-ass-naked, then shooting them."

"Even if it's likely that the victim was into that kind of alternate lifestyle?" Skye hadn't thought of folks being scared. Only titillated with Palmer's kinky sexual practices. "Why would they think his murder is anything but a love affair that ended badly?"

"Because maybe he isn't the only one around here who participates in a little BDSM." Loretta's wicked smile sent a chill up Skye's spine. "Think how that could shake up this town."

"You did not make me feel better." Skye crossed her arms. "Wally will have a cow when I impart your little suggestion."

"Make sure you share that tidbit with him right

before bedtime." Loretta's tone was satisfied. "Why should my marriage be the only one that's shaken up?"

"We're planning on telling folks that Palmer's death was a result of a burglary gone wrong. With the American Legion break-in and the catnapping, it makes sense to lump the murder in with those."

"If that's the story you're going to stick with"—Loretta swung open the massive mahogany door—"tomorrow should be an extremely interesting day."

Skye made a face, then hugged her sister-in-law good-bye and walked to her car. As she drove home, Loretta's words of doom echoed in her head.

CHAPTER 13

I gave an order to a cat, and the cat gave it to its tail.
—CHINESE PROVERB

On her way home, Skye stopped at the supermarket, so when she got back to her house, Wally's cruiser was already parked in the drive. From the sound of Bruce Springsteen's "Born to Run" pouring down the stairs, Skye deduced that Wally was in the gym that he'd installed in one of the extra third-floor bedrooms.

After putting away the groceries, she climbed the steps and found him lying flat on the weight bench. He was wearing low-riding nylon shorts and not much else.

Leaning against the doorjamb, Skye observed his chest and shoulder muscles flexing as he repeatedly lifted a barbell with a hundred-pound plate attached to each end. She admired the way the silver at his temples emphasized the midnight blackness of the rest of his hair and how his smooth olive skin stretched over his high cheekbones. He was such a handsome man that sometimes, when her insecurities surfaced, she wondered why he was with her.

Unwilling to go down the dark spiral of jealousy again, she pushed aside her self-doubt and smiled at Wally as he sat up, wiped his face with a towel, and grabbed a Dasani from the floor. Skye watched the strong column of his throat as he swallowed nearly half the water in one swig.

He put down the plastic bottle, got to his feet, and came toward her. "You're home." He kissed her cheek. "How was your visit with Vince and Loretta?"

"Surprising." Skye's grin was amused. "She's expecting again."

"Oh?" Wally raised his brows. "I didn't realize she and Vince were planning to have children so close together."

"They weren't. And I'm not sure when they'll announce it, so mum's the word."

"Don't you mean 'no mum'?" Wally asked. "As in 'don't tell May'?"

"Exactly." Skye gestured to the rest of the equipment. "Are you done?"

"Yeah." Wally picked up a remote and cut off the music. "I was just about to grab a shower." He shot her a seductive gaze. "Want to join me?"

"I'd love to. Another time." Skye didn't meet his eyes. "But it's getting late. How about I warm up supper instead?"

"Did Dorothy come over after all?" Wally walked across the rubber tiled floor and picked up the empty water bottle and dirty towel.

"No." Skye followed him down one flight of stairs and into the master bedroom.

"So what are you going to reheat?" Wally stripped off his shorts and underwear. He threw his discarded clothes and the towel in the hamper. "Did you pick up a pizza or something in town?"

"Nope." Skye shook her head. "Dorothy sent her designated hitter, who washed our windows and left dinner in the fridge."

Wally walked into the bathroom and turned on the water in the shower. "Your mother?" Wally asked, a note of concern in his voice.

"Yep." Skye waved as she hurried away. "I'll tell you all about it while we eat."

By the time Wally came downstairs, dressed in cargo shorts and a T-shirt, Skye had their salads on the table and the chicken parmesan and garlic bread in the oven. He poured a can of Caffeine-Free Diet Coke over ice for Skye, and uncapped a Sam Adams for himself.

Once they were seated, Wally picked up his fork, but paused as he lifted it to his mouth and asked, "So what did your mother have to say?"

As they ate, Skye summarized May's visit, omitting the part where Skye had turned into a suspicious, insecure puddle of raging hormones.

"Sounds like she was okay," Wally said cautiously. "Not too overbearing."

"Actually, she was sort of great." Skye got to her feet, took the chicken and garlic bread from the oven, and placed them on the table. Adjusting hot pads beneath them, she added, "Once I played the baby card and drew a line in the sand, she backed off and we had a really good mother-daughter moment."

"That's terrific." Wally slid a chicken breast onto Skye's plate. "I know confronting your mom is hard. I'm really proud of you."

"I am, too." Skye tore off two hunks of garlic bread, handing one to Wally. "And since Dorothy didn't let the cat out of the bag about Palmer's state of undress, I managed not to tell Mom that he was naked and tied up."

"That's great." Wally took a drink of beer, then added, "Right now, the only ones who know about the circumstances of the vic's body at the time of discovery are the crime scene techs, Reid, Dorothy, Lynch's mother, and us, but I doubt that's anything we can keep secret for too long. Best-case scenario, no one finds out until after the *Star* comes out on Wednesday."

"I did tell one person . . ." Skye had wanted to wait until after dinner to share her sister-in-law's theory, but couldn't ignore this opening. "I hired Loretta as my lawyer, so she's sworn to confidentiality. I wanted her take as a criminal attorney on the situation."

"Which was?" Wally asked. His tone was mild and he continued to eat.

"Loretta suggested that there might be a whole set of people in Scumble River that shared Palmer's unusual tastes," Skye explained. "And that those folks might be our suspect pool."

"I'm pretty dang sure if there was that type of club in town, I'd know about it." Wally frowned and took another swig of beer.

"Well, not necessarily," Skye said slowly, reluctant to bring up the incident when she'd snuck into a house she wasn't supposed to be in. "How about that kinky scene I witnessed at the Kesslers' after Barbie and Ken Addison were murdered? Those people liked to dress up in weird outfits and swap wives. Tony Zello had on some sort of black rubber suit that made him look like a giant condom and Nate Turner threatened me. You didn't know about those parties."

"You told me that the folks in that group claimed that Ken forced them to participate in the sex parties," Wally reminded her.

"Correct," Skye admitted. "But who knows if they were telling the truth."

Wally was quiet as he finished his meal, but when they were doing the dishes, he said, "I've been thinking about Loretta's idea."

"And?"

"You did say that Zello and Turner were talking about Lynch after church."

"Right." Skye rinsed the last pan and screwed up her face. "And as I mentioned, both those guys were a part of that kinky sex group that Ken Addison started."

"That moves them way up on my list of interviews for tomorrow."

"Is Virginia still your number one suspect?" Skye asked, wringing out the dishcloth and hanging it over the faucet.

"She is." Wally followed Skye into the sunroom and joined her on the wicker love seat. "But I'd like you to be in on that session so I'll ask her to come in after school."

"Who are you going to talk to while I'm working?" Skye asked.

"As soon as I get the preliminary ME report, I'll go over and see Charlie, then decide the batting order from there." Wally put an arm around Skye and cuddled her to his side. "There's a message for you on the answering machine from him, but don't answer his calls before I speak to him." Wally's jaw tightened. "No doubt, May has already filled him in on what she knows, but I don't want anything else to slip out from you."

"I hope he doesn't track me down at school." Skye worried her lower lip with her teeth. "He'll be fuming that I haven't returned his call."

"I'm hoping that by tomorrow morning the ME will have some information for me, and I'll speak to your godfather right after that." Wally brushed his lips over the top of her hair. "If Charlie gets to you before I can talk to him, use the same tactic with him that you used with your mother. Play the baby card."

"Yeah." Skye stroked her belly. "That will work on Charlie, but it won't work on Trixie. How much can I tell her about the murder?"

Trixie had been writing a mystery for what seemed like forever so she was particularly fascinated by Skye's involvement in real-life cases. She was persistent and clever, with better sources than the police. Trixie would come knocking on Skye's door as soon as she found out another murder investigation was under way.

"Dodge her if you can," Wally suggested. "But if she corners you, just make sure you avoid telling her about the bondage aspect of the investigation." He paused then said, "See if she's heard anything about the American Legion break-in or the catnapping."

"I was thinking that I'd try to find some time tomorrow to hang out in the faculty lounge." Skye wrinkled her nose. "Palmer's murder and that break-in should be the hot topics of conversation."

"Okay." Wally drew his brows together. "But don't let anyone know that you're particularly interested." He kissed her cheek. "We don't want the killer to see you as a target."

In a way, it was a shame Skye wasn't scheduled to be at the elementary school on Tuesday. It would have been interesting to see Virginia's demeanor. Was she distraught over Palmer's death or unaffected? On the other hand, Skye didn't have to worry about running into the teacher and making small talk, then seeing her at the police station and feeling like she'd misled the woman about her interest in the case.

With that in mind, when Skye finished doing her laps in the high school pool, instead of stopping by the grade school, Skye spent the rest of the morning at the junior high. She chaired five back-to-back annual reviews, and then at eleven thirty she headed to the Pupil Personnel Services meeting.

The session was scheduled for that time to take advantage of the double lunch hour. Teachers were able to attend during their free period. Unfortunately, since Skye was there for the entire gathering, it meant she missed eating altogether unless she could manage to gobble a sandwich in the five minutes it took her to walk across the campus to the high school.

This wasn't one of those days. While she hiked across the grass, she dug through her tote bag, but came up empty. She must have left her ham on rye at home.

As she pushed through the high school's glass front doors, her stomach growled and she felt light-headed, reminding her that she could no longer skip a meal without feeling the effects of the missing nourishment. She sure hoped she hadn't depleted her emergency cookie stash and forgotten to replace it.

She was trying to remember the status of her Pepperidge Farm supply when she heard a sarcastic male voice say, "Skye, so happy you could squeeze us in today."

Uh-oh. Homer sounded even more belligerent than usual. What sin had she committed? Surely he couldn't fault her for taking a personal day?

Homer Knapik had been the high school principal for as long as anyone under the age of forty could remember. Every May, for the past several years, he'd announced that he was stepping down. But like the taste of a bad burrito, he had always returned in the fall.

No one was quite sure how he managed that since the Illinois Teacher Retirement System required extensive paperwork to begin the retirement procedure, and once the forms were signed, it was difficult if not impossible to reverse the process.

After his last miraculous reappearance, the faculty was taking bets that should Homer pass away, the school board would have a life-size cardboard cutout placed in the chair behind his desk. Sadly, the only one who would be able to tell the difference would be his secretary, who would no longer have to fetch Homer pastries from the Tales and Treats café. Because as far as the running of the school went, the staff couldn't quite pinpoint what he did to contribute to the students' education.

She looked in the direction of the aggravating principal and her chest tightened. Why was the superintendent here? He rarely visited the schools, preferring to force everyone to come to his intimidating office for any meetings with him. This couldn't be good.

Taking a deep breath and hoping the superintendent was on his way back to his lair, Skye said, "Good afternoon, Dr. Wraige, Homer."

"Get your keister into my office immediately!" Homer bellowed.

"I can come back when you and Dr. Wraige are through," Skye offered. What in the world had she done to rile up the principal this time?

"Shamus is the one who wants to speak to you," Homer sneered. "Now, do you want to do this here in the lobby or in private?"

Skye dragged her feet as she reported to the principal's office. With each step, her anxiety soared. She'd been so worried about how she'd manage her job with a baby, maybe that wouldn't be a problem. School psychologists weren't covered by the teachers' contract so she didn't have tenure. The administration could literally get rid of her anytime they chose.

Skye paused at the threshold to Homer's office, allowing the men to enter first. Homer plopped down behind his massive desk, but didn't invite her to take a seat. Dr. Wraige chose to stand, glaring at her as she shifted from foot to foot feeling like she was about to get expelled.

In his late fifties, Shamus Wraige was a solidly built two hundred pounds. His red hair had faded, giving it the appearance of a rusty steel wool pad. And his personality was about as warm. He towered over Skye, using his size and position to try to intimidate her.

After several long seconds of silence, the only sounds in the room Homer's giant slurps from his can of orange soda, Dr. Wraige gestured for Skye to sit in one of the visitor chairs. Once she complied, he moved in front of her and leaned his rear end against Homer's desk. His knees were a hair's width from hers and she could smell his anger.

"Mrs. Boyd," Dr. Wraige began.

"Actually," before Skye could stop herself, she blurted out, "it's Denison-Boyd." When she saw his pale brown eyes narrow, she added weakly, "But, sir, why don't you just call me Skye."

"Mrs. Boyd." Dr. Wraige stared at her, daring her to object again.

Skye bit her tongue. The superintendent might not be a complete male chauvinist pig, but he certainly had his share of swine empathy.

When she kept quiet, Dr. Wraige's mouth rose in a self-satisfied smirk and he continued, "I just had an interesting visit from your husband."

"Oh?" Skye's heart skipped a beat. Why hadn't she asked Wally to warn her before talking to the superintendent? "About Mr. Lynch's murder?"

"No, about the price of hamburger at Walter's Supermarket," Dr. Wraige snapped. "Of course it was about Palmer Lynch's murder."

"Was he notifying you because Mr. Lynch was a member of the school board?" Skye decided this was a darn good time to play dumb. She was sure Wally wouldn't have identified her as the stool pigeon who overheard the superintendent's exchange with Pru.

"Yes." Dr. Wraige tilted his head as if assessing Skye's true knowledge of the situation. "But while Chief Boyd was there, he mentioned a discussion I supposedly took part in with Ms. Cormorant."

"Someone lied about a conversation?" Skye strove to keep her expression neutral, then shrugged and said, "Unfortunately, I'm not surprised. Scumble River seems to run on gossip in the same way most cars run on fossil fuel. Too bad, unlike crude oil, there appears to be an unending supply of rumors and insinuations."

"Then you don't know anything about this alleged chat?" Dr. Wraige inched closer and Skye scooted back in the chair. "I thought I saw you at church on Sunday. Did you notice anyone eavesdropping on me?"

"So you did talk to Pru?" Skye injected a note of innocence into her voice.

"We may have chatted briefly after Mass." Dr. Wraige's face flushed. "But we certainly didn't conspire to kill Palmer Lynch."

"Is that what the police were told?" Skye asked, knowing it wasn't.

"It was implied." Dr. Wraige abruptly straightened and strode toward the door. He paused with his hand on the knob and said to Homer, "I hope you'll warn your staff that scandalmongering can be very damaging to careers."

Once the superintendent disappeared, Homer slapped down the file he'd been leafing through and snarled, "Why the hell do you keep finding bodies?"

Homer's short stature and very round shape reminded Skye of an extremely hairy beach ball.

"I didn't," Skye protested. "I arrived afterward."

"You're still involved."

"Of course I am." Skye crossed her arms. "As you well know, I'm the police psych consultant." She winked. "And I sleep with the chief."

"Don't be a wise guy with me."

"I'm not trying to be." Skye cringed at his expression and vowed to keep her mouth shut. She had to remember that Homer had no sense of humor and his skylight was a little leaky.

"Then stop it."

"Okay." Skye felt as if she were starring in *Groundhog Day, Part Two*. She and Homer had had this conversation before. Actually several times.

"Okay?" The hair growing out of the principal's ears bristled. "Like I'm going to believe you'll follow my orders for once?"

"I've never purposely disobeyed your instructions," Skye protested. "But sometimes what you tell me to do is illegal or immoral or both."

"The others don't have a problem with the way I run this school." Homer's face turned a mottled red. "Just shut your mouth and do what I tell you."

"I'm afraid I can't agree to that." Skye refused to let someone who not only resembled Chewbacca but probably had a lower IQ than the Wookie, interfere with the ethical performance of her profession. "If your directives aren't within best practices, I won't follow them."

Homer stood, knocking over his chair, and pointed to the door. "Quit causing waves and quit interfering."

Skye turned to escape, but Homer yelled, "Wait! I forgot. You need to talk to Pru Cormorant ASAP. Dr. Wraige is concerned that she might be upset from your husband's interrogation. And we all know a disturbed Pru is not something that we can ignore." He winked. "Especially now that she's going through the change. There's no telling what kind of mood she'll be in."

"Women going through menopause are not moody," Skye corrected him. "There are merely some times that they are less disposed to put up with men's nonsense."

"Whatever." Homer snorted. "Just go talk to her."

Skye cowered. "Why me?" The English teacher had been at Scumble River High nearly as long as Homer. She was a law unto herself and she didn't like Skye.

"Because you are the freaking psychologist." Homer harrumphed. "If you're going to throw around words like *ethics* and *morals*, you need to be prepared to practice what you preach, Mrs. La-di-dah Denison-Boyd."

Shoot! He was right. Skye mutely walked out of Homer's office, checked the master schedule, and headed to Pru's classroom. Was this what it felt like marching to the guillotine?

CHAPTER 14

Curiosity killed the cat, but satisfaction
brought it back.
—ENGLISH PROVERB

As Skye trudged down the hallway, she rubbed her forehead. Pru Cormorant had the current period free, which gave Skye seventeen minutes to smooth the irritating teacher's ruffled feathers. By the time the next bell rang, the distasteful task would be over and Skye could get back to her real duties. The ones that actually involved helping the students.

"Corny," as most of the staff called her behind her back, had one of the best classrooms in the building. It had actual walls instead of folding accordion partitions, windows, and even an exterior door. Because of this, it was a well-known fact that if the weather was nice, Pru usually spent her planning periods on a lawn chair outside her room tanning.

True to form, Skye found the aggravating English teacher stretched out on a chaise lounge with a magazine covering her face. Skye took a moment to study her. Corny's gaunt limbs stuck out at awkward angles from her egg-shaped body, and her too-small head appeared in danger of tumbling off her neck if she made any sudden moves. She looked a lot like the stick figures that six-year-olds produced when Skye asked them to complete the Draw-a-Person test. One with alligator-like skin after all her years chasing the perfect shade of bronze.

Clearing her throat, Skye said, "Hi. Are you enjoying the sunshine?"

"Yes, I'm so glad that it isn't too hot to lie out today." Pru's watery blue eyes were malicious. "Are you aware that my room is one of only three with an exterior exit? Only the most valued faculty members are assigned these premier spaces. Your office doesn't have a door to the outside, does it, dear?"

Skye bit the inside of her cheek, then forced a pleasant expression on her face and said, "No, it doesn't."

They'd had this conversation before and it took all her self-control to refrain from retorting that *she* was too busy to care about the amenities. *Heck!* She was lucky to have an office to herself, let alone any extras.

"I don't see *you* very often." Pru raised an overplucked eyebrow.

"I guess not." Skye pasted a fake smile on her lips. "I don't get to the teachers' lounge much, at least not at lunchtime, and since you don't have any of the children on my caseload in your classes, there isn't much of a reason for me to stop by here."

"The students you deal with aren't able to cope with the high-level subjects that I teach." Pru pursed her thin lips. "Not too long ago, one of yours was mistakenly put into my class. But then he told me that the word *trouser* was an uncommon noun because it's singular at the waist and I had him transferred." She tsked. "When I started at Scumble River High School, those children would have been in a separate facility."

Skye dug her nails into her palms to stop herself from asking what it was like to teach during the Revolutionary War, and instead said, "That was a different era in education and thankfully we've moved past that kind of thinking."

"That's a matter of opinion." Pru patted her stringy dun-colored hair. "We need to stop coddling these students and their helicopter parents. No Child Left Behind is a travesty. Anyone with the slightest knowledge of the bell curve knows the largest portion of students will be average, then there's going to be a certain amount who are gifted, and sadly, there are going to be an equal amount who are as dumb as the deposit my dog made on the lawn this morning. The sooner everyone accepts that not every youngster is going to Yale or even finish twelfth grade, the better."

"I disagree." Skye had been letting Corny ramble, having heard her opinion on the subject before, but it was time to put the brakes on her rant. "While No Child Left Behind certainly needs some serious revisions, there isn't a single reason in the world for anyone to drop out."

"Piffle." Pru waved her skeleton-like hand. "Like I always say, *Cogito eggo sum.*"

"I think therefore I waffle?" Had Skye heard Corny right?

Skye couldn't help snickering. The haughty teacher considered herself an intellectual, but was prone to misquote well-known sayings.

Ignoring Skye's sarcastic question, Pru said, "If you aren't here to discuss one of your little darlings—and you'd better not suggest I add any of them to my roll— why are you here?" She lasered a look at Skye's stomach. "Perhaps you're seeking some parenting advice."

Are you out of your freaking mind? Skye barely swallowed the words. When she was sure she could control herself, she said, "Actually, Homer asked me to stop by. Dr. Wraige mentioned to him that he was concerned you might be upset about some of my husband's questions."

"And of course, Homer is afraid to speak to me himself." Pru's mean smile was filled with satisfaction. "That man should retire before he has an aneurysm."

"He does turn an alarming shade of magenta," Skye murmured, for once agreeing with Pru's sentiments. "It can't be good for him."

"Heliotrope," Pru corrected. "His color is closer to heliotrope."

"I'm sure you're right." Skye wasn't about to stand around arguing the finer points of Homer's apoplectic complexion. "So then you're not upset about Wally's conversation with you this morning before school?"

"I understand my duty as a good citizen." Pru's tone was completely insincere, then she added, "But your husband didn't have to be so rude."

"Hmm." Skye attempted to be conciliatory. "I'm certain he didn't mean to be. Sometimes, especially with a murder investigation, there's no nice way of proceeding."

"Nonsense." Pru levered the back of the lounger until she was sitting upright. "You and your spouse both enjoy poking your noses in other people's personal business entirely too much. It's vulgar." She shuddered. "And to top it off, Chief Boyd threatened me."

"Come again?" Skye's pulse raced. Pru had seemed okay when she arrived, but now she was agitated. Why hadn't Skye left after saying hi?

"Your husband warned me that if I didn't reveal what Shamus and I were referring to in our discussion Sunday after church, we would be continuing our interview at the police station. And he might even charge me with obstructing an investigation." Pru's voice rose. "I had to tell the chief things I promised never to reveal."

"That must have been scary," Skye murmured.

She wasn't sure if Wally truly could arrest Pru, but if he couldn't, clearly to the self-centered teacher, the threat had been enough. Pru always put her own best interests first. Anyone who trusted her to do differently was a fool.

"It was extremely frightening." Pru nodded regally. "Thank you for your understanding." She looked at Skye through her sparse lashes, and demanded, "I suppose you want to know what I disclosed."

"Only if it would be helpful to you in dealing with what happened." Skye couldn't believe her luck. Wally would share the information, but it was so much better to hear it from the source.

"Don't think I don't know that your husband will tell you anyway," Pru sneered. "This way, he won't be able to twist what I said."

"Wally will only share pertinent facts in my capacity as the police psych consultant," Skye assured her. "And I will keep whatever I hear to myself if it doesn't concern Mr. Lynch's death."

"Fine." Pru glanced at her watch and frowned. "My seventh period class will be here in five minutes, so I won't beat around the bush."

"That's probably best." Skye couldn't figure out why the woman was so intent on divulging information to her that Corny had resented telling Wally—probably to twist the facts and make herself look good—but far be it from Skye to stop her. "Whenever you're ready, please go ahead."

"Shamus's mother and my father were second cousins," Pru announced.

"I didn't know that," Skye said. So Pru and Dr. Wraige were related. That explained a lot. "Do you have other family in the area?"

"No." Pru's pointy nose twitched, making her look

like a possum hunting for a tasty tidbit. "And because my mother died when I was six, Shamus's mom watched me while my father was at work. We were essentially raised like brother and sister."

"I understand."

"Which is why I'm so apprehensive for him." Pru nibbled a ragged cuticle, sighed, and blurted out, "He and Palmer shared a certain . . . *proclivity*." She peered at Skye. "Do you get my meaning?"

"Are you referring to their love lives?" Skye asked, carefully trying not to leap to a conclusion that would offend Pru or divulge details Wally hadn't revealed to the teacher.

"Precisely."

"Oh." Skye cringed inwardly. She so didn't want to know this kind of thing about the superintendent. How would she ever look at him without visualizing him in a bedroom with whips and handcuffs?

"There are a few men in the area who enjoy that sort of thing and they attend a private club in Laurel," Pru went on, staring at her feet. "They don't discuss it outside of that social establishment."

"How does that apply to what you and Dr. Wraige were saying Sunday?"

"As you can imagine"—Pru's tongue snaked out and licked her dry lips—"finding women who are amenable to the men's tastes isn't always easy. Often once the men's wives or girlfriends discover their penchants, the women opt out of the relationship."

Skye clamped her mouth shut, chanting silently, *Don't, don't, don't.* It would be so easy to make a smart-alecky remark, but she finally managed to swallow her response and said, "Understandably."

"I agree. Why anyone would allow themselves to be subjugated is beyond me." Pru's face had a disapproving look on it. "However, the ones that do are not my problem. It's the ones who refuse that concern me because what happens if they tell someone?"

"Is that what happened with Virginia Elders and Palmer Lynch?" The pieces came together and Skye asked, "Were you and Dr. Wraige discussing the fact that Mr. Lynch had told Virginia too much?"

"Yes." Pru puffed out her cheeks. "Palmer tried to get her to play his games and she refused. Shamus had warned Palmer not to reveal his preferences until he was sure Virginia would be open to them, but he jumped the gun and she knew his dirty little secret."

"Just in time for the school board president election." Skye shuffled her feet, thinking. "Did Virginia threaten Mr. Lynch?"

"Not that I'm aware of." Pru sent a quelling look in Skye's direction. "But she didn't have to. She just called him a disgusting pervert and then refused to see him again. Why wouldn't she tell people rather than allow a man she thought of as a degenerate to have a position of authority involving children?"

Ignoring Pru's question, Skye asked one of her own. "Did Mr. Lynch have any plans to do something to stop Virginia from blabbing?"

"He was going to let her cool off for a couple of days, then apologize and try to convince her it had been a joke."

"Did that work?"

"I don't know." Pru wrinkled her brow. "When Shamus and I spoke after church on Sunday, he said that he planned to call Palmer on Monday morning to find out if he had managed to pacify Virginia. However, since I understand from your husband's questions that Palmer was murdered on Sunday night, Shamus wouldn't have been able to reach him."

Skye heard the bell and realized that any minute kids would be pouring into Pru's classroom so she took a breath and asked the question she wished she didn't have to bring up. "Did Dr. Wraige intend to say anything to Virginia to ensure her silence?"

"Are you obtuse?" Pru's irritation with Skye was obvious. "Virginia has no idea about any of the other men. Shamus would never take the chance of exposing himself to save an ass like Palmer. It would have been nice to have an ally as the president of the school board, but certainly not worth that kind of risk. Palmer was on his own, and he wouldn't reveal the other club members. They all signed a confidentiality agreement."

"Well, that's good," Skye said evenly. Pru's assertion made sense. Like his cousin, the superintendent was well known as a man who looked after number one and no one else. "Wally and I will keep Shamus's tastes confidential as long as it doesn't concern the murder."

Just as the first student entered, Pru marched into her classroom, followed by Skye.

Stopping short, the English teacher scowled. "See that you do."

"You have my word." Skye headed for the hallway.

Before she could escape, Pru grabbed her wrist and hissed into her ear, "And don't even think of trying to use this against either Shamus or me. Trust me. You will not come out on top."

"I wouldn't dream of it." Skye nearly choked, but managed to keep her expression neutral. "I don't break confidentiality unless someone is a danger to themselves or others. As long as what Dr. Wraige does is consensual, safe, and mutual, I don't care."

"That better be the case. Now"—Pru glanced pointedly at Skye and released her arm—"unlike you, I have a class to teach. So if you'll excuse me."

As soon as Skye got to her office, she phoned Wally, but he wasn't at the PD and didn't answer his cell.

Shoot! She wanted to compare notes and to ask if Dr. Wraige and Pru had alibis. Not to mention, she wanted to find out what Uncle Charlie had to say. She crossed her fingers that her godfather had someone who could account for his whereabouts during the time of death.

The rest of the afternoon whizzed by. In between counseling sessions and writing reports, Skye tried to reach Wally several times, but they ended up playing phone tag. Finally, she gave up and left a message that she'd see him at the police station after work.

A few seconds after the final bell rang at three twenty-five, Skye's office door crashed open and Trixie Frayne dashed through. Skye hurriedly finished the notes she'd been making, tucked the documents into their folder, and filed it away. She hadn't had a chance to hang out in the faculty lounge, so despite Wally's warning to dodge her best friend, she was glad to see her.

Trixie would have the inside scoop on what the gossips were saying about the murder, catnapping, and the break-in. In addition to being the school librarian, cheerleading coach, and co-sponsor of the student newspaper, she kept her finger on the heartbeat of the school and was all too happy to administer CPR if things got dull.

As Trixie rushed toward her, Skye smiled fondly at her friend. Trixie always reminded Skye of a brownie— not the Girl Scout kind, the forest imp variety. She had short nut brown hair and cocoa-colored eyes, a size 4 body, and extremely high spirits.

Trixie dropped into one of Skye's metal visitor chairs, leaned forward, and demanded, "Where have you been hiding all day?"

"Mostly seeing kids and writing psych reports." Skye raised a brow. "You know, doing the stuff the district pays me to do."

Unfazed, Trixie continued, "Why didn't you return my calls and texts yesterday?"

"Sorry," Skye apologized. "There were so many messages, I was overwhelmed. It was a madhouse. Wally and I had supper and went to bed early. We were both exhausted and knew today wouldn't be much better."

"Exhausted or frisky?" Trixie's grin was lascivious. "That man of yours is hot."

Skye inwardly frowned. During her first trimester she'd been turned on all the time. This second trimester? Not so much. Which was the complete opposite of what she'd read and damn annoying. Wally hadn't said anything yet, but she could tell he was disappointed when she went to sleep rather than return his advances. She needed to do something about that before Chantal started looking good to him.

"Hot isn't my number one criterion for a good husband. Right now being a good father is a lot more important," Skye said dryly, then wrinkled her brow.

Although Trixie had seemed happy for Skye and Wally when they'd announced their blessed event, she and Skye had never really discussed Skye's pregnancy. How did her friend feel about the upcoming blessed event?

Clearing her throat, Skye pointed to her belly and said, "This doesn't exactly make me feel in the mood."

"I feel ya," Trixie said. "I sure never want to blow up like a balloon."

"So you and Owen haven't changed your mind about raising a family?" Skye asked.

"Nope." Trixie shook her head. "For a while there we were talking about whether to have a baby or buy a dog. But we decided we'd rather make a mess of our rugs than our lives." She smirked. "For me and Owen, kids would be God's punishment for having sex."

"So you think I'm being punished and ruining my life?" Skye was hurt by Trixie's words.

"Not at all!" Trixie smacked herself on the side of the head, jumped up, and hugged Skye. "You and Wally will be wonderful parents. Me and Owen, not so much." Trixie bit her lip. "But I do worry that things might become different between us. That you'll want to hang out with other moms instead of me."

"Never." Skye hugged her back. "We don't have to change friends as long as we recognize that friends change."

"Awesome!" Trixie returned to her chair, snatched a piece of leftover Easter candy from the jar on Skye's desk, and examined the wrapper. "So tell me about the murder."

"Can we talk about something else, like the break-in at the Legion?"

"Sure." Trixie crossed her legs and dangled her bright yellow high-heel sandal from her toe. "But no one really has any theories about the break-in, except the obvious one. It's common knowledge that there's a lot of cash there for the taking."

"Shoot!"

"Now let's discuss the murder." Trixie smoothed her yellow and black polka-dot skirt over her thighs and tilted her head. "Spill."

"Fine," Skye agreed, then gave Trixie the lowdown on the homicide, without revealing the bondage aspect. When she'd finished, she said, "Any idea why Palmer would have a stolen cat in his garage?"

"None." Trixie peeled the foil off a miniature egg. "From what you told me, he dislikes animals, so cat-napping would seem out of character." She popped the chocolate in her mouth and licked her fingers. "And the drug angle doesn't really compute either. I only met Mr. Lynch a few times, but he sure didn't look like a user to me."

"Me either." Skye watched her friend eat another

candy, resisting the urge to join her. Although Trixie never gained an ounce, Skye could feel the fat forming just looking at the sugary treat. "But you really can't tell. People aren't always what they seem."

Skye closed her eyes thinking just how different Palmer and Dr. Wraige were from the way they presented themselves to the world. She'd bet that the other men in that private club of theirs were the same.

Her lids flew open. Confidentiality agreement aside, if Palmer told the superintendent about his problem with Virginia, he might have told the other guys. Could one of them be so enraged at his indiscretion that he killed him? And who exactly were these men?

Whoever they were, they probably had as much to lose as Palmer and Dr. Wraige. An alternative lifestyle might not be cause for too much concern in Chicago, but in Scumble River those kinds of choices could ruin you.

CHAPTER 15

*A cat may go to a monastery, but she still
remains a cat.*
—ETHIOPIAN PROVERB

Ten minutes later, failing to wheedle any more details about the crime out of Skye, Trixie jumped up from her seat and said, "I'd better get my rear in gear. I haven't done laundry in two weeks, and if I don't wash it tonight, I'll be wearing my bikini as underwear tomorrow." She giggled. "And it's been nearly as long since I've been to the grocery store. I don't have a thing in the fridge to cook and Owen is threatening to whip up a batch of his infamous roadkill stew if he has to eat cereal for supper again."

Chuckling, Skye waved good-bye to her friend, and she hurried out to her car. As she drove to the station, she considered who else might be a part of the private club Pru had mentioned. And which of those men would Palmer be likely to go to for help.

Sifting through the likely candidates from among Scumble River's male population, Skye almost missed her turn into the PD parking lot. The department was housed in a two-story red-brick structure. Accessible from two streets, the police station occupied half the main floor, with the chief's office above and the lone jail cell in the basement. It was bisected by a massive double-deep three-door garage and the city hall took up the other side of the building, with the town library inhabiting its second floor. All three spaces were too small for the growing town, but no one wanted to spend the money to expand, so there was a continuous fight for square footage.

When Skye arrived at three forty-five, the city hall and library were bustling. Both closed at four thirty, and Scumble Riverites hurried to complete last-minute business.

Cars jammed the shared lot and Skye had to circle several times, waiting for someone to pull out. Finally a sleek black Miata vacated its spot and she was able to maneuver her Bel Air between the white lines.

In order to avoid being delayed by her mother, who would be manning the dispatcher's desk, Skye went into the garage and used her key to enter through the door that connected the garage to the station. May would want to chat, and Wally had mentioned that he planned to pick up Virginia as soon as school was out. Knowing her mother, if Skye stopped to talk to her, she wouldn't have time to question Wally about what he'd found out while she'd been busy at school before they had to interview the teacher.

On her way to the stairs that led to Wally's office, Skye passed the coffee/interrogation area. Officer Zelda Martinez and Virginia sat at a long rectangular table. Zelda was staring at the woman as the teacher graded papers. Every time Virginia inked a check mark next to a wrong answer, the young officer flinched and fingered the gun on her belt.

Smiling at Zelda's reaction to the dreaded red pen, Skye climbed the steps to the second floor. She knocked on Wally's closed door, then cracked it open and stuck her head inside.

Wally was on the telephone, but he gestured Skye

over to the visitor chair across from his desk. He smiled at her, then put the phone on speaker, flipped open a folder, and grabbed a pen.

From what Skye could make out, the medical examiner was summarizing the preliminary results of Palmer Lynch's autopsy.

Finally, Wally said, "So what you're saying, Doc, is that the vic was shot in the heart with a forty-five at close proximity somewhere between eleven and midnight?"

"Yes." The ME's voice was hollow as if he, too, had his phone on speaker.

Wally made a note, then continued, "And your conclusion is that Lynch was already tied to the bed prior to being shot?"

"From the marks on his wrists and the powder marks on the skin of his chest, that would be my conclusion." The ME's voice got fainter as if he'd moved away from the microphone on his phone.

"How about drugs or alcohol?" Wally asked, raising a brow at Skye.

"No drugs showed up on the typical tests, and only a small amount of alcohol was in his system."

"Did you check for ketamine?"

"No. But I can," the ME said, then asked, "Any other unusual drugs?"

"Not at this time," Wally answered, then asked, "Is the bullet in good enough shape to make a positive ID if we find a weapon?"

"Yes."

"Thanks, Doc," Wally said. "When can I expect the full report?"

"Give me twenty-four hours." The ME hung up without saying good-bye.

Skye waited several seconds until Wally finished writing and looked up from the file, then asked, "Anything from the crime techs yet?"

"Nothing helpful." Wally rubbed the stubble on his jaw. "I spent the day talking to a few suspects, but didn't get too far. You'll be relieved to know that Charlie has an alibi. He had a plumbing problem in one of the units at the Motor Court and the plumber vouched for his whereabouts from ten until well past midnight."

"Thank goodness!" Skye fanned herself in relief. "Who else did you question?"

"Wraige and that Cormorant woman. Both of whom unfortunately also have alibis." Wally hesitated, then warned, "You may not want to know what they had to say. It could be hard to work with the superintendent once you get that picture into your head."

"Too late." Skye wrinkled her nose. "Pru already told me, and yuck. Then again, it did give me an idea. If Palmer went to Dr. Wraige for help with Virginia, isn't it likely that when the superintendent turned him down, he approached another one of the club members?"

"You might be right," Wally agreed. "The problem will be learning their identities. Ms. Cormorant didn't know any names, and I suspect Wraige won't be as forthcoming as his cousin. I doubt if I can scare him into talking."

"Maybe Virginia would know," Skye offered. "Or I'm still half convinced that either Nate Turner or Tony Zello might be involved."

"I tried to reach both of them today." Wally consulted his notebook. "According to his staff, Zello is at a medical conference in Chicago, and Turner was somewhere up north near Bolingbrook on a big landscaping project. I left a message for both men that I needed to speak to them."

"Which probably means tomorrow at the earliest." Skye got up and walked around the desk. "I guess that leaves Virginia." She took Wally's hand and kissed his cheek. "Let's go talk to her."

As Wally allowed Skye to tug him to his feet, he

winked and quoted one of her favorite movies, "As you wish."

Smiling, she led him to the door, and down the stairs. The minute Skye and Wally entered the coffee/interrogation room, Zelda jumped to her feet.

Not quite saluting, the young officer said, "Chief."

Wally tipped his head at Zelda, then asked, "Has Ms. Elders been read her rights?"

"Yes, sir."

"Did she sign the acknowledgment form?"

"Yes, sir."

He dismissed the young woman and turned to Virginia and asked, "Do you wish to have a lawyer present during questioning?"

"No."

"Okay. I'm Chief Boyd." From the cabinet next to the sink, he took an old-fashioned tape recorder, pushed a button, and said, "Please state your full name and address for the recording."

Virginia complied then flicked a glance at Skye. "What are you doing here?"

Before Skye could speak, Wally explained her status as the psych consultant, adding, "Skye will be sitting in on your interview."

"I . . . uh . . . it might be a little awkward since we're friends."

Skye took the chair next to the teacher and put her hand on her arm. "Nothing you say here will be shared with any member of the school staff. The only reason the content of this interview will ever be made public is if you go to trial for Palmer's murder."

"You can't imagine that I . . ." Color drained from Virginia's face. "We'd broken up. I wasn't even seeing him anymore. What reason would I have to kill him?"

Skye opened her mouth but closed it, not sure how to answer.

Wally ignored Virginia's question, sat across from her, and said, "Why don't we start with why you were no longer dating Lynch?"

Virginia looked down at the table and mumbled something Skye didn't catch.

"What?" Wally asked, leaning forward. "You need to speak up."

"He and I didn't have as much in common as it first appeared." Virginia shook her head sadly. "He wasn't who I thought he was."

Skye wrinkled her brow. Clearly, it wouldn't be easy to get Virginia to talk about her boyfriend's sexual preferences. Glancing at Wally, Skye silently requested permission to take over the questioning. He gave a slight nod and sat back in his chair.

"How was Palmer different than the man you believed him to be?" Skye asked.

"It took me a while to discover it, but his views and mine were diametrically opposed." Virginia avoided Skye's gaze and straightened the pile of homework that she'd been grading. "I knew there were some things we disagreed on, but not the extent of our differences."

"I see." Skye turned so that she was focused entirely on the teacher. Mentally she flipped through several counseling approaches, then settled on Rogerian. She would try to understand how Virginia saw her boyfriend and restate what she was saying about their breakup. "So at first, although you and Palmer weren't in complete accord, the dissimilarities were minor?"

"Exactly." Virginia's brown eyes softened. "And he was willing to discuss those issues." She shook her head. "But when push came to shove, his stance was that it was his way or the highway."

"So when the stakes became larger, Palmer refused to compromise?"

"Yes." Virginia twisted a strand of hair. "The more

important the issue, the more stubborn he became." Her voice faltered. "I . . . I thought I could put up with that. I was so tired of being alone."

"You were willing to overlook some concerns, but not fundamental ones?"

"Uh-huh." Virginia thrust out her chin. "Some things are nonnegotiable."

"And what were those things?" Skye asked. "The non-negotiable ones?"

"Just philosophical differences." Virginia crossed her arms.

"You mentioned that Palmer really liked to be in control," Skye said, recalling their previous conversation about Virginia's boyfriend. "Did that attitude play a part in your decision to break up with him?"

"In a way." Virginia busied herself putting the homework pages in a file and tucking the folder into her canvas tote bag. "There was only so much power that I was willing to cede to him."

Wally's foot nudged Skye's calf and she glanced at him. He was retaking the reins of the interview. She turned her chair to face the table and waited.

"This type of control was too much for you?" Wally tossed down the crime scene photos of Palmer Lynch naked and bound to the bed.

Virginia flinched and tried to push the pictures away from her. When Wally held the snapshots in place, she covered her eyes.

"Don't pretend you were unaware of Lynch's un-usual appetites." Wally raised an eyebrow. "We have a statement from a reliable source that your boyfriend tried to entice you into the lifestyle."

"Then you understand why I broke up with him." Virginia's cheeks were red. "When he suggested spicing up our love life with canes and handcuffs, I told him in no uncertain terms that we were through and gave him back his key."

"So you're saying that Lynch's sexual preferences were the 'philosophical differences' that ended your relationship?" Wally tapped the photos with his fingernail, clearly challenging the woman's statement.

"Yes." Virginia lifted her chin. "There was no way I could be with a man who expected me to surrender myself to his every desire."

"I understand that Palmer apologized and told you it was a joke," Skye said.

She couldn't remember if she'd told Wally that part of her conversation with the English teacher and felt it was an important enough point to interrupt his interrogation.

"Not quite." Virginia shot Skye a puzzled glance, no doubt wondering how she knew so much. "Palmer did apologize for frightening me, but then he attempted to convince me that the submissive had all the power in the relationship and the dominant one would only push as far as was pleasurable for his partner.

"He claimed that he was offering me the ultimate safety and protection. He wanted me to go with him to some kind of private club in Laurel so I could see for myself, but he wasn't willing to tell me who the other members were, so why should I trust him?"

Skye exchanged a glance with Wally, but was silent. She was unsure how to react and didn't want to break whatever fragile trust she had with Virginia.

When neither Wally nor Skye responded to her statement, Virginia continued, "I told Palmer that was double-talk. In the relationship he described, he would have the final say in practically every decision. He expected me to hand over control to him."

"And you were unwilling?" Wally tilted his chair on

its back legs, balanced for a moment, then came down with a thunk and asked, "Is that why you killed him? He wouldn't take no for an answer?"

"Absolutely not!" Virginia squeaked, then took a breath and said, "I told him that I wasn't interested, and that unless he was willing to continue the way we were before his big reveal, we were through."

"And?" Wally's voice reflected his growing impatience, and when Virginia didn't immediately continue, he snapped, "What happened?"

"Palmer said that he could no longer become aroused with vanilla sex." Virginia shrugged. "He'd been having trouble in the bedroom for a while so I wasn't exactly surprised. He asked that I not tell anyone about his preferences, and since I certainly didn't plan to discuss my sex life"—she shot Wally a glare—"I agreed."

Wally flinched and Skye bit the inside of her cheek to stop a giggle. Her husband was a gentleman through and through, and found it difficult to be as hardnosed with female suspects as he could be with men.

Clearing his throat, Wally asked, "When did all this take place?"

"He initially showed me his 'toys' a week ago today." Virginia shrugged. "Then he appeared at my door Sunday evening and asked me to reconsider. I said no."

"What time did he arrive and what time did he leave?" Wally asked.

There was a slight hesitation, then Virginia answered, "He got there a little before six and left about twenty minutes later."

Wally raised an eyebrow at Skye, who shrugged. Virginia's explanation sounded right.

"Did anyone see Lynch arrive at or leave your house?" Wally asked.

"When I opened the door for Palmer, I waved to my next-door neighbor, who was sweeping her porch,"

Virginia offered. "But I don't know if anyone saw him leave."

"Where were you from eleven p.m. to midnight on Sunday?" Wally asked.

"In bed."

"Was anyone with you?"

"Of course not." Virginia's eyes slitted. "I had just ended a monogamous relationship. I certainly didn't hop right into the sack with another man."

CHAPTER 16

There are two means of refuge from the miseries of
life: music and cats.
—ALBERT SCHWEITZER

Wally asked several more questions, but Virginia's answers never varied. Finally, he got up and said to Skye, "Time for a break." He motioned her through the door and called for Zelda to stay with Virginia.

Once Wally and Skye were back in his office, he asked, "What do you think?"

"Everything Virginia said sounds plausible." Skye eased into a chair and kicked off her pumps. Lately she'd been retaining water and every pair of shoes she owned seemed to shrink by late afternoon. "And Virginia's not stupid, so she knows it will be easy enough to check with her neighbors to see if she's telling the truth about Palmer coming by her place when she said he did."

"Yep." Wally scooped up the telephone, pushed a button, and said, "Have Anthony talk to Virginia Elder's neighbors and find out if any of them saw Palmer Lynch at her house Sunday night."

When Wally hung up, Skye said, "Pru did tell me that Palmer planned to approach Virginia and try to repair their relationship. Or at least make sure she didn't talk about his unusual tastes."

"Yeah." Wally walked in front of Skye, leaned against the edge of his desk, and lifted her foot into his lap. "Wraige mentioned that, too."

"Palmer was killed in his bedroom, right?" Skye asked, then moaned in pleasure as Wally rubbed her toes. "His body wasn't moved?"

"That's right." Wally continued to massage as he spoke, his thumbs pressing into Skye's heel.

"So the question then becomes, why would Virginia follow him to his house and kill him?" Skye sighed as Wally's fingers caressed her ankles. "If they quarreled during his visit and she killed him in anger, wouldn't she have done so during the fight?"

"That certainly would be more logical than the whole elaborate setup in his bedroom." Wally returned Skye's left foot to the floor and placed her right in his lap. "The thing that bothers me the most is what motive would Virginia have to murder Lynch?"

"If he tried to force her into a type of sexual relationship she didn't want, that could be a reason to kill him, but just asking her if she'd participate doesn't seem like enough."

"I agree." Wally circled Skye's ankle with his fingers and tightened his grasp. "I did a little research today, and it appears the whole BDSM lifestyle is based on consent rather than force."

"What kind of research?" Skye teased. "Will we need to have Justin clear your computer history before the mayor starts building a case against you? You know Uncle Dante is still out to get you."

Skye's uncle, her mother's brother, was the mayor of Scumble River. And ever since his get-rich-quick scheme to farm out the city's law enforcement needs to the county was thwarted, he'd had a vendetta against the police department in general and Wally in particular.

"I was careful." Wally winked. "I called a buddy of mine from college."

"You have a friend who is . . ." Skye trailed off suggestively.

"Who knows?" Wally smirked. "But I called him because he's a professor of human sexuality."

"Ah." Skye smiled. "Which leads us back to a lack of motive for Virginia."

"That it does." Wally released Skye's ankle and gently put her foot on the floor. "Unless Virginia was so outraged by Lynch's suggestion, she really doesn't have any reason to murder him."

"And if women killed men due to unwelcome or repugnant propositions, a good portion of the male population would be dead."

Wally and Skye had continued to question Virginia after their conference in his office, but didn't discover any new information. Virginia restated that Palmer wouldn't tell her who else belonged to the private club and that he'd left her house Sunday evening after she turned down his attempt at reconciliation.

When her neighbors corroborated her statement regarding Lynch's arrival and departure the night of the murder, Wally told Virginia she could go.

Watching Virginia leave, Skye asked, "Are we talking to anyone else tonight?" It was past seven thirty, but she tried not to let the exhaustion show in her voice.

"Dr. Quillen is next on my list, but I want to wait until the forensic results are in." Wally slipped an arm around Skye's waist. "Let's head home, get some dinner, and you can put your feet up."

"When will the crime scene techs have a report for you?" Skye allowed Wally to guide her out of the station, through the garage, and into the parking lot.

"They promised the summary no later than tomorrow

noon." Wally opened the passenger door of Skye's Bel Air and helped her inside.

As Wally slid behind the wheel, Skye asked, "What about your car?"

"You can drop me at the PD on your way to school." Wally drove the Chevy onto the street. "I want to come in early anyway."

After feeding Bingo, they made a quick meal of the leftover chicken parmesan and garlic bread, cleaned up the kitchen, then curled up on the sunroom's sofa to watch television. Skye sat in her husband's arms and rested her hands on her baby bump. They had both almost dozed off when a painful spasm radiated through Skye's calf.

Jumping to her feet, Skye ran to the kitchen and tiptoed on the cold tile floor. Wally followed, a look of concern marring his handsome face.

As the cramp eased, Skye hobbled back into the sunroom and sank back down on the couch. Wally sat next to her. Brushing a curl behind her ear, he silently began massaging her calf and thigh.

When she relaxed and laid her head back, he asked, "Better?"

"Much." The pain had started her adrenaline pumping, and now wide awake, she said, "Hey, I forgot to ask you about the American Legion break-in. Is there anything new on that investigation?"

"Someone reported seeing an old Buick Regal in the Legion's parking lot after closing time," Wally said. "No license plate number, but they said the paint job was mostly primer and Bondo."

"You know who has a car like that, don't you?" Skye raised a brow.

"No." Wally frowned, then groaned. "Earl Doozier." Wally sighed, "Great. I need to squeeze in a visit with him tomorrow, too."

Skye bit her lip thinking about her firsthand knowledge of Earl's family. "The Dooziers don't usually resort to breaking and entering. Their MO leans toward swindling folks rather than out-and-out robbery."

"True. Except for the occasional brawl, they generally walk that fine line between legal and illegal." Wally pursed his mouth. "The Dooziers may have a permeable view of reality, but they aren't downright delusional."

"Maybe I should talk to him," Skye offered. "Earl's a lot more likely to come clean with me than you. Something about your uniform triggers his natural inclination to lie."

Earl Doozier was the head honcho of the Red Raggers, a group that was hard to explain to anyone who hadn't grown up in Scumble River. The RRs were the crowd that your mother was referring to when she told you not to go into certain parts of town.

They were the folks who were most often the subject of complaint in the newspaper's "Shout Out" column—although they were never mentioned in any letters with signatures, because no one was foolish enough to purposely get the Red Raggers sore at them.

In short, the Dooziers and their clan had family trees that didn't so much branch out as they twisted inward, until all that was left was a Gordian knot of genetic mistakes. Forget survival of the fittest. The Red Raggers were more survival of the sneakiest.

Skye had a special relationship with the Dooziers. She protected them from the bureaucratic school rules, and they protected her from her tendency to be too trusting and believe that there was good in everyone. Normally, she didn't like to press her luck, all too aware that the whammy could hit at any minute, but she knew that things would go better for both Wally and Earl if she was the one to ask why the family's

Regal had been spotted at the scene of a crime. And if Earl had an alibi.

"I don't want you to go to the Dooziers alone," Wally cautioned.

"They'd never hurt me." Skye was fairly sure the only Doozier she had to worry about was Earl's wife, Glenda, who hated her guts.

"Still. I should come with you." Wally's voice was firm. "What if they've changed their methods and now really are into burglary?"

"How about I ask Trixie to come along?" Skye countered. When Wally frowned, she added, "We can casually stop at the Dooziers' place so Trixie can discuss his daughter, Bambi. She's in that club Trixie sponsors, and I understand she's up for an end-of-the-year award."

"Fine." Wally narrowed his eyes. "But if you feel the least bit threatened, grab Trixie and get out of there. No second-guessing. Earl isn't the harmless pet you think he is. He may be dumber than your old cell phone, but stupidity can be dangerous."

"I understand, sweetie." Skye yawned, rose from the sofa, and said, "I'm pooped. Is it too early for you, or are you ready for bed, too?"

Wally got to his feet, slipped an arm around her, and murmured huskily into her ear, "I'm always ready to join you in bed."

"Uh . . ." Skye stuttered. "The thing is, I'm really tired . . ." She trailed off.

Wally pressed openmouthed kisses along her neck. "Want me to carry you?"

Heck! Skye mentally screamed. He wasn't getting the message and she really couldn't blame him. Up until a few weeks ago, she couldn't get enough of her handsome husband. She'd wanted him so often, she'd been half afraid that she would wear him out.

But now, her libido seemed to be in the permanent OFF position. And when she crawled into their king-size four-poster, all she wanted to do was sleep. Unfortunately, she hadn't quite gotten up the nerve to let Wally in on her feelings. How do you tell your husband of less than five months that you aren't interested in sex?

Great! Now Wally was looking at her funny. Realizing she hadn't answered him, Skye stepped out of his embrace, poked him in the chest, and said, "No Rhett Butler moves for you, mister. It's only been a few days since you hurt your back, and with this baby, I weigh a ton."

"I can still sweep you off your feet." Wally grinned and reached for her.

Before he could swing her into his arms, she darted away and said over her shoulder, "Make sure the lights are out and the door is locked."

"This isn't over," Wally warned, his voice fading as Skye trudged up the stairs.

Knowing she had only a few minutes, Skye hurriedly changed into her nightshirt, washed her face, brushed her teeth, and climbed into bed. As her eyelids drifted shut, she vowed to call her doctor and ask if there was anything she could do to jump-start her sex drive. Or at least get an ETA as to when it might be back.

The next day, after dropping Wally off at the police station, Skye headed for the grade school for another session of pet therapy. When Wally had said he wanted to talk to Dr. Quillen that afternoon, she'd forgotten the vet would be with her in the morning. She should have asked if there was anything she should try to find out.

A quick text to Wally and she had her answer—a

resounding no. Wally didn't want Dr. Quillen to have any warning before he interviewed him.

The pet therapy session went smoothly, and Skye walked the vet to the front office. He tried to ask Skye about the murder investigation, but when she explained that she wasn't at liberty to discuss any details, he nodded and said, "Whatever else happens, at least Belle is back safe and sound."

Skye's afternoon at the junior high was jammed with annual reviews, but she took a few seconds to call Trixie. A promise of a lengthier explanation to come, and her friend agreed to arrange the meeting with Earl and meet Skye in the high school parking lot as soon after the dismissal bell sounded as possible.

Getting Glenda out of the way was a bit trickier, but Trixie said she had a plan. Skye didn't get a chance to ask for details, which was probably for the best. Her friend's schemes were frequently convoluted, but more often than not successful, so it was best to go along, but not necessarily know all the particulars.

The afternoon dragged on, and by the time the final annual review ended, Skye was sick of the words *Individualized Education Plan*. After a crucial bathroom stop—Baby Boyd seemed to be doing a tap dance on her bladder—Skye hurried across the campus to the high school.

Rushing toward the parking lot, Skye was relieved to see Trixie leaning against her Honda. If she wanted to talk to Earl *and* get to the PD in time to help Wally with interviews, Skye needed to streamline the upcoming Doozier encounter.

As Skye skidded to a stop, her friend straightened and tucked the cell phone she'd been holding into her pocket. Today Trixie wore skinny ankle-length floral slacks with an asymmetrical celery green shirt. Skye smoothed her own boring black and white checked maternity top over her stomach, fingered her wrinkled black slacks, and grimaced. She looked like the ugly stepsister.

"Get in." Trixie slid behind the wheel, and after Skye maneuvered into the passenger seat and fastened her safety belt, she turned on the engine and sped out of the lot. Once they were rocketing down the road, Trixie said, "Fill me in."

"Earl's car was spotted in the American Legion parking lot the night of the break-in and I figured he'd tell us more than the police," Skye summarized, then asked, "Were you able to get rid of Glenda?"

"Yep." Trixie grinned. "She has to go claim her prize this afternoon or she loses it." When Skye made a continue motion with her hand, Trixie explained, "I asked a pal of mine who sells Lady Ladonna cosmetics to call Glenda and tell her she'd won a free demo."

"Smart." Skye beamed at her friend. "It's a win-win situation. We don't have to deal with the wicked witch and she gets some much-needed makeup tips. Who knows? Maybe Glenda will even stop going for the raccoon look with her eyeliner and mascara."

"We can only dream." Trixie smirked, then asked, "So what's the plan? I told Earl that I wanted to discuss Bambi's GIVE award."

"Get Involved, Value Everyone" was the service club Trixie had recently established as one of the high school's extracurricular activities. Much to her and Skye's surprise, Earl's youngest daughter had joined and become one of the leading freshman members.

"I don't have a plan per se," Skye admitted. "More like a beginning, middle, and I hope an end that doesn't involve Earl's shotgun."

"Sort of like how I write." Trixie laughed. "I hate outlines. Which might be why it's taking me forever to finish this dang book."

"I love outlines." Skye crossed her arms. "But I didn't have time to come up with one for this project. Winging it is so not how I like to do things, but I figure we'll start out with the award stuff." Skye glanced at Trixie. "You do have that worked out, right?"

"Sure."

"Phew." Skye blew out a long breath. "Then I'll casually mention the Legion's break-in and try to steer the conversation toward Sunday night."

"So far, so good." Trixie nodded her approval. "But what's the ending?"

"Once Earl admits he was at the Legion, I'll ask him what time he left and why his car was there after the place was closed."

"And if he doesn't have a good answer or refuses to say?" Trixie prodded.

"That part is harder to figure out." Skye chewed her bottom lip.

"Well, you better do it soon." Trixie spun the wheel and pulled into a rutted driveway. "Because we're here."

CHAPTER 17

One cat just leads to another.
—ERNEST HEMINGWAY

Marching up the Dooziers' weed-choked sidewalk, Skye was relieved to see that Glenda's Chevy was gone. There were various vehicles scattered in and near the ramshackle garage, but the prickly woman's prized 1974 baby blue Monte Carlo—a car no one but Glenda was allowed to drive—was conspicuously absent.

When Skye first returned to Scumble River, she and Glenda had an argument about Glenda's kids throwing rocks at the glass marquee in front of Vince's hair salon. The annoyed mother hadn't taken Skye's intervention well and had never forgiven her for interfering with her God-given right to ignore her children's bad behavior. It didn't take a very big person to carry a grudge, and if Glenda's shoulders could lug around her double-D boobs, they certainly could support her vendetta against Skye.

Shaking her head at the bleached blonde's pigheadedness, Skye studied the Doozier house. It was far more dilapidated than the shacks she'd seen as a Peace Corps volunteer in Dominica. Random tufts of crabgrass grew between cars up on cinder blocks and in the front yard; old appliances were scattered around like lawn ornaments.

A new hand-lettered sign had been added since the last time Skye had visited. Tacked to a tilted wooden stake near the front of the house was a poster that read, KEEP OUT. SHYSTERS COST 2 DAMN MUCH SO WE SHOOT 2 KILL. She was impressed that all of the words were spelled correctly and wondered if Bambi had been enlisted as Earl's ghostwriter.

In the warm humid air, Skye could smell animals, and the growls and snarls coming from the backyard were anything but welcoming. She was trying to remember just how many dogs the Dooziers owned and if the pen holding them was a sturdy one when Junior burst out the side door.

He had a red crew cut, and a wide jack-o'-lantern grin lit up his freckled face. "Miz F, Miz D, what are you two doing here? You okay, Miz D?" He had come to her aid on more than one occasion, and now considered himself her personal guardian angel.

"I'm fine, thanks." Skye smiled. "How have your sophomore classes gone?"

Skye hadn't seen too much of Junior during the school year and she hoped that was because he was doing well in school. The boy had average intelligence, but he had a severe learning disability and often gave up trying to learn because he felt stupid.

"Okay." Junior dug his sneaker-clad toe in the dirt. "My SpEd teacher says that I might make all C's if I do okay on—finals."

"That's awesome!" Skye would have loved to hug the boy, but touching a student was a dangerous idea. Too many innocent educators had been falsely accused or hit with groundless lawsuits to risk an embrace. Instead, she held up her hand for a high five. "You come see me when you get your report card. If you get all C's or above, I'll have a reward for you."

"What kinda reward?" Junior asked. "Not some stupid old sticker?"

"Nope." Skye shook her head. "It's a surprise, but I promise you'll like it."

Junior remembered the incentives Skye had given out when he was in grade school. Too bad that once the kids moved on to junior and senior high, the cost of prizes skyrocketed. Once the students entered their teens, she switched to McDonald's gift cards, which she had to purchase with her own money since the district refused to give her any type of budget.

"Wait until I tell Cletus. He ain't doin' half as good as me." Junior started to run off.

Skye called after him. "We're here to see your dad. Is he home?"

"Yeah." Junior skidded to a stop. "Ma went off somewhere to pick up a prize, but Pa's here." The boy motioned for them to follow him. "Come on."

Junior led Skye and Trixie through the side screen door, past a tiny entryway, up a few steps covered in peeling linoleum, and into the kitchen. Skye wrinkled her nose at the odor of stale beer and cigarettes hanging in the air, then cringed at the raised voices blasting from the other side of the room.

A chipped Formica-topped table had been shoved against a stained wall, and Earl Doozier had an extremely handsome man in his forties backed against the edge. Earl was heavily tattooed and wearing only a pair of camo shorts, while the other guy was dressed in crisp khaki shorts and a mint green polo shirt. One of the men looked out of place in the Doozier home, and it wasn't Earl.

Trixie elbowed Skye in the side and asked, "Who's the hunk?"

Skye jumped at her friend's touch. She'd been engrossed in trying to figure out what the men were arguing about. Most of what she could make out were either threats or cursing.

"That's my fiancé, Dr. AJ Martino," Yolanda Doozier answered, stepping between Skye and Trixie.

Yolanda was a raven-haired beauty whose lush curves made the twisting Scumble River look as straight as a telephone pole. Although not in the same class, the three women had gone to high school together. Yolanda was one of the rare Red Raggers with ambitions beyond Scumble River, and she made it a point to speak standard English instead of Doozierese.

"Congratulations!" Skye and Trixie said in unison.

"AJ and I are getting married as soon as he clears up a few technicalities." Yolanda thrust her left hand in their faces.

As Skye oohed and ahhed over the large diamond solitaire sparkling on Yolanda's finger, she wondered what sort of technicality was holding up the wedding. Could it be the same issue that had delayed Skye's own nuptials? Was the groom Catholic and waiting for an annulment? After all, the Dooziers might not worship anything except beer and guns, but that didn't mean their future in-law wasn't religious.

Suddenly, Yolanda grabbed Skye's wrist and said, "Yours is nice, too." Her thumb stroked the two-carat stone of the engagement ring and the baguette-studded wedding band. "I heard you did pretty well in the marriage sweepstakes."

"Wally is a wonderful husband," Skye agreed, knowing that wasn't what Yolanda meant. "I hope you and AJ will be as happy as we are."

"We will." Yolanda shot a pointed glance at Skye's midsection and patted her own slim waist. "But we'll be a heck of a lot more careful. No way am I ruining this figure by popping out a kid."

"Everyone has to make the right choice for them," Skye said, admiring Yolanda, as she did Trixie, for knowing that motherhood wasn't for all women.

"Choice?" Yolanda laughed. "Let's see. You got married the end of December, and you're what?" She gazed at Skye's stomach and pursed her lips. "Five, maybe six months pregnant? I'd bet that's an oops baby."

"Then you'd be wrong." Skye lifted her head. There wasn't a chance in hell that she was allowing that rumor to get started. "Wally and I have been open to conceiving since our engagement."

"Right." Yolanda sniggered, then shrugged. "Although at his age, I guess . . ."

Before the woman could start down another innuendo trail, Skye asked, "When did you get back in town, Yolanda? After Dr. Addison's death and your move into the city, I don't recall you visiting much."

Yolanda had been the office manager for Ken Addison's medical practice. When he'd been murdered, her job disappeared. Rumor had it that she'd decided to make a fresh start somewhere that no one knew her or her relatives' reputations.

"That's right." Yolanda crossed her arms. "At first I was too busy. I tried a lot of different kinds of work. Then a few months ago, I took a position at the Golden Mile Center for Cosmetic Surgery and fell in love with the boss." She beamed in the direction of her fiancé and said, "AJ is the owner of the clinic."

"So you brought AJ here to meet your family?" Trixie asked.

"Yeah." Yolanda fingered the rose tattoo peeking from her cleavage. "I put it off as long as I could, but AJ insisted on coming. A fraternity brother that he'd recently gotten back in contact with lives in Scumble River and he wanted to look him up." She jerked her chin at Earl and her fiancé. It appeared as if they were about to come to blows. "I bet AJ's sorry now he didn't listen to me."

"What's the problem?" Skye asked. "Doesn't your brother approve of the marriage?"

"Like I give a flying crap what he thinks," Yolanda snorted. "No. A few minutes after we got here Saturday afternoon, Earl ran over AJ's brand-new Porsche Boxster with some mutated bulldozer thingy he built. He smashed the entire driver's side and we've been stuck in this shit town ever since."

"Can't you rent a car?" Trixie asked. "Or have Earl drive you to Chicago?"

Before Yolanda could answer, Earl bellowed, "Iffen you didn't go parkin' in my blind spot, Ida never hit your goldang hotrod."

"Nevertheless, you're liable for the damage." AJ adjusted the Rolex on his wrist. "And since you have no insurance, you need to make it right."

"They've been going at it for the past four days." Yolanda shook her head. "Earl said that he had a friend who could fix the damage. The guy came Saturday night and picked up the Porsche. He promised that we'd have it back by Tuesday, but still no sign of it."

"Which friend?" Skye tensed, fearing that AJ's Porsche was in some distant chop shop, resting in pieces.

"No idea." Yolanda bent to adjust the gold bracelet around her ankle. "And Earl claims to have lost the guy's phone number."

"Shit!" Trixie yelped, then glanced at Junior and put her hand over her mouth.

"AJ refuses to leave until he has his car back." Yolanda poked out her bottom lip. "Which means our Disney vacation is ruined. I had reservations to eat breakfast with Cinderella and everything."

"You were on your way to Florida and figured a quick stop in Scumble River would be a good idea?" Skye guessed. "That way just one night, introduce him to the family and a swift departure down the highway?"

"Twenty-four hours in and out was how AJ talked me into it." Yolanda stalked over to Earl and tugged him away from her fiancé. "Instead, I'm trapped in this hell-hole."

As Yolanda manhandled her brother or half brother or stepbrother or however they were related—the Doozier lineage was tough to follow—Skye grimaced. Except for a modest beer belly that hung over the waist of his shorts, Earl was as thin as a snake, but she feared what would happen if Yolanda pushed him too far.

Scumble Riverites knew you didn't put your hands on a Doozier, even kin, without his permission. Obviously, several years away and four days held hostage in the Doozier compound had made Yolanda forget.

Earl's face was now redder than the Miller High Life trucker cap on his head, and he windmilled both arms around wildly, nearly hitting Yolanda in the face. "You tell your highnmighty feeunsay that my friend ain't no thief. He'll get that fancysmancy car of his back here as soon as it's fixed."

"Couldn't Earl drive it back to the city?" Skye asked. "Then you and AJ could fly to Orlando."

"AJ doesn't like airplanes." Yolanda rolled her eyes. "He claims they trigger his asthma."

"Maybe you two could take Earl's Buick, and on your way back from Florida you could pick up the Porsche," Trixie suggested, pulling Yolanda away from her brother.

"I'm not driving that piece of shit." AJ moved next to Yolanda.

"Hell no!" Yolanda crossed her arms. "It didn't even make it back from the bar Sunday night."

"It was fine when we left here." Earl sputtered. "Some-body must've messed with it when we were inside." He shrugged. "Anyways I always says that the most interestin' trip starts with a broken fan belt and a leaky tire."

Trixie wiggled her brows at Skye, indicating this was their opening. Skye nodded and cleared her throat. Three pair of eyes swung in her direction.

"So you all went out Sunday night," Skye said cheerfully. "Where did you go?"

"Some hole-in-the-wall American Legion post," AJ sneered.

"Did your frat brother tell you about it?" Trixie asked.

"Uh. Yeah." AJ shot her an irritated look. "He was busy so we couldn't get together, but he said that there was an interesting contest called the King of Diamonds and suggested it might be fun to give it a try. But once I saw how the game was set up, I immediately figured out the only big winner would be the house."

"And the car broke down?" Skye ignored AJ's tantrum. "How did you get home?"

"One of Yolanda's friends gave everyone else a lift." AJ screwed up his face.

"But not you?" Trixie's expression was flirtatious and she tapped his arm.

"No." AJ shuddered. "The proffered transportation was in the back of a dirty pickup." He scowled. "I wasn't risking my APO jeans."

"So you stayed with Earl's car?" Trixie asked. "That had to be boring."

"It wasn't fun." AJ shrugged. "But his friend, the one supposedly fixing my Porsche, finally showed up and got the beater running."

"What time was that?" Skye asked.

"Why do you ask?" Yolanda's thickly lashed violet eyes narrowed and she tilted her head. "What are you doing here anyway?"

"That's exactly what I want to know." An angry

voice shrilled from the doorway and Glenda Doozier stomped up to the group. Thrusting her face into Skye's, she sprayed saliva as she yelled, "You better not be accusin' anybody in this family of nothin'."

"Of course not." Skye's pulse rate increased and she crossed her arms protectively around her baby bump. "Mrs. Frayne and I just stopped over to tell you about Bambi's award and invite your family to the final GIVE meeting to see her accept it."

"What in the hell is Bambi doin' now?" Glenda clutched a huge purple and green purse to her ample chest. "We ain't givin' nobody nothin'."

"GIVE stands for Get Involved, Value Everyone," Trixie rushed to explain. "It's a service club. We promote community welfare and goodwill."

"We ain't donatin' to Goodwill either." Glenda scowled at Yolanda. "All this la-di-dah stuff is your doin'. You're a bad influence."

From her stiletto-heeled gold sandals to her knock-off Paris Hilton blond wig, Glenda was the quintessence of Red Ragger womanhood. And Red Raggers did not help their fellow man. They helped themselves to their fellow man's property and considered it a good deed.

"But . . ." Trixie struggled to explain, looking at Skye, who shrugged. Finally Trixie said, "Remember the rubber duck race? The club organized it to save the no-kill animal shelter. Our members didn't give anything but their time and the kids had fun."

"See, honey pie," Earl, beaming like the proud owner of a blue ribbon hog, rushed over to her and put an arm around her waist. "It didn't cost us nothin' and Bambi's takin' a real likin' to the club."

Glenda stared at Earl. "When did you start carin' what the kids liked?'"

"In the olden days daddies jest worked and provided

for their family." Earl lifted his nonexistent chin. "But now they neuter their kids, too."

Skye's eyes widened until she translated. Earl had to mean "nurtured."

"What are you talkin' about?" Glenda growled.

Earl looked down and mumbled, "Now, baby cakes, yous knows I love the young'uns."

Glenda cuffed him on the side of the head. "You tryin' to make me look bad?" Her blowup-doll-size bust heaved and her fake lashes fluttered.

Earl, taking his life in his own hands, said, "You're doin' a mighty good job of that without my help." He straightened his scrawny shoulders. "Bambi and Yolanda ain't like the rest of us, but they're still kin."

Skye and Trixie gasped. Glenda had the personality of a wolverine and Earl had just offered his throat to her razor-sharp teeth.

Glenda glared at her husband and screamed, "If you know what's good for you, Earl Doozier—"

Once again thrusting himself into the lion's den, he cut her off. "Accordin' to you, I ain't never before, so why should I start now?"

Trixie whispered in Skye's ear, "When did Earl grow a pair of—"

Skye shushed her and turned her attention back to the quarreling couple.

"It's a good thing for you that I don't wanna break a nail, or I'd teach you to sass me." Glenda waved the red talons on the end of her fingertips. "I'm goin' to take a bubble bath." Glenda crushed out her cigarette in an overflowing ashtray on the kitchen table. "And when I'm through, you better have your skinny butt ready to make this all up to me. You hear?"

"Get along with you." Earl had a stubborn expression on his usually slack-jawed face. "Miz Skye and Miz Trixie is our guests and you ain't bein' polite to 'em. I'm goin' fetch 'em a beer and we's goin' conversate about Bambi and how first-rate she's doin' at school."

Glenda grabbed Earl by the shirt. "You're lucky I'm in a good mood." She tugged at the crotch of her spandex shorts, her halter top exposing a large expanse of chalk white skin. "But these two better be outta my house by the time I get through with my bath."

Earl looked from his wife to Skye and back. "You gots a deal."

CHAPTER 18

The cat who frightens the mice away is as
good as the cat who eats them.
—GERMAN PROVERB

Skye and Trixie took a seat at the kitchen table, but refused Earl's offer of refreshment. Earl seemed puzzled when Skye said she couldn't have a beer because of the baby. And when she tried to explain, Trixie elbowed her in the ribs and shook her head. Skye clamped her lips shut. Her friend was right. What was the point?

Yolanda and Earl pulled up chairs and joined Skye and Trixie, but when they all looked in AJ's direction, he muttered something about needing to check in with his clinic and slammed out the door.

Earl narrowed his beady eyes and said, "That guy is more full of shit than a Porta-Potty after the Chokeberry Days chili-eatin' contest."

Yolanda's face turned an alarming shade of purple and Trixie quickly spoke to Earl. She went over how his daughter had earned the service club's award, then handed him a sheet of paper with the time and place of the meeting where Bambi would be honored.

Finished with the purported reason for their visit, Skye knew she had only one or two questions left before their presence would become questionable. And no one wanted to outstay their welcome at the Dooziers. Not even someone they considered a friend.

Pasting a casual smile on her face, she turned to Earl and said, "By the way, that pal of yours who fixes cars, what's his name?"

"Cooter somethin' or other?" Earl lifted his cap and thoughtfully scratched his head. "I don't rightly recollect the rest."

"Why do you want to know?" Yolanda asked, suspicion shining from her eyes.

Skye thought fast and said, "Wally and I are thinking of getting a new car before the baby comes and I want to have a few dents and scratches fixed on my Bel Air before we try to sell it."

"If Cooter ever returns AJ's Porsche, I'll ask him to call you." Yolanda's smirk told Skye that she didn't believe her story.

Earl immediately started to whine, "Cooter's real reliable-like. He'll get 'er done soon. I don't know why AJ is so upset. It weren't more than a little scrape."

"Right," Yolanda snorted, then poked her brother in the arm. "Speaking of the accident, what exactly was that thing you were driving?"

"My Doozier Dozer," Earl said, puffing out his chest. "I made it myself."

"Why do you need an armor-plated bulldozer?" Yolanda demanded.

"I'm gettin' ready for the end of the world." Earl took off his hat, revealing muddy brown hair that formed a horseshoe around a bald spot the size of a bocce ball. "Haven't you been watchin' TV? Lots of folks are goin' to be turned into zombies any day, and when they attack, they'll chew through any kind of regular vehikkle."

"Last time you brought out the Doozier Dozer, didn't you say that Reverend Alphonse told you that godless hordes from the Middle East were about to appear?" Skye asked.

"Well, yeah." Earl rubbed the dense tattoos covering his arms. "But they never showed up soes I put the dozer away. Then when I heard about the zombies, I fired her up again and she still runs just fine."

"I see." Skye had long ago given up attempting to make any sense of Earl's reasoning. Changing the subject, she said, "So you still had Cooter's number Sunday night when you phoned him for help with your Buick?"

"I must have." Earl blew his lips in and out for several seconds before finally adding, "Hows else could I have called him?"

He had a point. Skye abandoned that line of questioning and asked what she really wanted to know. "When did AJ get home from the Legion?"

"Let's see. The bar closed down and kicked everyone out at twelve thirty, and once we realized the Buick wouldn't start, it took us a bit to find a ride so it was pretnear one by the time we got back here." Earl furrowed his brow. "I musta passed out before Prince AJ got back."

"AJ got home about half an hour or so later." Yolanda smiled thinly. "You may fool my brother, but I heard about the break-in at the Legion and even you aren't crazy enough to think a successful plastic surgeon would risk going to prison for a measly thirty-two thousand dollars."

Skye opened her mouth to reply but Yolanda held up her hand. "That kind of money is chump change to a man like AJ. A drop in the bucket." She spread her arms wide. "He makes more than that on one boob job."

Earl had been silent while the women talked, but now he scratched his crotch and said, "Miz Skye, if I remembers Cooter's number, I'll call you."

At that, Glenda charged into the kitchen and whacked

Earl on the head with a hairbrush. "You best not be cal-
lin' any females but me."

Skye said quickly, "Glenda, you don't have to worry
about—"

"You better pray that's the truth." Glenda bared her
teeth.

Skye's lips quirked as she tried to hide her grin.
Maybe the Doozers were more religious than she
thought. Or more likely, the Red Ragger Queen had
gotten off the crazy train a few stops short of her intended destination.

Grabbing her husband's ear, Glenda pulled him out
of his chair and screeched, "I keep tellin' you to stay
away from that woman."

Skye stood up and said, "Thanks for taking the time
to talk to us." As the Kenny Rogers song advised, it
was time to fold 'em. "Have a good evening."

"See you at the awards ceremony." Trixie rose to
her feet and followed Skye to the door. "Bring the
whole family. Afterwards, we're serving punch, and
Orlando from Tales and Treats is baking his famous
shortbread cookies. They are scrumptious."

As the two women drove away, Skye looked at her
friend and said, "You do realize just how many Doozier
kin there are, right?"

"Oops!" Trixie grinned. "I better ask Orlando to double the cookies."

"More like triple it," Skye muttered, then smiled. "At
least the Doozers are clear for the Legion break-in. I
knew that wasn't their style."

"How about Yolanda's fiancé? You said the break-in
was around two a.m.," Trixie asked as she turned into
the school parking lot and pulled next to Skye's car.
"His alibi is shaky."

"I'll certainly tell Wally about him," Skye said, getting out of the Honda. "But Yolanda's right. Why would

a successful doctor attempt burglary? To him that amount of money would be peanuts."

Trixie shrugged, waved good-bye, and drove away. Settling behind the wheel of her Bel Air, Skye dug out her phone and checked to see if she'd missed a message from Wally as to whether he had anyone at the police station that he wanted her help in interviewing.

Shoot! It was still on vibrate. She'd forgotten to turn on the sound after work. Although the new district policy allowed staff to use cell phones, they had to be muted during the school day. Sighing, she scrolled through her texts. There was one from Wally saying he was on his way to Dr. Quillen's veterinary clinic and asked her to meet him there.

She checked the time and saw he'd left the message only a few minutes ago. Fastening her seatbelt, Skye fired up the Chevy, pulled out of the lot, and headed south of town to join her husband.

Skye pulled into Dr. Quillen's lot and parked next to the squad car. Getting out of the Bel Air, she stepped toward the cruiser and felt its hood. It was still warm. Wally couldn't have arrived too long ago.

When she walked through the double glass doors, the waiting room was empty, but a few seconds later a huge man with acne-scarred skin and a crew cut lumbered into sight. He wore jeans and a T-shirt with the clinic's name and logo printed across his massive chest. His muscular arms were decorated with tattoos and his ear was pierced.

He marched behind the front counter and growled, "We're closed."

"I don't need your professional services," Skye said, indicating her lack of pet. "My husband, Chief Boyd, asked me to meet him here."

"He's with Dr. Q." The guy jerked his thumb over his shoulder. "Follow that hallway."

"Okay." Skye held out her hand. "By the way, I'm Skye Denison-Boyd."

The man eyed her palm as if it were holding a live grenade, but finally gripped her fingers for a nanosecond and muttered, "Name's Cal."

"Are you Dr. Quillen's assistant?" Skye didn't recall seeing him when she'd brought Bingo for his yearly checkup a few months ago.

"Doc hired me to keep an eye on the place." Cal crossed his gigantic arms.

"After the catnapping?" Skye asked, and when the man nodded, she said, "I bet Dr. Quillen feels much better about his animals' safety with you around. Do you work for a security company?"

"Freelance," Cal answered, then pointing to the corridor he'd already indicated, he repeated, "Your husband and Doc are that way."

Recognizing a dismissal when she heard one, Skye thanked the taciturn man and followed the passageway to the back of the building until it ended at an alarmed exit. To her right was a closed door marked DOGS and on her other side was one marked CATS.

Hmm. Cal hadn't said which kennel area Wally and Dr. Quillen were in, but since Belle had been the one taken, Skye went left.

Dr. Quillen and Wally were standing in the center of the aisle. On either side were six-by-six-foot rooms with sliding glass gates. All of the spaces had a cushion, water bowl, and food dish on the floor. And behind a privacy screen, Skye could just make out a litter box. Felines of every size and color occupied the luxurious quarters.

As Skye walked toward the men, Wally turned and smiled at her. Taking her hand, he said, "How did your visit to the Dooziers go?"

"Interesting." She squeezed his fingers. "I'll give

you the scoop later." Gesturing around her, Skye said, "Dr. Q, this is quite a setup."

"I had it remodeled when I bought the practice." The vet frowned. "The old cattery consisted of three levels of stacked cages." He grimaced. "No animal in my care would live like that."

"I take it the dog kennel got a similar makeover?" Skye asked.

"Of course." Dr. Quillen beamed. "Would you like to see it?"

Skye looked at Wally, and when he nodded, she said, "Sure. Lead the way."

After they crossed the hallway and Skye admired the clinic's canine accommodations, she asked, "I don't think I ever heard. In addition to Belle, was anything else stolen during the break-in?"

"We were just discussing that before you arrived," Wally said.

"Yes." Dr. Quillen wrinkled his brow. "Nothing else was disturbed. I've had drugs stolen before so I keep the pharmaceuticals on a mobile cart that I secure in a walk-in safe."

"It would seem that the bad guy's sole intent was to take an animal to use for coercion purposes," Wally said. "You were only contacted by the catnapper that one time, right, Dr. Quillen?"

Wally had his cell phone out and Skye peeked at the screen. He'd brought up information on ketamine, but from her angle she couldn't read the small print.

"Correct." The vet nodded. "He or she demanded five hundred bottles of liquid ketamine or Belle would be delivered to me in pieces. The extortionist said something about his usual supplier being permanently unavailable."

"What size bottles?" Wally asked, tapping the screen of his cell to bring up the calculator app.

"Five hundred milligrams."

Wally whistled. "Street value on that would be half a million dollars."

"Oh. My. God!" Skye gasped. "Why is a veterinarian drug so valuable?"

As a school psychologist she was certainly familiar with marijuana, cocaine, methamphetamine, even heroin, which were the drugs of choice for the kids in Scumble River, but beyond knowing that ketamine was referred to as Special K, she was in the dark.

"The physical effects of ketamine are similar to PCP crossed with LSD, but the trip lasts an hour or less," Wally answered. "Lower-dose experiences are reported to be smooth and very colorful. But higher doses often cause a near-death-like experience."

"Don't forget," Dr. Quillen added, "due to ketamine's dissociative effect, it's also become popular as a date-rape drug."

"Just what the world needs," Skye muttered. "Another way to sexually assault women." She frowned.

Hmm. Was Palmer intending to use the ketamine on Virginia to ensure her participation in his bondage games? But then why would he need so much?

"I know the street price is a thousand dollars a bottle, but what would a bottle cost you?" Wally asked the veterinarian.

"Usually around eight bucks," Dr. Quillen answered. "But requesting that quantity would have set off red flags. I don't have a track record of doing enough procedures to warrant that large an order."

"What was your plan?" Skye asked. "I know you weren't going to just let them mutilate Belle, so you must have had something in mind."

"I ordered as much as I could without arousing suspicions." Dr. Quillen shrugged. "I was going to give the catnapper what I could get and hope it would be enough."

Skye moved closer to the vet and patted his slumped shoulder, but the smell of the disinfectant Dr. Quillen used caused her to feel queasy and she swayed.

He immediately gripped her elbow and suggested, "Why don't we sit in my office?"

"Good idea." Wally put his arm around Skye's waist and pulled her away from the vet.

Once the three of them were seated at a table, Dr. Quillen, a look of concern on his handsome face, asked, "Skye, would you like some ginger ale? Or maybe some tea?"

"No thanks." She smiled at him. "I'm already feeling better. I think it must have been whatever you use to wash your hands. I've read that during pregnancy strong odors can bring on transitory nausea."

"It's no trouble at all to get you a drink," he persisted.

"That's very sweet of you, but I'm fine." Then without thinking, Skye blurted out, "Are you seeing anyone, Dr. Q?"

Wally shot Skye a fiercely possessive look and she quickly explained, "I was talking to our school nurse, Abby Fleming, and she was saying how hard it is to meet a nice guy. It just dawned on me that the two of you might have a lot in common. Not to mention she's gorgeous."

"I'm not dating anyone right now." Dr. Quillen's voice was cautious. "I think Abby might have brought her dachshund in for a knee problem. Is she a tall blonde with blue eyes and an athletic build?"

"Yes. That's her. She's a really good tennis player." Skye beamed. "If you like, I could set up you two."

"Well . . ." The vet hesitated, then swallowed hard and said, "Actually, I play quite a bit of tennis, too. So, sure."

Tilting his head at Skye, Wally raised a brow and said, "If you're done matchmaking, I have a few more items to discuss with Dr. Quillen."

"Be my guest." Skye wrinkled her nose at him. "Sorry to interrupt."

Wally asked the vet several questions about the break-in and Skye listened carefully to the men's conversation. All the fingerprints in the area of the crime had been matched to Dr. Quillen, his staff, or the cleaning crew. The blackmailer's call had been traced back to a disposable phone. And currently, the only lead was finding the missing cat in Palmer Lynch's garage. But there was no evidence that proved Lynch had been the catnapper.

Skye blew her lips in and out, then asked, "Why do you think that the burglar took Belle as opposed to one of the other animals?"

"My guess is that it was because she was the focus of the article in the newspaper." Dr. Quillen sighed. "The piece stated that Belle was a pedigree and trained for my pet therapy practice, so I would assume the catnapper figured she was the most valuable animal here."

"But her therapy partner had a pedigree and was highly trained, too," Skye said thoughtfully. "And he was in the *Star* as well."

"True." Dr. Quillen nodded. "And now that you mention it, the dog kennels have an exterior door, so it's easier in and out than the cattery, which has no exit other than the one into the clinic itself."

"I noticed that the kennels only have a latching system, but the sliding doors to the cat's quarters have a keypad," Skye added. "Which means he or she had to force his or her way through two entry points."

"The glass to Belle's door was smashed to smithereens," Dr. Quillen confirmed. "The repairman just fixed it today."

"So why choose the cat?" Wally murmured, tapping his pen on the table.

"Maybe because the catnapper was deathly afraid of dogs?" Skye murmured. "Virginia told me that Palmer's mother bred prize-winning German shepherds, and that one day when he and his mother were having some sort of argument, a couple of her dogs attacked him."

"Considering that Belle was found in Lynch's garage, I'm now inclined to believe that Lynch probably was the catnapper." Wally stood and started pacing. "Which leads us to the question of what did he want with so much ketamine?"

"If he planned to sell it, how was he going to distribute the drugs?" Skye pursed her lips. "The amount he demanded would be a lot for a small town to absorb."

"Maybe he had a partner." Wally shoved his hands in his pockets. "Maybe more than one."

CHAPTER 19

Scalded cats fear even cold water.
—THOMAS FULLER

After Wally and Skye said good-bye to Dr. Quillen, they walked from the clinic into the parking lot. Skye slid a peek at her silent husband's profile. His jaw was clenched and the muscles in his arms were rigid. Something was definitely bothering him; she just wasn't sure what.

Wally opened Skye's car door, but before she could slip inside, he slid one arm around her waist and used the other to cup the back of her head. Instead of the usual tender kiss they exchanged in public or the passionate ones they shared in private, this time his lips branded her as his.

Skye was surprised by his sudden possessiveness, but she leaned into her husband's embrace. Was her pregnancy causing him to have some of the same insecurities that she was experiencing?

Several breathless minutes later, Wally settled her behind the wheel of the Bel Air, stroked her hair, and said, "Let's go grab some supper and catch up on our day. It feels like forever since this morning."

"Where shall we go?" Skye asked, glancing at her watch. "It's past six, so the Feed Bag shouldn't be too crowded."

"It will be a zoo." Wally shook his head. "The Chamber of Commerce is meeting there, and I want an hour with you to myself before I have to go back to work."

"Do you have other suspects to talk to tonight?"

"Yep. I need to do one more interview before calling it a day." Wally leaned his forehead against Skye's. "I really don't have time to drive somewhere out of town, which leaves fast food as our only option." He frowned. "I'm sorry we can't go to a nice restaurant."

"I don't mind at all," Skye reassured him, pressing a soft kiss to his chin. "In fact, I'm glad for the excuse to indulge in McDonald's French fries. I've had a craving for them for weeks."

"Why didn't you swing by the drive-thru and get some?"

"Because I'm trying not to gain any more weight than necessary for the baby to be healthy." She puffed out her cheeks and looked ruefully down at her stomach. "I already feel like a beach ball with legs and I still have over four months to go."

"You look beautiful." Wally rubbed his knuckles along her cheek. "I've always had to fight to keep men away from you, but now I need to use my nightstick to keep them off. One more longing glance from that damn vet and I was ready to throw him in jail just on principle."

"Seriously?" Skye snickered incredulously. "Dr. Q is about as interested in me as Bingo is in attending obedience training."

"He kept touching you." The muscle in Wally's jaw tightened.

"He's a caregiver and was concerned about me because of the baby," Skye explained. "Did you see his reaction when I suggested fixing him up with Abby? He lit up like a Roman candle." She tilted her head. "Seriously, who are all these guys you think were interested in me?"

"Simon." Wally held up a finger. "And your ex-fiancé." He added a second finger. "And what's his name?" A third finger joined the other two. "That private investigator who pretended to be a reporter for the newspaper."

"Kurt. And he was using me," Skye protested. "Then there's Luc, who only came back to get my signature. Neither guy was really attracted to me." She shrugged. "Not to mention that Emmy seems to have helped Simon recover pretty darn quickly from his heartbreak."

"She's a diversion." Wally crossed his arms. "He's still in love with you."

Considering Simon had said something similar to her on the day of her wedding, Skye decided to ignore Wally's statement. Instead, maybe this was her chance to vent a little of her own jealousy.

"Well, I heard that Monday morning after the Legion break-in, Emmy's friend Chantal had trouble keeping her hands off of you," Skye retorted.

May hadn't quite said that, but it would be interesting to see Wally's reaction to the accusation. With most people, her husband had a good poker face, but Skye could always tell when he was hiding something from her.

"Chantal was hysterical." Wally's cheeks reddened. "I made it clear I was happily married." His back stiffened. "It was nothing personal on her end, and I turned her over to Quirk as soon as I could."

"I see." Skye would have to quiz her mother a little more thoroughly. May hadn't been nearly as explicit as she should have been. "Then I guess we're even." Skye's mild expression didn't reveal her thoughts. "We both need to work on our trust issues."

Being a smart man, evidently Wally recognized a truce when one was offered. Leaning in for another quick kiss, he changed the subject and said, "I need to pick something up at the station. I'll meet you at Mickey D's."

Five minutes later, Skye swung into McDonald's, parked the Bel Air between two empty spots, and twisted the rearview mirror toward her. The car's air-conditioning wasn't working, and in order to cool off, she had to roll her window down. As a result, her curls were a tumbleweed of snarls and she quickly brushed her hair into a ponytail. While she was at it, she applied concealer under her eyes and added a light coat of pink gloss.

Getting out of the car, Skye tried to smooth the wrinkles from her slacks and maternity top, but it had been a long day and the creases wouldn't budge. Her rubber-soled loafers, the only shoes that didn't make her ankles swell, squeaked annoyingly as she crossed the asphalt and she grimaced.

She certainly sympathized with Loretta, who wasn't happy about being pregnant again so soon. She really couldn't wait to be able to get back into her regular wardrobe. It may not be high-end, cutting-edge fashion, but it looked better on her than what she was currently forced to wear.

Maybe she needed to expend a little more effort in finding maternity clothes in her size that were more flattering. She knew they existed. She'd seen pictures in magazines. But she'd probably have to shop closer to Chicago to find them.

The glare blinded her when Skye pushed open the door, but once her eyes adjusted, she made her way to her favorite rear corner booth. While she waited for Wally, she dug a pencil stub and a crumpled receipt out of her purse. Flipping over the slip of paper, she itemized what she wanted to tell him. Then she made a second list of questions to ask him.

Just as she finished writing, she heard the automatic door swoosh open and saw him stride into the restaurant.

Hurriedly, she slid out of the booth and met him near the front.

They placed their order and the girl behind the counter took the twenty that Wally handed her and said, "Ms. Denison, I heard you were having a baby. Congratulations."

Skye recognized the clerk from the high school, but couldn't remember her name. "Thanks. Are you ready for the end of the year?"

"I guess so." The girl's face reddened, and she mumbled as she turned to get their food. "But Ms. Cormorant is failing me. I know I'm not as smart as a lot of the kids in her class, but she seems to have it in for me."

Normally, Skye wouldn't automatically believe that a teacher was showing favoritism. However, knowing Pru, the girl might have a point. Corny was famous for being harder on some students than others.

Touching the teen's hand, Skye said, "If there's one thing I've learned, it's not to compare myself to the best that other folks can do. Instead, I measure myself against the best that I can do."

"That doesn't help me pass the course." The girl's chin sank to her chest. "I'll probably have to go to summer school unless I ace Ms. C's final essay."

"That's too bad." Skye made a sympathetic face. "But maybe you'll pull through in the end." She bit her lip. She really didn't have time to take on anything extra, but she just couldn't ignore the girl's predicament. Mentally rearranging her schedule, she said, "Do you want me to take a look at your paper before you turn it in? I was pretty good in English."

"That would be awesome." The girl's eyes brightened as she filled their order. "Can I drop it by your office tomorrow morning?"

"Of course." Skye moved out of the way as Wally reached around her to grab the heavy tray. "Stick it under my door. I won't be at the high school until the afternoon."

Waving good-bye, Skye headed back to the table she'd claimed earlier, slid into the booth, and glanced across at Wally as he joined her. In the harsh fluorescent lights, the skin around his eyes was papery looking, and deep lines bracketed his mouth. He was clearly exhausted.

She reached across and squeezed his hands. "How are you holding up?"

"Murder investigations are always tough." He shrugged. "The first few days are so crucial, but with limited resources, there just aren't enough hours in the day to pursue every lead in a timely manner."

"And my being pregnant isn't helping matters." Skye blew out a breath. "You really don't have to worry about me. I won't overdo it."

"Right." Wally grunted his disbelief, then added, "Still, nothing is more important than you and the baby."

"I know. But I don't want to get in the way of your job." Skye took a napkin and wiped off the tabletop. "Forget about me."

"Never." He looked at her with a goofy smile. "I couldn't if I wanted to."

"Aw, me, too. About you, I mean," Skye assured him, then said, "Look, there's no reason for you to take off work and go to the doctor's with me tomorrow morning. It's just a routine appointment and I can get Mom to go with me."

"No way." Wally ran a knuckle down her cheek. "Dr. Johnson is doing an ultrasound and said she'd be able to confirm your due date this visit. I'm not missing that."

"Well, if you really want to, you know I'd rather you were there than my mother." Skye blew Wally a kiss, then said, "Let me tell you about my visit with the Dooziers." Before he recovered his usual mild expression, she saw

disappointment flash in his eyes and realized that he had
wanted to take a break from the case, so she hurriedly
added, "Unless you want to eat first."

"Nah. You're right." Wally leaned forward, his forearms on the table. "I need to get to Dr. Zello's house
before it's too late. His wife said he had to leave for an
important appointment in Laurel at eight."

Skye put Wally's Big Mac, fries, and soda in front of
him, then lowering her voice, she said. "Do you think
Dr. Zello's going to that private club Pru mentioned?
Maybe we should follow him."

"If I'm not satisfied with his answers, I plan to." A
line formed between Wally's brows. "I want to get a
court order for the membership list. But when I talked
to Wraige again, he wouldn't even tell me the name, let
alone the address, of the place. And I don't have enough
to legally compel him to answer my questions about it."

"How about Palmer's phone?" Skye opened the wrapper of her Quarter Pounder, moved the sandwich over,
then squeezed a packet of ketchup onto the makeshift
plate. "Maybe you could find the club's number on it."

"Martinez went through both his home and cell records." Wally peeled the paper from a straw and
shoved it through the plastic lid. "There was nothing
that indicated the club even has a phone."

"Shoot!" Unable to resist any longer, Skye selected
a fry, dragged it through the ketchup, and took a bite
of the salty goodness.

"Nate Turner has an alibi and he claimed he had no
idea what I was talking about when I brought up Lynch's
club." Wally took a long drink of his Coke. "And unless
Turner is a much better actor than I give him credit for,
he was surprised at Lynch's sexual taste and was telling
me the truth."

"Well, hell!" Skye wiped her fingers on a napkin

before picking up her burger. "Did the crime scene techs find anything useful?"

She bit into the Quarter Pounder as she waited for his reply. The greasy indulgence was heavenly. She licked her fingers and stared at Wally expectantly.

"No unexpected prints at the scene," Wally reported. "It will be quite a while before we get the DNA results from the tissue under Belle's claws. The lab the county uses is cheap and slow."

"Did the crime scene techs check Belle's collar?" Skye asked.

"For trace," Wally answered. "But there wasn't anything there."

"That wasn't what I meant." Skye wrinkled her nose. "I meant maybe something had been concealed inside the collar." When Wally raised a brow, she shrugged. "Hey. I saw it on a TV show."

"I'll ask them to take a look, but I'm sure they already did." Wally finished his Big Mac, washed it down with a slug of soda, then added, "And that other guy Turner and Zello were talking with after church was clueless." Wally gave Skye a twisted smile. "Both figuratively and literally."

"Who does that leave?" Skye asked, playing with the straw in her drink.

"The vic's ex-wife." Wally polished off his last few fries. "And his employees."

"Anything on the Legion's break-in?" Skye dabbed her lips with her napkin.

"You tell me." Wally pushed the debris from their meal to one side of the table. "What did you and the next Agatha Christie find out at the Dooziers?"

Skye picked up the wrinkled receipt that she'd used to make notes and grimaced. What was wrong with her? She sure wasn't her usual organized self. That Skye would have had a fresh legal pad, her favorite pen, and index cards.

Dismayed by the change, Skye said, "Yolanda is in town. She's engaged and she brought her fiancé, AJ Martino, who is also her boss, to meet the family. They were only supposed to be here one night, but Earl drove his Doozier Dozer over AJ's new Porsche."

"Quite a welcome to the family." Wally couldn't quite hide his grin. "Did you find out why Earl's car was in the Legion's parking lot after it closed?"

"The Regal wouldn't start. Earl claimed it had to have been messed with because it was running perfectly when they got there," Skye reported. "They called for a crony of Earl's to come to get it going, and hitched a ride home from some friends."

"Did anyone stay with the car?" Wally asked, glancing at his watch.

"Yeah." Giggling, Skye buried her face in her hands. "Evidently, AJ refused to ride in the bed of a pickup, so he stayed."

"What time did the fiancé make it back to the house?" Wally asked, getting to his feet.

"According to Yolanda, AJ rolled in round one thirty, but I wasn't able to really question him directly."

She frowned. She probably should have tried harder to talk to AJ alone.

As if reading her mind, Wally said, "I'll have Quirk get ahold of him and ask if he saw anything." Wally jotted a note on his pad. "Chantal wasn't too precise about when the break-in actually occurred. She said it was around two, so he might have still been there when it happened."

"Odd that Chantal doesn't know exactly what time it was," Skye murmured.

"She doesn't wear a watch and her cell was in her purse," Wally said.

Skye raised a skeptical brow. Wouldn't Chantal have glanced at the clock when she heard the first sounds of the break-in? Was she somehow connected to the attempted robbery? No. That didn't make any sense. If it was an inside job, she would have made certain that they got the money. Unless the cash wasn't what they were after. But what else could someone want at the Legion?

Skye opened her mouth to share her thoughts, but Wally looked at his watch again and said, "I need to go or I'll miss Zello."

"Sure. I'll see you at home." Skye scooted to the edge of the booth, but with a full stomach, she couldn't quite gain the momentum to get up.

"I should be back around eight or nine." Wally reached down and helped Skye stand. "I'll walk you to your car."

Looking down at their intertwined hands, she shivered. She loved him so much.

They deposited their trash in the bin and walked outside, where Wally opened the Bel Air's door for her and said, "Get some rest."

"Don't work too late." Skye stared into his eyes. "You need rest, too."

"I'll be home as soon as I finish with Zello." Wally leaned down and gently pressed his lips to hers. "Maybe if you take a short nap, you can stay awake a little longer once we go to bed." He pinned her with a sharp look. "Or we can talk about why you don't want to."

Without waiting for her response, he turned and walked away.

CHAPTER 20

When the rats infest the palace, a lame cat is better
than the swiftest horse.
—CHINESE PROVERB

Two hours later, Skye heard the front door open. Putting aside the book she'd been reading, she transferred Bingo from her lap to the cushion of the sunroom sofa, then hurried to greet Wally in the foyer. The minute that he spotted her, his warm brown eyes lit up and he quickly met her halfway down the hall.

Folding her in his arms, he ran his hands up and down her back and murmured, "You look amazing. When did you get the new nightie?"

"When I went shopping with Trixie. She insisted that I buy it."

Wally pressed his lips to hers and whispered, "Thank her for me."

As soon as she had gotten home from McDonald's, Skye had scoured the Internet searching for information on how to rev up her libido. It was time to either solve the problem or talk about it. She preferred the former to the latter.

One blog written by a woman who experienced a similar issue during her pregnancy had really resonated with Skye. The site had listed all the reasons women's desire waned when she was expecting. It had explained that the constant fatigue of sleepless nights and carrying around extra pounds took their toll. As did feeling unattractive and worrying about hurting the baby.

During the time Wally had been busy interviewing Tony Zello, Skye had taken the blogger's advice. She power napped, showered, and then curled her hair. Slipping on her new black mesh baby doll nightgown, she felt sexy for the first time since she'd really started to show.

Wanting to retain that feeling, Skye read a few chapters of a great new romance she'd just picked up at Tales and Treats. The book was about a good girl who was determined to be bad, and the love scenes were smoking hot. It also didn't hurt that the cruise setting reminded Skye of her honeymoon and her own sizzling experiences.

Now as Wally deepened his kiss, she returned it with a wild abandon that she hadn't felt in months. He pulled her closer, her new curves molding to his muscular body. She could smell the sweat of his hard day's work and it turned her on even more than his usual scent of woodsy aftershave and spicy shampoo.

Blood rushed south and she gasped for air. As Wally rocked Skye's world with his fingers and tongue, the radio attached to his epaulette crackled.

The disembodied voice said, "Officer Martinez reports that the subject is pulling into the Laurel Hospital. Please advise if she should follow him into the building or keep an eye on his car."

Skye stiffened in Wally's arms. Her mother's words were like a cold shower. Too many memories of teenage kisses interrupted by May switching on the front porch's floodlight and announcing it was time to come inside made it difficult for Skye to ignore her mom's voice.

Wally swore, then tugging Skye closer, he continued to caress her as he unclipped the radio from his shirt and pressed the button to talk. "Have Martinez stay with the vehicle." Raising a brow at Skye, he said, "I doubt that Lynch's private club is inside a hospital." He frowned. "Zello's meeting must be legit."

"I agree," Skye said, then trying not to lose the mood, she nuzzled his neck as he unbuckled his leather utility belt, loosened his collar, and took off his tie. "But let's forget about the case."

"Works for me." Wally bent his head to nibble at her earlobe.

"And that works for me," Skye sighed as a shiver raced up her spine.

"How about this?" Wally pressed openmouthed kisses down her throat as he fumbled with the halter tie of her baby doll nightgown.

"Oh, yeah." Skye breathed, adoring the feeling of her husband's lips and fingers exploring her body. "That's good, too."

When Wally slid his palm down her stomach and edged beneath the elastic of the baby doll's matching bikinis, Skye took his hand and towed him up the stairs. There was no need to stand around in the drafty foyer when they had a king-size four-poster with the covers turned down ready for anything they might like to try.

Skye dimmed the lights and hit the remote. Soft music poured from the sound system that Wally had recently installed, and as Coldplay's "Yellow" washed over them, Skye helped Wally shed his clothes. He made quick work of her panties, which was all she still had on, then he stretched out on the bed and drew her on top of him.

She nibbled from his pecs down to his waist, then raised her head to look into her husband's eyes. His lids were at half-mast as he watched her trace the smooth olive skin stretching over his abs. Purring her pleasure, she continued her journey southward.

He shivered as she nuzzled the sensitive skin there. Finally, Wally growled and reversed their positions so that she was lying on the mattress, and after that, Skye lost track of time.

Much later, when Wally and Skye lay sated, cuddling under the sheet, she asked, "How did your interview with the good doctor go?"

"He seemed cooperative." Wally traced circles on her bare shoulder.

"What did he say about Lynch's false promises?" Skye laced her right hand with Wally's left. "Did he admit to knowing about the private club?"

"Zello claimed that he had never heard of it." Wally turned on his side and spooned Skye against him. "As to Lynch's campaign promises, the doctor seemed convinced that the guy would choose his pet cause to support."

"Did you believe Dr. Zello was telling the truth?" Skye wiggled until her entire backside was pressed against her husband's front.

"It's a moot point since Zello had an alibi for Sunday night." Wally stroked Skye's stomach. "He had receipts for a weekend trip to New York. He was speaking at some medical convention."

"Mmm." Skye had almost dozed off when she forced her eyes open and said, "We're running out of suspects. I sure hope it isn't the ex-wife. From what Palmer's mother said, she's had enough troubles."

The next morning, the late nights and stress-filled days caught up with Skye and Wally and they slept through their alarm. Lucky for them, Bingo jumped on the bed demanding his breakfast or they might have stayed in dreamland until noon. When Skye saw how late it was, she asked Wally to take care of the hungry feline, while she got ready to go.

In under twenty minutes, Skye showered, scraped her hair into a ponytail, and threw on one of her new maternity dresses. Wally had beaten her time by half and they were in his Thunderbird speeding toward Kankakee by eight fifteen.

Skye had chosen the obstetrician's first appointment of the day hoping to be back at school by lunch. Now she wondered if they'd make it to the doctor's office by nine o'clock.

As they drove, Skye applied concealer, blush, and lip gloss. There was no way she was letting Dr. Johnson see how pale and tired she looked. Finished with her primping, she glanced away from the vanity mirror at Wally and smiled, happy that he'd insisted on accompanying her. May would have been thrilled to take her, but Skye didn't want to hear her mother's opinion of her weight, dress size, or other figure flaws.

There was a slight chance May wouldn't criticize Skye's appearance. She had been very supportive during their last conversation. But Skye wasn't betting any money that the change in her mother was permanent. Years of nitpicking wouldn't be reined in overnight.

Thanks to Wally's speedy driving—he seemed to forget he wasn't driving a squad car in hot pursuit of a criminal—they arrived at the medical office with a few minutes to spare. Skye was given a specimen cup and sent to the bathroom. After producing the required sample, not a problem since it seemed she had to pee every five minutes, she and Wally were shown into an examination room.

Once they had all squeezed into the tiny space, the perky nurse said, "Let's get your weight."

"Let's not," Skye muttered under her breath, glancing at Wally. Could she ask him to step out? Heck. It wasn't as if he hadn't heard how fat she was on their last visit to the obstetrician. Surely, she hadn't gained that much.

The nurse shook her head and pointed to the scale. "No need to be shy."

"Easy for you to say since you're probably a size 2," Skye retorted, then kicked off her shoes, stepped on the scale, and sucked in her stomach.

Yes. She knew holding her breath wouldn't make her any lighter, but she couldn't fight the impulse. She watched the digital numbers shoot upward at an alarming speed. When they finally stopped, she was relieved that she'd only put on two pounds.

Phew! Dr. Johnson should be okay with that.

The nurse took Skye's blood pressure and temperature, then after entering all the information she'd gathered into the exam room's computer, she handed Skye an ugly turquoise gown and said, "Once you've changed, flip the switch by the door to indicate that you're ready. The phlebotomist will come in to draw your blood, and the doctor will be with you after that."

As soon as the nurse left, Skye quickly removed her dress, put on the gown, and said to Wally, "Go ahead and flip the switch."

Skye sat on the examination table and Wally stood next to her holding her hand. She took a deep breath and tried to calm her nerves. She loved her obstetrician, but having any kind of medical exam still made her nervous.

He ran his thumb over her knuckles and said, "How're you holding up?"

"Apart from my iatrophobia"—Skye wrinkled her nose—"I'm fine."

"Why do you think that you're so afraid of doctors?" Wally asked.

"Mostly because they always yell at me about being

too fat." Skye narrowed her eyes. "Whatever issue I go in to see them about from a cold to a broken bone, they blame the problem on my weight."

"But you said that Dr. Johnson wasn't like that."

"She isn't." Skye blew out a breath. "It's just the years of being chewed out have conditioned me to expect the worse."

"You don't have to worry." Wally winked. "I'll protect you."

Before Skye could respond, the phlebotomist arrived to draw her blood, and as she left, Dr. Johnson walked into the room. The obstetrician was an attractive woman in her early forties with short blond hair and warm blue eyes. She wore a cute pair of black and white capris and a black T-shirt under her white jacket.

"Skye, Wally, good to see you." She moved to the sink and washed her hands. "Everything going okay? Any problems or concerns?"

"Juniorette and I are doing great." Skye smiled and patted her baby bump.

"Junior," Wally teased, "might be fine, but Skye's been having painful charley horses. Is there anything you can give her to help with that?"

"Hmm." Dr. Johnson threw her used paper towel in the trash and approached Skye. "I'll check your calcium, magnesium, and potassium levels, but if they're okay, it's probably muscle fatigue. Make sure you don't get dehydrated since that will increase the spasms."

"Okay." Skye glanced at Wally and grinned. He had his memo book out and was taking notes.

"Please lie down." Dr. Johnson helped Skye recline, then said, "Today we're going to listen to your baby's heartbeat and measure your fundal height. The height of your fundus should roughly equal the weeks of your pregnancy."

"Will that tell us the due date?" Wally asked.

"It'll help, but the ultrasound will give us a more accurate estimate." Dr. Johnson warmed up her stethoscope, then moved Skye's gown aside and pressed the instrument to her stomach. After a minute she smiled and said, "Your baby's got a strong heartbeat."

"Are you doing the ultrasound just to determine the due date?" Skye asked. "Because remember, we don't want to know the sex."

"I'm going to check for any physical abnormalities and confirm the location of the placenta, as well as measure your baby, which will provide the best information about your due date."

"Okay. But even if there is a physical problem, we're carrying the baby to term." Skye glanced worriedly at Wally and he nodded his agreement.

"Of course, but in some cases we can correct an issue in utero," Dr. Johnson reassured her, then said, "I'll be right back."

The doctor stepped out of the room and a few seconds later she returned followed by a woman wheeling a portable ultrasound. The sonographer stopped by the examination table, introduced herself, then squirted Skye's stomach with a clear gel. As the tech moved the wand, Dr. Johnson pointed to the screen and explained what Skye and Wally were seeing.

Once the test was finished and the sonographer left, Dr. Johnson said, "Everything looks fine and our best estimate is that you're twenty weeks along."

"So that means I'm due . . ." Skye counted on her fingers. "The end of September, right?"

"That would be full term," Dr. Johnson agreed. "But first babies rarely keep to the schedule." She smiled. "Speaking of which, have you two signed up for childbirth classes yet?"

"No." Skye and Wally exchanged a guilty glance, and Skye said, "We'll do that once school is out."

"I highly recommend that you do." Dr. Johnson raised a brow. "The lessons will teach you about the stages of labor, as well as relaxation and pain management techniques."

"It's on my summer to-do list," Skye assured the doctor.

"See that it's checked off that list soon." Dr. Johnson pointed her pen, then grinned. "Next visit we'll do a vaginal culture to screen for beta strep infection and a glucose screening test to check for gestational diabetes." As she walked out the door, she said, "Call me immediately if anything changes."

"Will do," Wally said.

Skye re-dressed and she and Wally headed for the parking lot. As she slid into the car, Skye's stomach growled. They hadn't had time to eat and she was starving.

"I think Junior wants breakfast." Wally grinned. "How does Bakers Square sound?"

"Perfect." Skye checked her watch. It was only nine forty-five. Plenty of time to eat and still be back at work before noon. "Juniorette worked up quite an appetite performing for us during the ultrasound."

"That's my baby." Wally chuckled and squeezed her hand.

His expression was so loving that Skye's throat closed. Tears of happiness welled up in her eyes. This was it. They were really having a baby

When Skye returned to work after her OB-GYN appointment, she was in a good mood, but then idiots happened. After solving the crisis du jour at the grade school, she hurried over to the high school to assist the clerk from McDonald's with her final English paper.

Before calling the girl down to her office, Skye had looked through her file. And as she'd suspected, the only class the teen wasn't doing well in was Pru's. Her previous English grades had been A's, and when questioned, the girl assured Skye that she had no missing assignments or low test scores, so there was no reason she should be struggling to pass this year.

That is, unless the teacher had some sort of prejudice against the girl. Skye didn't have time to figure out what that bias might be, and frankly probably couldn't do much about it if she knew. With Corny, it could be as simple as the student's low social economic status or as complex as a grudge against a family member.

Although frustrated with her inability to right all the wrongs in the school system, Skye had to settle for cautioning the teen not to mention to Pru that Skye had helped her. With a final admonishment to the girl to keep quiet, Skye hurried to her next appointment.

When she arrived at the junior high for the school's afternoon annual reviews, Neva Llewelyn met Skye at the door and directed her to clear her schedule. She told Skye that she had to attend an emergency meeting regarding a student named Grant Paulk. Without giving her any other details, but with a warning that the matter would end up in the hands of the law, the principal had ordered Skye to accompany her to a parent conference.

Neva led Skye to the art room. It was in an isolated area, allowing for more privacy than any other spot in the school. Which was why they always used it for this kind of session. Unfortunately the odor of turpentine was overwhelming, and Skye prayed that the smell wouldn't make her deposit her hastily consumed lunch on Neva's shiny beige pumps.

Breathing through her mouth, Skye glanced at the other three women sitting around the paint-stained table waiting for Grant Paulk's folks to arrive. The trio looked as if they wished they were anywhere else.

Determined to shake her bad mood and make the best of the situation, Skye leaned to her right, lowered her voice, and said, "Abby, do you remember the other day we talked about how hard it was to meet a nice guy?"

"Uh-huh." The school nurse nodded cautiously. "Who do you have in mind?"

"Linc Quillen, the vet who owns the animal clinic just outside of town," Skye whispered. "When I saw him yesterday, it dawned on me that he'd be perfect for you. He's single, handsome, and has a good job. Plus, you both are in the medical field."

"Hmm." Abby wound a strand of white-blond hair around her finger. "He is cute. And I really liked how sweet he was when I brought Hasselhoff into his clinic. He had a really soothing bedside manner."

"Shall I give him your number?" Skye asked, then flinched when the art room door banged open and Mr. and Mrs. Paulk marched inside. "I mentioned you to Dr. Q and he was definitely interested."

"Sure." Abby's aquamarine eyes twinkled. "I'm ready to shake up my love life."

"Great." Skye turned her attention to the hostile faces of Grant Paulk's parents. Neva was seated to her left, and Skye could feel the principal's anxiety.

Neva waited until the Paulks sat down, then said, "Thank you for joining us on such short notice. I'm afraid we have a serious situation with your son Grant that needs our immediate attention."

"This is ridiculous," Barney Paulk raged. "We just spoke to Grant in your office. He has assured us he's innocent and is being set up."

His wife, Posey, screeched, "I can't fathom why you would believe some little tramp, rather than an out-standing boy like our son. We'll sue."

"Of course you will," Neva muttered under her breath, then said aloud, "At lunch today, Grant snuck out of the cafeteria and lured one of his female classmates into the woods behind the athletic field."

"Grant says he was only walking the girl home." Mrs. Paulk gripped the edge of the table. "She didn't feel well and Ms. Fleming refused to allow her to call her parents." Mrs. Paulk scowled at Abby, who remained expressionless. "The girl became disoriented and panicked."

Skye watched in hypnotized fascination as a drop of sweat hovered above Posey Paulk's lips. Outside, temperatures were nearing the ninety degree mark and the junior high wasn't air conditioned.

Neva continued as if Mrs. Paulk hadn't spoken. "Luckily the girl was able to break free and got away." Neva glanced at her notes. "When she stumbled back to the school, she told the cafeteria supervisor what happened." The principal gestured to a woman wearing a white apron over a pair of jeans and a T-shirt that read, THE 3 C'S OF BEING A CAFETERIA LUNCH LADY ARE COOKING, CLEANING, AND CARING. "Mrs. Owenton immediately brought the girl to me and I summoned Ms. Fleming."

"That little hussy made all this up so she wouldn't get into trouble." Barney Paulk swung his oversized head toward the principal and pinned her with his feverish glare. "Grant is the victim here."

"The girl was never *in* trouble, and Ms. Fleming has no record of her ever requesting to go home due to illness." Staring at the hulking man, Neva continued, "When the young lady was brought to my office, she still had the can of soda your son had given her."

At Neva's statement, all the fight went out of Mrs. Paulk. She hunched down in her chair and covered her face with her hands.

Obviously, Grant's mother knew something his father didn't because Mr. Paulk huffed, "So what. Giving someone a pop isn't a crime."

"It is when the drink has been drugged." Neva's tone was firm.

Skye felt sorry for these parents. Like many others, they couldn't let themselves believe that their child might do the awful things of which he was accused. Some, like the father, were unaware, and others, like the mother, chose to ignore whatever they suspected.

"What the hell are you talking about?" Mr. Paulk roared. "Are you crazy?"

"Because of the girl's disoriented state and the gaps in her memory, Ms. Fleming suspected that something had been added to the can of soda," Neva answered. "She and I searched Grant's locker and found this."

Neva displayed an open shoe box. Skye noticed that a very famous athlete's name was printed on the side of the bright red carton.

"Those aren't my son's," Mrs. Paulk said. "We never bought him those."

"Nevertheless they were in his locker. And this is what we found inside the shoes." The principal reached into the sneaker's toe and held up a baggie containing a tiny vial of white powder. "As a courtesy," Neva continued, staring at the Paulks, "we asked you to come in so you could be with Grant when the police arrive. You may wait with him in my office while I telephone the station."

"But . . . wait a minute," Mr. Paulk stuttered. "Nothing happened and the girl is fine. Can't we handle this without the cops?"

"Sorry." Neva shook her head. "It is a school board policy that any time a crime is committed, the police need to be informed." She crossed her arms. "We have no choice in the matter."

"You people should never have started this whole thing. Grant is being framed by some slut who is mad that he dumped her," Barney Paulk shouted. He leaned forward toward Neva and yelled, "You bitch! You had no right to search his locker without a warrant."

"Yes, we did." Neva narrowed her eyes. "At the beginning of the school year we sent home a notice stating that the principal has a master key to the lockers and periodic searches for contraband would be conducted. You initialed, indicating you read and understood the document."

"That's bullshit!" Mr. Paulk bellowed and pounded the tabletop.

Abby glanced at Skye, obviously frightened. Neva and Mrs. Owenton were staring at Grant's father as if he were a cobra about to strike and they were too hypnotized to get out of the way.

Skye's chest tightened. This was why Neva wanted her at the meeting. It was tough being the one to attempt to persuade parents to see their children's problems, but in this situation it was her job.

"He tried to kidnap a girl and was found with drugs in his possession," Skye said firmly. "You need to recognize that he has a problem and get him help now before he succeeds in raping someone. Next time, the girl might not get away, and who knows what could happen afterwards."

Posey Paulk started to speak, but was interrupted by her husband when he lunged across the table. His face within inches of Skye's, he wordlessly growled his rage.

Desperate to escape his deranged stare, Skye struggled to push her chair back. But it stuck to the old linoleum floor, and before she could get it to budge, Paulk grabbed her upper arms.

His breath smelled like road kill as he hissed, "My son is innocent." Giving Skye a shake as if to emphasize his point, the man screamed, "My boy doesn't do drugs and no one is saying that he does!"

Not waiting to see what the crazed man would do next, Skye thrust her lower arms up between his and knocked his hands away. Freed from his grasp, she hurriedly put as much space as possible between her and the lunatic.

Everyone in the room, including the man's wife, froze.

Skye's breath was coming in shallow gasps and she felt light-headed, but she lifted her chin and said, "That was assault, Mr. Paulk. And don't think for a minute that I won't press charges."

Barney Paulk stepped closer and threatened, "You better watch yourself, missy. I'm a close personal friend of the mayor's. This whole business will be thrown out as soon as I call Dante."

"Perhaps." Skye forced her voice to remain steady. "But the mayor's my uncle and I'm married to the police chief." Pointing to her stomach, she said, "And this is his baby."

"So? Men don't care as much about that as you bitches think we do. It's not as if we can't make another one." Paulk stomped to the door. "Let me make myself clear. Either this all goes away or the whole bunch of you will be sorry."

CHAPTER 21

Time spent with cats is never wasted.
—SIGMUND FREUD

Unlike the time when Skye had been attacked by a parent at the high school, Neva fully supported Skye's decision to make a formal complaint regarding Barney Paulk's assault. While Homer had threatened Skye with immediate dismissal if she pressed charges against the man, Neva stated that she fully intended to see if there were any charges the school could bring against Mr. Paulk to support Skye's claim.

As Neva and Skye walked to the office, she asked, "Do you ever feel like you're one knucklehead away from insanity?"

"All the time." Skye chuckled.

Stopping by the empty secretary's desk, Neva indicated the phone and said, "Do you want to call the police, or should I?"

"It would be best if you did it and didn't mention my involvement." When Neva raised a questioning brow, Skye said, "All we need is for one of my concerned relatives to show up and try to defend me."

Lucky for Mr. Paulk, Wally was busy with the murder investigation and had put Martinez on the daytime shift. When Zelda arrived at the school, Neva outlined what had led up to the Paulk meeting and what happened during the conference. She then informed the young officer that Mrs. Paulk was with Abby and Mr. Paulk was with his son in Neva's office.

Although clearly outraged at Paulk's laying his hands on Skye, Zelda didn't appear inclined to beat the crap out of the man, which might not have been the case if Wally had been the officer on the scene. However, when Paulk refused to open the door, claiming he was waiting for the mayor to return his call, Zelda's faced reddened and she fingered her weapon.

Skye tapped her on the arm and whispered, "Dante's on a cruise with my aunt. He won't be home for a couple of days, and I seriously doubt he's checking his voice mail."

"That's probably a good thing." Zelda may have been the newest member of the force, but she had quickly learned that the mayor was no friend of the police department. Gesturing to Neva to come closer, she asked softly, "Do you have a key for your office?"

"It's in my purse, which is in my desk drawer." Neva's tone dripped with frustration. Stepping over to the intercom, she pressed a button and said, "Aiden, I need your passkey." A second later, she added, "Right away."

A couple of minutes passed before the custodian arrived. He silently tossed a ring of keys at Neva and left. Aiden had been hired at the beginning of the school year and Skye couldn't recall ever hearing the man speak.

Zelda motioned for Skye and Neva to stand back, then she quietly turned the key in the lock. With her gun at the ready, the officer stood to the side and twisted the knob.

Charging into the room, Zelda shouted, "Barney

Paulk, you are under arrest. Place your hands on the wall and spread your legs."

Skye couldn't see what was happening, but she heard the rattle of handcuffs and Zelda reading Paulk his rights. Suddenly, there were the sounds of a scuffle. Worried that the young officer was in trouble, Skye crept closer.

When she saw that Zelda had Grant Paulk against the desk and was securing his wrists with a zip tie, Skye blew out a relieved breath. Evidently, the Scumble River police had only one set of metal cuffs and the plastic version as backup. She was thankful that the cops were so well prepared. That had to be Wally's doing.

Because it was against policy to transport two prisoners in the same cruiser, once Zelda had the Paulks under control, she radioed for a second squad car. A few moments later, Quirk arrived and father and son were taken away.

As soon as Neva notified Mrs. Paulk that her husband and child had been arrested, she stormed out of the building. Skye assumed the woman would follow her family to the station. But there was an odd look in her eye so there was the off chance she'd had enough of the two bullies in her life and was heading home to pack and leave town.

Skye turned to Neva and announced, "I'd better go to the PD so I can make my statement."

"Abby and I will be there as soon as school is over to give ours." The principal nodded. "Now, I need to deal with the girl's parents. I've had them waiting with Ursula in the band room to avoid any run-ins between them and the Paulks."

"Oh." Skye wasn't sure how to respond to that statement.

With the teachers all occupied with students they

couldn't leave unsupervised and Abby and Skye needed at the Paulk meeting, Neva had little choice. But the school secretary, Ursula Nelson, wasn't exactly the warm and cuddly type.

Shrugging her shoulders, Skye retrieved her purse from her desk and headed to her car. Ursula's lack of tact was Neva's problem, not hers.

While Zelda and Quirk had been handling Barney and Grant, Skye sent a text to Wally outlining what had happened. She'd assured him she was fine and would see him soon. But she knew that he'd be worried, so before driving to the PD, she sent him a message that she was on her way and would meet him in his office.

May wasn't scheduled to be at work until four, but with Thea on vacation, Skye wasn't certain when her mother's shift started. Unwilling to take the chance that May was already on duty, Skye once again entered the station through the garage and snuck upstairs.

Wally was waiting in the second-floor hallway and swept her into his arms. After he had reassured himself that she and the baby hadn't been injured, he led Skye into his office and settled her on a chair.

Once they were both seated, he said, "Tell me what happened. Until I got your text, all I heard was that there was an incident at the junior high and Martinez had been sent to deal with it."

She recounted both Grant's actions leading up to the meeting and his father's behavior during the conference, then said, "I wonder if the drugs that were found in the boy's locker are ketamine."

"My thoughts exactly." Wally had kept ahold of her hand and now he squeezed her fingers. "I had Martinez sign them over to Anthony, and he's already on his way to Laurel to have them tested along with the soda can that Grant gave the girl."

"I sure wish we knew what Palmer had been up to." Skye chewed her lip.

"And I sure wish he was around to interrogate." Wally rolled his neck, then sighed. "Considering that I want to kill Paulk for touching you, I thought it best to let Quirk process him and his son." Wally frowned, obviously wishing that he were the one locking up his wife's assailant. "Are you up to taking a ride to the Dollar or Three store with me?"

"Which one?" Skye asked. "Didn't we say there were four of them?"

"Let's start with the closest." Wally pulled her up from the chair and wrapped an arm around her, keeping her close to his side. "I want to talk to Ruben Ramirez, the chain's manager, but no one can tell me which store he'll be at when. Evidently, he likes to surprise his staff. Says it keeps them on their toes."

Once they were out of the station and in the squad car, it only took a few minutes to drive to the Scumble River Dollar or Three store. It was located at the edge of town in a struggling strip mall a couple of miles from the I-55 overpass.

The only other occupied buildings held a cigarette shop and a nail salon. A Mexican restaurant's window held a tattered notice that read, COMING SOON, but that sign had been there for at least a year.

Skye had never been inside the Dollar or Three store and was impressed at the variety of merchandise on display. Everything from hardware to jewelry to pantry staples such as cereal and potato chips. It was the only place within a half hour where some of the nongrocery items were available.

The Dollar or Three parking lot was jammed, and Skye wasn't surprised to find the store full of jostling shoppers. While Wally waited for the clerk to finish ringing up a customer, she examined the shelves.

Squeezing through the congested aisles, she listened to children whining for candy and toys and husbands whining to go home. Skye took her time studying the assorted products. There were a few brand names mixed with the generic labels, but most of those looked as if they were either seconds or discontinued items.

Noticing a section of school materials, Skye headed in that direction. She always kept a stash of pens, pencils, notebooks, and glue sticks in her desks at the various buildings for students whose parents might not be able to afford to buy them.

The prices were really good, and Skye was planning a trip back to restock her supplies when she spotted a display of tennis shoes. Maybe she could pick up a cheap pair that would fit her swollen feet.

Unwilling to spend a lot of money on shoes that would be too big in a few months, she bypassed the red boxes containing the pricey sneakers endorsed by a famous athlete and instead she scanned the other possibilities. Torn between the pink high-tops and the more practical traditional white tennies, she didn't hear Wally's approach. When his hand landed on her shoulder, she jumped and let out a tiny shriek.

"Sorry, darlin'." Wally's tone was amused. "I didn't mean to scare you. I forgot how focused you get when you're shopping."

"If you don't start making more noise before you come up behind me, I'm going to put a bell around your neck. I have one on a nice pink collar that Bingo refused to wear." Skye swatted his arm and asked, "Is the manager here?"

"No." Wally's mouth thinned. "The clerk thinks he might be at the Clay Center store."

"Let's go find out." Eager to see what kind of merchandise might be available at their next stop, Skye laced her fingers with Wally's and headed for the exit.

An hour later, Ruben Ramirez wasn't in Clay Center or Brooklyn, and Skye still hadn't purchased a pair of sneakers. She kept thinking there might be something better at a store they had yet to visit.

As they returned to the squad car for the third time, Skye said, "I don't think you ever told me where the fourth store was located."

"Laurel." Wally blew out a disgusted breath. "Of course, the manager would be at the farthest one. And of course, he doesn't answer his cell phone. This guy is harder to find than a teenager when it's time to do the dishes."

Wally was silent as they drove to the county seat. Skye could tell that he was stressed by his white-knuckled grip on the steering wheel. Between Paulk's attack on her and the time they'd wasted trying to locate Mr. Ramirez, Wally's last shred of patience was just about gone.

When he nearly rear-ended a car moseying along below the speed limit, Skye tried to distract him. "Hey. Since we're going to be in Laurel anyway, maybe we could stop at the crime lab and see if they know whether the drugs in Grant's locker were ketamine like we suspected."

"It's too soon." Wally's jaw tightened and he ground his teeth. "Which is all I ever hear from the crime techs or the ME."

"Then we could treat ourselves to dinner at Harry's," Skye suggested, determined to divert his attention to a more pleasant matter. "You love their prime rib."

"Sounds like a good idea." Wally's lips twitched. "And if we get a lead from Ramirez, I'll even treat you to that dessert you like."

"I shouldn't." Skye glanced down at her ever-expanding waistline.

"I wish you wouldn't worry about that." Wally stroked

her thigh. "How about I order the French silk pie and ask for two forks?"

"Deal." Skye caressed his hand, then raised hers and pointed to the right. "And there's the Dollar or Three next to Dunkin' Donuts."

Wally made a sharp turn into the lot, pulled into an empty spot, and helped Skye from the car. Following him inside, she ignored the wonderful chocolate smell wafting from the doughnut shop.

Like the other Dollar or Three stores, this one was situated on the outskirts of town. But Skye had noticed that while all the stores carried similar products, specific items varied from location to location.

Wally zeroed in on the front counter, but Skye strolled down the aisles. One area in particular was mobbed, and she scooted into a space vacated by a large man clutching something red to his chest.

What in the world were all the folks fighting to get? Peeking over a woman's shoulder, she saw a wall of sneakers. Apparently there was some sort of sale on a particular brand, and it was a very popular one. Most items in the place were under ten bucks, but the sign above these shoes read, $50.

Before she could ease away from the horde and allow someone else to take her spot, a boy next to her said, "What size are you looking for?"

Skye turned and saw the speaker, a twelve-year-old with sandy hair, sincere brown eyes, and a shy grin. Although she recognized him from Scumble River Junior High, she couldn't recall his name.

She smiled back and said, "I'm not. These are too pricey for me."

"But they're Konan Laborie's," he explained. "The shoes he endorses sell for two to five hundred bucks. These are the cheaper ones, but still at seventy-five percent off, they're a steal."

"Oh." Skye knew that Konan was a famous basketball player, but not much else about him. "What I don't understand is why people are struggling to get them. I've seen a few pairs in all of the Dollar or Three stores."

"Yeah." The boy shrugged. "Usually they sell some of Konan's shoes that are seconds, but these are perfect."

"Are you getting a pair?"

"No." His cheeks turned red. "Mom can't afford to buy 'em for me." He crossed his arms, then obviously parroting something he'd heard, said, "She works too hard to spend that kind of money on sneakers."

"That's very grown-up of you to understand." Skye wished she could buy the boy the shoes. But before she could figure out a way to do it, she spotted Wally gesturing for her to meet him. Turning to the preteen, she said, "I've got to go. My husband's waiting for me. Nice talking to you."

Wally was standing next to a man with dark black hair and deep brown eyes. When she reached his side, he said, "Mr. Ramirez, this is Skye, the police psych consultant."

"Nice to meet you, ma'am." He shook her hand. "How can I help you?"

"We'd like to ask you some questions about your boss." Wally rested a hip on the counter, giving the impression of a casual conversation. "What happens to the stores now that Mr. Lynch is gone?"

"I think Mrs. Lynch will take over." Ruben shrugged. "She is half owner."

"His mother?" Skye asked.

"No." The manager shook his head. "His ex."

"Did she get the interest in the business in the divorce settlement?" Skye asked, shooting a questioning look at Wally.

Wally leaned forward and murmured in Skye's ear,

"We're still waiting for a court order to examine Lynch's financial records."

Nodding her understanding to Wally, Skye asked the manager, "How are the stores doing? Are they in the black?"

"Yes!" Ruben nodded emphatically. "I am a first-rate manager."

"I'm sure you are," Wally said, then asked, "Was Mr. Lynch a good boss?"

"Sure." Ruben shoved his hands in his pockets. "As good as any."

"Do you know of any employees or customers that were angry at Mr. Lynch?" Wally asked.

"He mostly left things to me." Ruben frowned. "Except for okaying the merchandise orders, he rarely got involved in the day-to-day operations of the business. As long as I followed policy, he didn't interfere."

Wally continued to question the manager. When it was clear there wasn't anything more the man could or maybe would tell them, he said, "Thank you for your time, Mr. Ramirez. Please call me if you think of anything that might be relevant to Mr. Lynch's death."

Ruben accepted Wally's card, tucking it into his shirt pocket, then escorted Skye and Wally to the exit. Just before she left, Skye dug in her purse until she located the emergency fifty-dollar bill she kept behind her driver's license.

Adding a ten to it, she pressed the money into the manager's hand and pointed at the kid she'd been chatting with, then said, "This is for a pair of those Laborie shoes for that boy. Give him whatever change there is and tell him it's because he acted so mature."

Wally raised a brow, but didn't say anything. And Skye shrugged. Now that she was no longer buried under a mountain of debt, when she saw the opportunity, she enjoyed helping out others.

As they walked toward the squad car, Skye came to an abrupt stop. Something niggled at her brain. What was she trying to remember? She gazed back at the store. It was something she'd just seen.

"Wait." Skye faced Wally and put her hand on his chest. "I think I know how the ketamine Palmer was trying to get from Dr. Q was going to be distributed."

"How?" Wally wrinkled his forehead.

"Inside designer athletic shoes."

"Go on," Wally encouraged.

"Grant Paulk's drugs were found in the toe of a box of shoes that he had in his locker. Shoes just like the ones that I've seen in every Dollar or Three store." Skye took a breath. "Plus Mrs. Paulk said she didn't buy those shoes for her son."

"And?"

"I read about this somewhere." Skye pursed her lips. "I bet Palmer used kids to sell the drugs and paid them with these expensive sneakers that they all want but their parents won't or can't afford to buy for them. Then he sold the rest of the shipment out of his stores." She frowned. "Now all we have to do is prove it."

CHAPTER 22

*A countryman between two lawyers is
like a fish between two cats.*
—BENJAMIN FRANKLIN

Skye and Wally were in a hurry to get back to the
police station and talk to Grant Paulk about the
drugs they'd found in his fancy tennis shoes, so instead
of a leisurely meal in Laurel's nicest restaurant, they
had a quick bite to eat at Culver's and headed to Scumble River.

While Skye loved Culver's crispy chicken sandwich
and crinkly fries, the fast food just didn't compare to
prime rib. Although the caramel cashew sundae that
Wally had insisted she order almost made up for missing Harry's perfectly seasoned beef.

On the drive home, Skye was quiet as she mulled over
the break-in at the Legion. Something was nagging in the
back of her mind. Something she'd heard at the Dooziers'.
Who had said what? Something about Yolanda's fiancé
wanting to visit a friend in Scumble River.

A spark of an idea fluttered through Skye's head,
and before she lost it, she turned to Wally and asked,
"Did Quirk ever talk to Yolanda's fiancé?"

"No." Wally frowned. "He was on his way to Earl's
when Martinez called to transport Barney Paulk from
the junior high to the PD."

"What if the break-in at the Legion had nothing to do with the money?"

"What else would be the motive?" Wally glanced at Skye.

"I think it might have been connected with the new manager, Chantal." Skye closed her eyes and continued, "Both you and Mom said that she was hysterical, but something seems wrong about that picture. First, the thieves didn't hurt her, and second, why did it take her so long to come out of her hiding place and call for help?"

"I wondered that myself." Wally rubbed the back of his neck. "But she started crying when I tried to ask her, so I figured she was just high-strung."

"Or hiding something." Skye tapped her fingers on the armrest. "Yolanda's fiancé insisted on coming to Scumble River. He claimed he'd recently reconnected with a frat brother from here and wanted to visit."

"Chantal may have gone to college." Wally raised a brow. "But she's certainly no one's fraternity brother."

"Well, AJ could hardly tell Yolanda he wanted to see another woman." Skye barely resisted rolling her eyes. "However, he was also the one who suggested the family go to the Legion. And when Earl's car mysteriously broke down, he was the one who volunteered to stay with it. In fact, I think he did something to the Buick so that it wouldn't start."

"Okay." Wally's tone was quizzical. "But if AJ and Chantal have some sort of a relationship, why was the door smashed? Why wouldn't she just let him in?"

"Maybe the relationship ended badly. Maybe Chantal is hiding in Scumble River," Skye suggested.

"We need to talk to those two." Wally scrubbed his face with his hand. "But we also need to talk to Grant and his father about the drugs. I've been looking forward to a little face time with the asshole who dared to put his hands on my wife and endangered my child."

"Look"—Skye patted Wally's arm—"why don't you let Quirk interview the Paulks? The sergeant is good with obnoxious guys like Mr. Paulk and smart-alecky kids like his son." She was afraid if Wally was in the same room with Barney, he might kill the man. "We should get Chantal and AJ together and goad them into telling us the truth."

Reluctantly agreeing to Skye's plan, Wally radioed Quirk to question the Paulks about Skye's drug theory. Luckily, Barney Paulk was still in the holding cell waiting for an officer to escort him to the county jail, and his son was still with Zelda, who hadn't yet transported Grant to the juvenile facility.

Finishing with Quirk, Wally spoke to Martinez and ordered her to pick up Chantal and AJ and bring them to the station for questioning. Once she'd delivered the suspects, she was to get hold of the junior and high school principals and conduct a building-wide locker search for red shoe boxes. Any boxes found should be dusted for fingerprints, and that included the one that had previously been discovered in Grant Paulk's possession.

Skye sighed. She knew that the legality of locker searches depended on the students' reasonable expectations of privacy. And that all students were notified at the beginning of each school year that the principal had a master key to their lockers and periodic searches for contraband would be conducted.

Nevertheless, she wished there were another way. The students would be upset. And it would be hard for the staff to rebuild the trust the kids would feel had been violated.

Thirty minutes later, when Skye and Wally entered the PD, Grant and his father were in the coffee/interrogation room. As Skye walked past, she heard Barney stuttering and Grant crying. Evidently, Quirk was making excellent progress.

Chantal and AJ were seated in the lobby, pointedly ignoring each other. Wally introduced himself to the plastic surgeon and Skye to the Legion manager, then ushered the pair upstairs. The police station didn't have a second interrogation room, but since it was after business hours, Wally had asked that the city hall conference room be opened up and equipped with a tape recorder.

He waited until Chantal and AJ settled on one side of the table, then gestured Skye to the seat across from the plastic surgeon. Wally sat facing the Legion manager, and as he pushed the button of the old fashioned tape recorder, he asked her and the doctor to state their full name and address.

While the formalities were being handled, Skye noticed that Chantal edged her chair away from AJ's and refused to meet his gaze. The plastic surgeon stared at her, then smirked and looked away.

Wally allowed the couple to squirm for several long minutes, then abruptly asked, "How long have you known each other?"

"Three—"

"We've never met before today," AJ cut off Chantal with a glare.

"Not even Sunday night at the Legion?" Skye asked, feeling a little like Nero Wolfe as she laced her fingers over her baby bump.

"Of course not," AJ simpered. "I only had eyes for my fiancée."

"Another woman you promised the moon and who will end up with nothing," Chantal muttered. She peered at Wally from beneath her lashes and teased, "Chief, do you know the one thing that all men in singles bars have in common?"

Wally shook his head.

"They're married." Chantal's giggle had a hysterical edge to it.

"Be quiet," AJ snapped. "I'll handle this."

"Like you handled the insurance company?" Chantal crossed her arms.

"Zip it!" AJ glowered at the woman next to him. "Try keeping quiet and proving your IQ is higher than your bra size."

"At least I fill up my bra," Chantal retorted. "We both know that isn't true for you and your briefs."

"Shut the fu—"

Wally interrupted the surgeon, snarling, "Do not use that word in front of my wife." After AJ snapped his mouth shut, Wally leaned toward Chantal and said, "You know it's in your best interest to tell the truth here." He waited until she gave a little nod, then continued, "We're aware that despite his fiancée's reluctance, Dr. Martino insisted on coming to Scumble River. We're also cognizant that it was his idea to go to the American Legion and that he stayed with a mysteriously disabled car after the bar closed."

"None of which is a crime." AJ looked down his too-perfect-to-be-real nose. "At least, not anywhere outside of Hooterville. What is it, Sheriff? Are you low for this month's arrest quota?"

"Yeah," Wally drawled. "One more criminal in custody and I get a widescreen TV." He glanced between AJ and Chantal. "Which one of you will it be?"

Neither suspect volunteered.

Returning his attention to Chantal, Wally said, "What did Dr. Martino want to talk to you so badly about? And why were you so afraid of him that he had to break into the building to do it?"

"I called my lawyer the minute that cop picked me up." AJ shot a silencing look at Chantal and commanded, "Don't you dare say a word until he gets here."

"Chantal." Wally waited until the woman acknowledged him. "Just remember, Dr. Martino's attorney won't represent your best interests."

Chantal gazed at AJ and asked, "Did you call a lawyer for me, too?"

"Not exactly," AJ mumbled. "Mine will look out for both of us."

"Right." Chantal snorted. "All you care about is you. I had a nice gig here. I like Scumble River. I was starting to make friends."

"You are so stupid, your hair should be platinum." AJ shook his head.

"Really?" Chantal bristled. "Do you know why all the dumb blonde jokes are one-liners?" Without waiting for an answer, she said, "So men like you can understand them."

"Seriously? I'm a freaking surgeon and you question *my* intelligence?" AJ huffed. "If you would have just answered your damn phone or your e-mail, I wouldn't have had to track you down. Imagine my surprise when I found you living in Yolanda's hometown."

"I met her the day I quit." Chantal sighed. "She came into the clinic looking for a job and she mentioned Scumble River. I remembered that my friend Emmy lived there and I thought it would be a good place to regroup and make a fresh start."

Skye smiled. A lot of people seemed to come to Scumble River looking for a clean slate. Or like she had, returned there in search of one. Noticing that Wally had paused in his interrogation, she glanced at him and he dipped his head slightly indicating he wanted her to take over.

"Chantal." Skye reached across the table and took the woman's hand. "You can still have that fresh start. We can help you. But you need to tell us the truth."

"Don't be a fool," AJ snarled. "These people are not your friends. You may have a crush on the chief, but he's obviously not into you." AJ jeered in Skye's direction, "Although what he sees in her . . ."

Wally's fist clenched, but Skye used her free hand to pat his thigh. Who cared what this smarmy creep thought about her or their relationship?

"As usual," Chantal straightened, "you didn't listen to me. I said the sergeant and I had gone out, not the chief." She glanced at Wally and smiled. "Not that you aren't a handsome guy, but"—she shot a pointed glance at AJ—"I've learned my lesson about married men."

"Oh?" Skye encouraged. "Was Dr. Martino married?"

"Still is, unless he decided he can live with his wife getting half of everything." Chantal wrinkled her nose. "At least, that was the excuse he always gave me for not divorcing her."

"Why don't you start at the beginning and tell us what happened," Skye suggested. "You'll feel so much better once it's all out in the open. After that, you really can get that fresh start."

"You're right." Chantal took a deep breath. "If I want to have what you and the chief have—a home, true love, a family—I need to get out in front of the lies and deceit. How could I even think of getting involved with a cop if my whole life is a sham?"

"Baby . . ." AJ's voice turned seductive. "I've missed you. I'll ditch the little redneck I came here with, divorce my wife, and you and I can be together. All you need to do is keep quiet. These two don't know anything."

"They know you're full of shit." Chantal stared at her hands and said, "I was AJ's office manager. The day I was hired, he started to wine and dine me. Before I knew it, we were engaged, which was kind of weird since he was still married. But hey, I believed him when he said that the minute he figured out how to hide his assets, he would get a divorce."

"Sometimes we believe what we want to believe," Skye assured her.

"Anyway, as soon as I was thoroughly hooked, he asked me to fudge a few of the insurance claims." Chantal's face reddened. "He said that the insurance paid so little that if we didn't massage the paperwork, we wouldn't even break even. And after all, the insurance companies could afford it."

AJ tried to interrupt, but Wally narrowed his eyes and fingered his gun until the plastic surgeon closed his mouth.

"Nonetheless, you knew it was illegal," Skye said softly. "So it bothered you."

"It did." A tear slid down Chantal's cheek. "But anytime I complained, AJ had an answer." She wiped away the moisture. "And I loved him."

"So what happened?" Wally asked. "Why did you quit and run away?"

"I was getting more and more worried." Chantal bit her lip. "The insurance companies were starting to question our claims and I told AJ we had to stop."

"Shut the hell up!" AJ bellowed.

"One more word and I'm locking you in the holding cell in the basement," Wally threatened.

The plastic surgeon mutely glared at his ex-fiancée.

Chantal turned her head and continued, "Finally, I told AJ that I wouldn't falsify the claims anymore, and he said that if I didn't, he'd turn the whole mess into the insurance companies' fraud department. He pointed out that his signature on all the paperwork was just a stamp and I was the one that submitted the documents."

"So you quit and disappeared," Skye said, then added, "But he found you."

"I wasn't exactly hiding." Chantal sighed. "I knew AJ wouldn't voluntarily put the insurance claims under scrutiny. After all, even if they held me legally responsible, he'd have to give back all the money."

"Good point." Wally tapped his chin, then asked, "What changed? Why was he suddenly so desperate to see you?"

"The idiot did the same thing with the next office manager." Chantal pressed her lips together in disgust. "He romanced her, got her to fiddle with the claims, and kept on cheating the insurance companies."

"And the companies wised up and he's being investigated for fraud," Skye guessed.

"Exactly. That's when he started calling and texting me. He was afraid that when the insurance investigators talked to me, I'd blow the whistle on him and his new fiancée." Chantal smiled meanly. "When I didn't respond to his messages, he threatened me. So when I saw him at the Legion Sunday night, I hid in the back until he left. But after everyone was gone, he broke the glass in the front door and came looking for me. I locked myself in the closet. I have no idea why there's a deadbolt on the inside, but I was sure glad it was there."

"She's lying!" AJ screeched.

"About what?" Skye was surprised it had taken the plastic surgeon so long to accuse Chantal of deceit.

"All of it." AJ crossed his arms. "And you can't prove otherwise."

"I bet we can." Wally turned to Chantal and cocked an eyebrow. "I'm thinking that you saved the threatening messages and probably some paperwork that incriminates Dr. Martino regarding the insurance scam. Is that right?"

"Of course." Chantal tilted her head. "I have everything tucked away in my safe-deposit box."

"You need to get yourself a good lawyer," Wally

advised. "Then turn everything over to the insurance investigators. We'll be charging Dr. Martino with breaking and entering, but the fraud will be handled by state or maybe federal authorities."

"I don't know any lawyers." Chantal's chin quivered and she jerked her thumb at AJ. "And I don't have his kind of money."

"You should have thought of that before you opened your big fat mouth, bitch," AJ sneered.

As Wally handcuffed the plastic surgeon and hauled him away, Skye slipped Chantal a business card, and said, "My sister-in-law is one of the top criminal attorneys in Illinois. Call her and tell her I sent you."

CHAPTER 23

Like all pure creatures, cats are practical.
—WILLIAM S. BURROUGHS

Skye told Wally she'd meet him in his office and hurried to the restroom. She'd had to go for the last hour, but there was no way she was disturbing the flow of the interrogation for a potty break.

Afterward she leaned against the sink and sighed. Things had gone much better with Chantal and AJ Martino than she had expected. It always surprised her when suspects spilled their guts. It had to be the feeling of catharsis from finally coming clean.

Walking into Wally's office, Skye was surprised to see Quirk pacing in front of the desk. The sergeant was scowling and so was Wally. *Uh-oh.* What had she interrupted?

"Are we through here?" Quirk snarled. "Chantal is upset and I'd like to get her home." When Wally frowned, the sergeant thrust his chin out and said, "I won't stop seeing her just because she made a mistake. She was a victim. That asshole threatened her."

Ah. They'd been talking about Quirk's budding relationship with the pretty American Legion manager. Maybe she should leave. Skye started to back away, but Wally glanced at her and gestured her forward.

"I'm not going to order you to stop dating her." Wally rubbed his neck. "We won't be involved in any charges that are brought against her, so it probably isn't a conflict of interest. But you should clear it with the city attorney because she is a witness in our case."

"Fine." Quirk's lips were pressed together in a tight line. "I'll make an appointment tomorrow."

"Okay." Wally picked up several sheets of paper from the top of his desk and straightened them into a neat pile.

"Can I go?" Quirk stood, obviously impatient to leave.

"Yes." Wally nodded, then as the man marched toward the door, he added, "Good job with the Paulks."

Once the sergeant was gone, Skye sat down and said, "I hope Quirk doesn't end up jeopardizing his career for someone he just met."

"Me, too." Wally sighed. "But some relationships are worth the risk."

"And some aren't." Skye wasn't sure how she felt about Chantal. "From what she said to me after you left with AJ, her track record with men isn't very good."

"Everyone's track record with the opposite sex is bad until they meet the one that makes it good." Wally shrugged. "Look at our past. You thought Luc was a good catch."

"True. And he turned out to be a fumble." Skye felt sorry for Chantal, but she'd made her own choices. Despite what Quirk wanted to believe, the Legion manager had knowingly got involved with a married man and committed fraud for him. She could have said no. "But being beautiful only gets a woman so far. After that she needs to have some substance and I'm not sure there's much beneath Chantal's surface."

When Wally didn't respond, Skye smiled. He was such a romantic. Changing the subject, she asked, "What did Quirk find out from the Paulks?"

"Pretty much what you guessed." Wally flipped through the documents he was holding. "Grant admitted that every couple of months, there'd be a message on a private Open Book group page. Anyone interested in earning a pair of the newest athletic shoes could pick up a box from the manager at one of the Dollar or Three stores. Inside were the drugs, different kinds depending what was currently popular. The boys would sell the dope, turn the money into the manager, and keep the shoes."

"Wow." Skye leaned back in her chair. How had all this been going on under their noses at school? "So I take it Ruben Ramirez is being arrested as we speak?"

"He claims he had no idea what was in the boxes he handed out or the envelopes the kids gave him to pass on to Lynch, but he's the sheriff department's problem, not ours." Wally shoved his fingers through his hair. "Since the stores are spread throughout Laurel County, it's better if they take jurisdiction in the matter."

"Then it wasn't just the Scumble River stores." Skye felt slightly better that other school districts had missed what was happening, too. "What did the locker search turn up?"

"Two more boxes at the junior high and five at the high school," Wally said. "And we found Lynch's fingerprints on three of them."

"Good." Skye tapped the arm of the chair with her nails. "That proves Palmer was involved. Maybe Mr. Ramirez is telling the truth."

"Could be. To be sure, the sheriff will have to see who the admin was for the Open Book page." Wally shrugged, then smiled at Skye and said, "At least we've solved the American Legion break-in." He tilted his head. "Or should I say you solved it, darlin'?"

"Nope, you were right the first time." Skye blew him a kiss. "It's always we."

"Now we just have to figure out which one of Lynch's drug connections killed him." Wally picked up three thick files. "These are the reports from the ME, the crime lab, and the neighborhood canvas. They're first on my agenda for tomorrow's reading. Since we have a better idea of the vic's extracurricular activities, I might be able to spot a clue."

"Is the ME releasing the body?" Skye asked.

"Yes." Wally rubbed his thumb along the edge of the manila folders. "He informed Mrs. Lynch this afternoon that she could make the funeral arrangements."

"She'll be relieved to finally be able to have some closure." Feeling the baby move, Skye shifted in her chair. "The wake will probably be Saturday. I'm guessing that if we haven't caught the killer by then, we'll be attending."

"At the rate we're going, we'd better count on making an appearance." Wally's voice was discouraged. "It'll take a long time to track down all his drug connections."

Skye was silent for several minutes, then said slowly, "You know, in view of how Palmer was killed, I really don't think that it was business related." Wally raised a brow and Skye added, "Even the criminal side of his business. The method was just too personal. Why would he let an employee tie him to the bed naked? And if he was forced to do so at gunpoint, why wasn't there any sign of a struggle?"

"Maybe he had taken a dose of ketamine. That would impair his judgment," Wally suggested.

"His mother claimed that Palmer was too much of a control freak to take drugs."

"One way to find out." Wally riffled through the ME's report, then said, "She's right. Nothing on the additional tox screen I requested."

"Interesting." Skye wrinkled her brow. "So if he was killed for a personal reason, that brings up another question. If Palmer was as much of a control freak as Mrs. Lynch claimed, wouldn't he be the one tying someone to the bed, not the one being tied?"

"So who would he allow to tie him up?" Wally asked.

"How about his ex-wife?" Skye's eyes widened.

"Son of a bee!" Wally thundered. "She's the one person we haven't talked to yet. She should have been first on my list."

"Why?" Skye hated seeing Wally blame himself for a decision he'd made before all the facts had been discovered. "Yes, she's his ex and he treated her badly in the divorce. But that was over a year ago. What reason would she have to kill him now? We concentrated on the suspects with more pressing motives." Skye added, "And I know it seems so much longer, but it's only been four days since Dorothy found the body."

"You're right regarding why we haven't talked to the ex-wife yet." The muscle in Wally's jaw jerked. "But since we're currently out of suspects, Felicia Lynch has become much more interesting."

"Where does she live?"

Wally checked the file and said, "When she and Lynch divorced, she moved to Naperville."

"It's past nine so we'd never make it to her place before ten or ten thirty," Skye mused. "And since we have no evidence to arrest her, I'm thinking showing up on her doorstep in the middle of the night wouldn't be the best way to get her cooperation."

"Agreed. I'll go first thing in the morning." Wally stood and stretched. "Now, we better go home so you can get some rest. You have to be up early for school."

"Shouldn't I be with you when you interview the former Mrs. Lynch?"

"That would be ideal." Wally grimaced. "But I don't want to wait until the afternoon. You can listen to the recording when you come to the station after work."

"I guess that's the best solution." Skye yawned. "Let's hit the road."

Once they were home and Skye had fed Bingo, she

trudged upstairs, so tired she could barely lift her foot to the next step. Wally was right. If she was going to make it through the next school day's endless meetings, she really did need to get some rest.

As she walked down the short hallway, soothing music flowed from the bathroom. Candlelight flickered, the smell of peppermint and rosemary floated in the air, and Wally beckoned her from the doorway.

He'd filled the soaker tub with hot water and her favorite foaming bath salts. Undressing her, he eased her into the bubbles, picked up her loofah, and starting at her feet, began to bathe her.

Nearly purring under his tender ministrations, Skye felt herself relax for the first time that day and drifted off to sleep.

Friday's high school annual reviews were brutal. Several mothers and fathers were not happy with their children's special education programs, and Skye had spent the morning acting as a mediator between the parents and the principal. Since Homer was anything but reasonable, she'd often found herself on the opposite side of the administration. Not a comfortable position to occupy.

Wally had promised to text Skye after he'd talked to Felicia Lynch, but when the group broke for lunch and she checked her phone, he hadn't contacted her. Did that mean he was still with Felicia? Or maybe he'd arrested her and was busy with the booking procedure.

Skye had decided to eat in her office so she could scan the next student's file while she ate, but before she'd even taken her sandwich out of the plastic bag, Trixie burst into the room.

"Bambi says, and I quote, 'Aunt Yolanda stole Pa's car and lit out of town last night like her tail feathers were on fire.' Do you have any idea why?"

"Wally put AJ Martino in jail for breaking into the Legion." Skye had half expected to find Yolanda waiting in her office when she'd arrived at school; now she understood why she'd been spared.

"Why in the heck did AJ do that?" Trixie demanded, snagging a grape from Skye's lunch.

"To talk to the manager. She was his former employee and ex-fiancée," Skye said, then explained about AJ, Chantal, and the insurance fraud.

"Wowie Kazowie!" Trixie squealed. "I thought he seemed shady."

"You said he was hot." Skye sniggered.

"Hot and shady. He seemed mighty fluent in hound dog." Trixie ate another grape then asked, "Do you think Bambi's aunt will be implicated? If Chantal said AJ got his new squeeze to keep doctoring the books, that would be Yolanda."

"My guess is the reason she left last night was to get rid of any evidence of her involvement," Skye commented. "Yolanda may not be the typical Doozier, but she still has the cunning that the rest of them have that keeps them out of legal trouble." Skye smiled meanly. "AJ is probably better off in jail than facing Earl now that he knows how AJ done his sister wrong."

Trixie giggled, then when the bell rang, she said goodbye and hurried back to the library. Stuffing the last bite of her sandwich into her mouth, Skye gathered the afternoon meeting folders and headed back into the trenches.

Ushering the final set of parents out at three fifteen, Skye looked at her cell. There was a text from Wally asking her to meet him at the station as soon as she could. She hastily deposited the completed paperwork in her file cabinet, locked it, and rushed to her car.

When she walked through the PD's front door, May told her that Wally was waiting in the coffee/interrogation room. Skye was surprised to find him there alone.

After kissing her cheek and pulling out a chair for her, he said, "Felicia Lynch had an airtight alibi."

"Oh?" Skye wrinkled her brow. If that was the case, why was Wally in such a hurry for her to get to the station?

"She was in an airplane flying home from Las Vegas with her brand-new husband." Wally drummed his fingers on the table. "She showed me the ticket to prove it."

"Well, that sucks." Skye exhaled. "Our last lead bites the dust."

"Not quite. I asked Felicia if she was aware of Lynch's sexual leanings. When she said that she was, I asked her who he'd allow to tie him up, rather than vice versa." Wally smiled and pushed the button on the tape recorder in front of him. "Listen to this."

A woman's voice said, "The only time he'd allow that is if he were trying to convince a first-time partner to play with him."

From the recorder Wally's voice asked, "So someone unaccustomed to the lifestyle?"

"Yes," Felicia answered. "He definitely wouldn't ever submit to a woman after that initial experience."

Wally turned off the playback. "What do you think?" he asked Skye, clearly having already formed his own opinion.

"Unless Palmer had another girlfriend ready and waiting after begging Virginia to take him back, which seems highly unlikely since he hoped she'd be going home with him, that means . . ." Skye trailed off, contemplating the likely scenarios.

"Virginia lied to us." Wally's expression was grim. "For some reason she decided to go to his house and give his kink a try."

"That seems to be the most logical answer," Skye said thoughtfully. "But then why did she kill him?"

CHAPTER 24

A cat has nine lives. For three he plays, for three he strays, and for the last three he stays.
—ENGLISH PROVERB

"We need to get Virginia back in here." Wally paced the length of the interrogation room. "But before we do, we have to figure out her motive."

"Do we have any witnesses of Virginia and Palmer quarreling?" Skye pulled a legal pad from her tote bag. "Maybe they had other issues in addition to their sex life."

"I never did get a chance to read all of the neighborhood canvas summaries." Wally returned to the table and flipped open a folder. "I was mainly interested in whether anyone had been observed entering or leaving the Lynch residence on Sunday evening, and both Martinez and Anthony said they hadn't."

"That's a quiet street, and considering the time of death is between eleven and twelve"—Skye chewed on the end of her pen as Wally scanned the reports—"I'm not surprised that the murderer wasn't seen."

"Here's something." Wally whistled. "A Mr. Cooperson stated that the Friday night before the murder, he saw the vic and Virginia Elders having a—and I quote—'lively discussion' on Lynch's back patio."

"Didn't Virginia say they broke up on Tuesday and she didn't see him again until he came to her house on Sunday?" Skye asked.

"Exactly." Wally narrowed his eyes. "That's the first lie that we can prove."

"Could Mr. Cooperson hear what Palmer and Virginia were talking about?"

Wally flipped through a couple more pages, then blew out a disappointed breath. "Unfortunately not."

"What else would help us prove that Virginia and Palmer had resumed their relationship?" Skye tapped her pen against the table edge, then snapped her fingers. "Let me see the crime tech's list of the contents of Palmer's bedroom and bath."

With a puzzled expression, Wally handed the documents to Skye. "What are you looking for?"

"This." She waved the inventory of Palmer's dresser, closet, and bathroom cabinets. "There were women's clothing, shoes, and toiletries."

"We know they dated and were intimate." Wally shrugged his shoulders. "She probably stayed overnight."

"But"—Skye pointed her finger at Wally—"if they truly broke up Tuesday, wouldn't she have demanded her stuff back?"

"She might not have gotten around to it yet." Wally shrugged again. "Or didn't want the hassle."

"Possibly." Skye wrinkled her brow. "But there are expensive items listed here." She read further. "And there was a laminated memorial card from her son's funeral in the pocket of one of the slacks." Skye shook her head. "Virginia often held that card when she was feeling stressed. That's something that she would have definitely missed and wanted back right away."

"Okay," Wally conceded. "We'll mark that down as likely evidence that they didn't truly break up."

Skye continued to read the reports, then glanced up and asked, "What about the gun? The ME said that the bullet was in good enough shape to make a match."

"True." Wally lifted a brow. "But first we have to find

the weapon before we can compare it. A forty-five wasn't registered to any of our suspects." He frowned. "But now that we're concentrating on Virginia, I could expand the search to include relatives."

"Check her son," Skye suggested. "I remember her saying she was upset that when Jameson turned eighteen, her ex-husband signed for him to get a permit for a gun. The boy insisted that they needed it because, with his dad living elsewhere, he wanted to be able to protect himself and his mom."

While Wally made the call about the weapon, Skye glanced at her watch. It was nearly six and she was starving. She needed to get something to eat soon.

Interrupting her hunger pangs, Wally clicked off his cell and said, "I reached out to a friend at the state police and he'll get back to us on the permit as soon as he can."

"I hate to be a bother, but can we get a pizza?" Skye asked. "My lunch was a long time ago."

"Of course." Wally cupped her cheek and brushed his lips over hers. "You are never a bother. Nothing is more important than you and the baby."

Skye took out her phone and placed the order, then as they waited for both food and information, she asked, "Will you be able to get a search warrant if Virginia's son had a forty-five registered to him?"

"I think so."

"Let's finish studying the reports," Skye suggested. "We have half an hour before the pizza gets here."

They'd finished both their dinner and their reading by the time Wally's friend at the state police got back to them. Wally listened, took a few notes, then thanking his contact, disconnected the call.

Turning to Skye, he said, "There's a permit for a forty-five owned by Jameson Elders. The address on the paperwork is the same as Virginia's."

"Does that mean you're ready to re-question Virginia now?" Skye asked.

She wasn't eager to confront her colleague, but she had no choice. If Virginia had murdered Palmer, justice had to prevail.

"First, I'll ask the city attorney to get the warrant." Wally dialed his cell. "When we serve it, we'll bring her in for interrogation."

Wally made his call, then said, "We're in luck. The city attorney is in Laurel at a local American Bar Association dinner, so he has his choice of judges. He said he should have our warrant to us in less than an hour."

"We still don't have a motive." Skye chewed on her thumbnail. "She'll be hard to crack without one."

Wally grunted his agreement and resumed his pacing.

Several minutes later an idea popped into Skye's head and she asked, "Did I tell you that Virginia's son died of a drug overdose?"

"I don't think so," Wally said slowly. "Are you thinking that Lynch might have been his supplier and Virginia just discovered that fact?"

"That hadn't occurred to me." Skye's expression was grim. "But it could be. What I really was thinking was that Virginia found out that Palmer was dealing and couldn't handle that she'd been sleeping with the enemy."

The city attorney had been as good as his word, and by eight thirty, the warrant had been served and Virginia was in the police station coffee/interrogation room. Sitting across from her, Skye studied the fourth grade teacher. Virginia was dressed in sweatpants and a ratty T-shirt, with her hair in a messy ponytail. Plainly, she hadn't been planning to go anywhere that evening.

Once the tape recorder was started, Wally said, "We know you killed Palmer Lynch." He waited, but when

Virginia didn't react, he confirmed, "You've been read your rights?"

"Yes"—Virginia's tone was clipped—"but I have nothing to hide. I haven't done anything wrong."

"Really?" Wally took his notebook from his uniform pocket. "Because we know you lied about your breakup with Lynch. Your possessions were still in his house, including one that Skye assures me you wouldn't have left behind if you didn't intend to see him again." Wally waited a full beat, then added, "What's more, we have a witness placing you at his house Friday night."

"I see."

Pausing before he delivered the coup de grâce, Wally leaned forward, plainly waiting for some subtle cue to continue.

When the muscle near Virginia's mouth twitched, he pounced. "*And* we know about your son's gun. The officers will find it, and the bullet in Lynch will be matched to it."

"How . . ." Virginia stopped, a flicker of panic in her eyes. "I mean, I threw that gun in the river the day after Jameson died."

Skye hated to do it, but the information wasn't confidential and she had no choice. No matter how sympathetic Virginia was and how awful Palmer had been, she couldn't allow the woman to get away with murder.

"Virginia, you told me you couldn't bear to part with a single item of Jameson's," Skye said gently. "You said you weren't even able to empty his wastebasket, which is why I'm certain that even after using the gun as a murder weapon, you didn't get rid of it."

"Uh." Virginia wrinkled her brow. "I, uh, that was different. I hate guns."

"Right." Wally's voice was knife-edged. "That's why you used one to kill your boyfriend." When Virginia remained silent, he continued, "You think you've concealed the gun so well my officers won't find it, but they know all the hiding places."

"I have no idea what you're talking about." Virginia's voice cracked. "I didn't—"

Skye interrupted. She was well aware that the more times a person said, "I didn't do it," the less likely they would confess.

"We know what an awful man he was." Skye patted her arm. "And I don't mean his sexual preferences. I'm not judging him on those. But he was involved in extortion and drugs. I'm certain there are extenuating circumstances for why you killed him and those will mean a much lighter sentence than usual for murder."

Virginia curled her lip.

Wally abruptly leaned across the table and grabbed Virginia's wrist. "I didn't notice this last time we talked, but I see now that your middle knuckle is swollen and you have a bruise between it and your index finger."

Virginia jerked her hand away from Wally's grasp.

"Those types of contusions are caused by an improper grip on a handgun," Wally explained. "A lot of first timers fire a gun the wrong way and are injured."

"That doesn't prove anything." Virginia crossed her arms. "I was making some repairs and hurt myself using a power drill."

"Felicia Lynch told us the only time Palmer would allow himself to be tied up without a struggle would be to reassure a new partner and persuade her to go along with his kink," Skye said. When Virginia's eyelids trembled, Skye asked, "Is that how you got him to cooperate? You said you'd give the whole BDSM thing a whirl if he let you tie him up?"

Before Virginia could respond, Wally's phone pinged and he glanced at the incoming text. Smiling grimly, he said, "We've got the gun." He glanced at Skye and added, "She had it hidden in a stereo speaker.

Virginia sagged.

"The weapon is on its way to the crime lab for ballistic testing and fingerprinting," Wally continued. "You might as well tell us your side of the story."

"You won't understand." Virginia slumped forward. "Maybe I do need a lawyer."

"That's your right." Wally hooked his thumb in his belt loops.

"I . . . I . . ." Virginia scrubbed her eyes with the heels of her hands and looked at Skye. "What do you think I should do?"

"Well, you do have a right to counsel, Virginia." Skye wrinkled her nose. "But the thing is, a lawyer probably won't allow you to tell us your side of the story. We won't know the mitigating circumstances of the situation." She paused, then asked, "Do you want to call an attorney?"

"No. I guess not." Virginia sniffed, a tear leaking down her cheek. She obviously realized she was running out of options.

"Well, you can anytime. But let me tell you what I think happened." She smiled reassuringly at the woman. "I think you missed Palmer and wondered if you could bring yourself to tolerate his sexual preferences. You went to his place Friday to discuss it with him and agreed to try it out Sunday night."

Virginia nodded.

"But between Friday and Sunday, you somehow found out about his drug dealing," Skye continued.

"When I left Palmer's Friday night, I forgot my car keys and went back into the house through the patio door to get them from the kitchen counter. I overheard him talking on the phone about a big supply of ketamine he was expecting. I left without confronting him, but I asked some of Jameson's friends about Palmer.

They confirmed that he was supplying drugs to the kids in the school."

"We know." Wally nodded.

As if guessing the next question, Virginia shook her head. "Palmer wasn't Jameson's dealer, but that didn't matter. He was poisoning other people's children just like Jameson had been poisoned."

"So when you didn't show up at his place Sunday, he came to yours." Skye waited until Virginia jerked her head up and down, then continued, "He suggested that you tie him up as a way to ease you into the situation, and you saw it as a way to talk to him about his drug dealing."

"Exactly." Virginia clenched her fist. "Once he was naked and tied to the bed, I took out the gun and told him if he didn't stop dealing drugs, I'd go to the police. He said that no one would believe me. That I had no proof." She straightened and spoke faster. "I never intended to kill him, just force him to stop dealing. But he taunted me. He said that drugs were an evolutionary device. The weakest people die."

"And you couldn't stand him making such a cruel statement about your son," Skye said, truly feeling sorry for the woman.

"When he said that, my finger just squeezed the trigger." Virginia's chin dipped to her chest. "I panicked, and after I left his house and was home, I just hid the gun and pretended to myself that it had all been a bad dream. Like the ones I had right after finding Jameson dead in the garage."

"So you admit you shot Lynch?" Wally asked.

"Yes." Virginia nodded. "But I didn't mean to kill him."

"You wouldn't believe how often we hear that." Wally blew out a loud breath. "But that doesn't mean much when a man is dead."

Virginia's head jerked up, then she collapsed against the back of the chair, a broken woman who clearly had nothing left to deny. Sobbing, she said, "I didn't want to hurt anyone. But he kept pushing and pushing. He didn't even pretend to be sorry about my son."

"What a jerk," Skye muttered.

Virginia wiped her cheeks with her palms. "Someone had to stop him." Her expression hardened. "He should have agreed to quit. He didn't need any more money, but he said he enjoyed the power that dealing gave him." She sank farther in her chair, muttering over again, "I took all the power away from him. Yes. I did. I took it all away just like his kind took my son away from me."

Skye and Wally exchanged a look, and he wrapped up the questioning. Three hours later, Virginia's case had been turned over to the city attorney and Skye and Wally were on their way home.

As they pulled into their driveway, Skye said, "Keeping the gun and not even wiping her prints off the thing, it was almost as if Virginia wanted to be caught so she could tell someone her story."

"Except for habitual criminals"—Wally's smile was grim—"most people find it hard to handle the guilt of what they did."

Skye was silent as they parked, went inside, and fed Bingo.

Finally, as they walked upstairs and into their bedroom, she said, "It's difficult to feel happy about putting Virginia away. She's a good teacher and a caring human being. She's a much better person than Palmer Lynch ever was."

"But we can't let murderers go free, even if we don't like their victims." From behind her, Wally slid his arms around Skye's waist. "Although it's tough to see someone like her throw away her life."

"You're right on both counts." Skye laid her head back on Wally's chest. "I bet in the end, Palmer Lynch was sorry he ever messed with a mother's love."

Wally rested his hands on Skye's stomach. "A lesson he should have learned a lot sooner."

EPILOGUE

Happy is the home with at least one cat.
—ITALIAN PROVERB

It was Friday night, three weeks since Skye and Wally figured out who had murdered Palmer Lynch. School had officially ended that afternoon, and to celebrate the beginning of summer break, Wally, Skye, Loretta, Vince, Abby, and Linc Quillen were all having dinner together at the Country Mansion in Dwight.

"You should have seen Trixie's face when the Dooziers arrived for the GIVE ceremony." Skye laughed, clutching Loretta's arm as they walked up the sweeping cement stairs that led to the restaurant's entrance. "Especially when they kept pouring into the gym. Just the amount of camo and cleavage was enough to make several parents change seats."

"I'm not surprised." Loretta chuckled. She waited for her husband to open the double glass doors, then swept inside, tugging Skye along with her. Leaning close, Loretta said, "From what I've heard, Bambi's award might be the first anyone in that family has ever won at school."

"Maybe she's the start of a new generation of Dooziers," Skye said, scanning the enclosed porch, where she and Loretta had paused to allow the rest of their group to catch up to them.

The white lace curtains rippled in the breeze of the open windows, and people sat on white wicker sofas and chairs relaxing until their tables were ready. Skye smiled at Wally as he guided her and Loretta through another set of doors, then along with Vince, he went to speak to the hostess.

While the men checked on their reservations, Skye glanced at Abby and Linc, who had lingered a few steps behind the rest of the group. The pair had been dating for a couple of weeks, and according to Abby, they were really hitting it off. Skye watched as they examined a beautiful wooden staircase, along with the half-oval antique china cabinet and old-fashioned oak icebox displayed against its rails.

"Ah." Loretta's gaze followed Skye's and she said, "I think those two might be on their way down the aisle soon."

"Seriously?" Skye snickered. "They've been on, like, three dates and you're ready to marry them off?"

"Must be the baby hormones." Loretta narrowed her eyes. "I usually couldn't give a crap about anyone else's love life."

"Right." Skye hid her smile. Her sister-in-law liked to pretend to be tough as nails, but Scumble River was softening her city girl heart.

Spotting the green crystal-stemmed goblets on the glass-enclosed shelves that hung on the opposite wall, Skye remembered that she'd noticed them the last time she was at the Mansion. There were a dozen similar ones in the china cabinet in her own dining room.

She'd inherited them along with the house from Mrs. Griggs and had meant to have them appraised to see if they were valuable enough to sell, but had forgotten.

Although maybe that was just as well. Mrs. Griggs's spirit had haunted her from the time she'd moved into the house until her wedding night. Once Skye and Wally returned from their honeymoon, the old woman's ghost hadn't reappeared, and her policy was to let sleeping poltergeists lie.

Nudging Skye out of her thoughts, Linc and Abby joined Skye and Loretta just as Vince and Wally walked over and Wally said, "Our table's ready."

An enticing aroma of cinnamon and freshly baked bread floated from the bakery as the six of them followed the hostess down a narrow hall. The Mansion was famous for its pastries and Skye had saved up her calories all day so she could splurge tonight.

They were led into a large room filled with diners and shown to a large corner table partially shielded by a folding screen on one side and a large floral arrangement on the other. Undoubtedly, just as he had on their first date, Wally had called ahead and arranged for the secluded spot.

Wally helped Skye into her chair, then sat next to her. Loretta took the seat on Skye's left, with Vince, Abby, and Linc completing the circle.

"Linc," Skye said to the vet, who was directly across from her. "I wanted to thank you again for helping me with my counseling group. The boys made a lot of progress thanks to your pet therapy."

"I enjoyed it." Linc twined his fingers with Abby's. "Thank *you* for fixing me up with such a wonderful woman."

"I enjoyed it," Skye echoed, then slipped her hand into Wally's. "When you're happy, you want everyone around you to be happy, too."

The waitress approached and said, "Hello, my name is Rhea Ann and I'll be taking care of you tonight. What can I get you all to drink?"

When both Skye and Loretta ordered soda, Abby raised a brow and said, "I understand about Skye, but Loretta, is there about to be another announcement?"

Vince hurriedly asked for a beer. Wally and Linc said that they'd have one, too. Giving up her questioning, Abby asked for a Mojito.

When the server left to fetch their drinks and appetizers, Linc said, "I wondered if there was anything more you could share about Palmer Lynch's murder and the drugs."

There was a brief, awkward silence, then Wally said, "I really can't say too much."

"All I want to know is if my animals are safe from future blackmail schemes," Linc assured Wally.

"I believe so." Wally buttered a roll. "The county prosecutor is satisfied that Ramirez was not involved in Lynch's drug business. He may have suspected that something wasn't on the up-and-up, but he never received any compensation for handing the shoes out at the stores or collecting the envelopes for Lynch."

Everyone was quiet as their waitress served their appetizers and drinks, took the order for their entrées, and refilled water glasses.

Once she left, Skye plucked a homemade toast point from those arranged around a small oval casserole dish, scooped a bit of the hot artichoke and crab dip onto it, and took a careful bite. All she needed was to have the appetizer spill down the front of her pale peach maternity dress and have to wear a food-spattered garment for the rest of the evening.

Abby followed suit with the dip, then asked, "Do you think poor Virginia will go to prison for the rest of her life?"

Skye opened her mouth, then glanced at Wally, who gave her a slight nod. Smiling at Abby, Skye said, "Virginia's been charged with second-degree murder."

"Which means what?" Abby and Linc asked simultaneously.

"It's not premeditated killing," Loretta explained, then added, "The sentence is usually between four and twenty years. Virginia has hired me to represent her, and I believe I can get the minimum once I finish negotiating with the prosecutor."

They were all silent as they processed Loretta's words. Once their salads arrived, the conversation turned to plans for the summer, which carried them through the entrée.

But as dessert and coffee were served, Skye touched Loretta's arm and said in a low voice, "I wanted to thank you for taking Chantal's case on a sliding fee scale. What do you think will happen to her?"

"She and Yolanda have both agreed to testify against AJ Martino." Loretta's smile was satisfied. "Since neither of them saw a penny of the money, in exchange for their statements, they won't be charged with insurance fraud."

"Wow!" Skye shook her head. "First, hope for the minimum sentence for Virginia and now this. You are an amazing lawyer."

"I am." Loretta grinned. "And I'm thinking that there actually may be enough business in Scumble River for me to open a branch of my firm here."

"That would be awesome." Skye sighed. "Whoever thought that when you first came to town to help my brother, we'd all be sitting here together?"

Skye glanced around the table. Vince looked happier than he'd ever been. Linc and Abby's relationship seemed to be going in a positive direction. And she and Wally were about to become parents.

Whatever the future held for them, as long as they were together, Skye was certain they would be all right.

If you missed out on Denise Swanson's
first book in the *New York Times*
bestselling Scumble River Mysteries,
keep reading for an excerpt of . . .

Murder of a Small-Town Honey

Available now!

When Skye Denison was forced to return to Scumble River, Illinois, she knew it would be humiliating, but she never dreamed it would be murder. It was embarrassing enough to have been fired from her first full-time position as a school psychologist, but then she'd had to beg for a job in a place she had described as a small town, full of small-minded people, with even smaller intellects. Skye only wished she hadn't said it to the entire population of Scumble River via her high school valedictorian address. Granted, the speech took place twelve years ago, but she had a feeling people would remember.

Nonetheless, she was back, and nothing had changed. Skye had arrived in Scumble River last Sunday afternoon, barely in time for the start of school on Monday. Her plan had been to slip into town unnoticed and remain that way for as long as possible. But it was only Saturday, and she'd already been suckered into participating in one of the community's most hokey events, the Chokeberry Days Festival.

Skye stood behind a huge table made from sawhorses and sheets of plywood. Spread across its surface

was a red-and-white-checked cloth on which were
lined up hundreds of bright pink bottles of chokeberry
jelly. The clashing colors made Skye dizzy, and the
idea of actually tasting the contents of all those jars
made her nauseous. How had she ever let herself be
talked into judging the chokeberry jelly contest?

Before she could make a bolt for freedom, a woman
dressed in a magenta-colored polyester pantsuit descended on the booth. "Skye, it's good to see you back
home where you belong. Though I do remember you
saying something when you left about Scumble River being too *small* for you."

"Aunt Minnie, what can I say?" She could think of
lots of things, but none that wouldn't get her in trouble.
Minnie was her mother's middle sister, and she would
be on the phone griping to Skye's mom in a minute if
she felt Skye had been rude.

"Did you hear about what happened Thursday night
at the high school band contest?" Minnie was also gossip central for their family. She was better at getting
the news out than Dan Rather.

"No, what?" Skye asked warily. Her aunt reminded
her of a Venus-flytrap, and Skye was always afraid she
was about to become the bug.

"Well, I thought you would've been there, since you
got that fancy job working for the schools." Minnie
smiled sweetly.

Swallowing the words she wanted to say—fancy job
and Scumble River School District did not belong in
the same sentence—Skye matched her aunt's smile and
said, "Gee, I didn't know you all were impressed by my
little job."

After a few moments of silence, Minnie went on as
if Skye hadn't spoken. "The problems started when
half the kids discovered their music had disappeared
and the other half claimed their instruments were

missing. Both were later found stashed in the shower stall next to the boys' locker room, but by then it was too late to go on with the contest."

Skye said, "Oh, my, I did hear some teachers talking about that yesterday in the teachers' lounge. There was a fight, too, right?"

"Right. The rival band members blamed each other for the missing items, and Scumble River's tuba player ended up with a broken nose. A drummer from Clay Center took home two black eyes."

"How awful. The poor kids had probably practiced for months for the competition." Skye narrowed her eyes. "A prank like that is just plain mean. Do you know if they found out who did it?"

Minnie shook her head.

"I wonder if the band director kicked any kids out of the band recently."

"Not that I heard of. But that's not all that's been happening," Minnie said and fanned herself with her handkerchief. "Yesterday at the catfish dinner, someone replaced all the salt in the kitchen with sugar. Seventy pounds of catfish, potato salad, and baked beans were ruined. The Feedbag was sponsoring the supper, so they're out a pretty penny."

Skye frowned. The Feedbag was Scumble River's only restaurant, other than the fast-food places along the road heading out of town. Like any small business, the Feedbag operated on a shoestring and couldn't afford a big hit in the cash register. "Why would someone do that?" she asked.

Minnie's face grew angelic. "Why, honey, you're the one with the degree in psychology. I'm just one of those people with *small intellects* you told us about in your graduation speech."

Skye felt her face turn the same color as her aunt's suit, and decided the better part of valor lay in switching subjects—quickly. "Chokeberry Days has certainly changed a lot."

"This year is different," Minnie said quietly. "There's a bad feeling in town. Half the people want the festival to grow bigger and bigger."

Skye hazarded a guess. "The ones in town who stand to profit from the crowds, no doubt."

"Yes. And on the other side are all the folks that just see it for a nuisance."

"Who's that?" Skye wrinkled her brow.

Minnie held up her hand and counted on her fingers. "The junior high principal, Lloyd Stark, is the prime instigator of the anti-festival campaign. He hates how it ruins the beginning of school. There are classes for three days, and then Chokeberry Days starts, and half the kids play hooky for the rest of the week."

"I wondered why things were so quiet on Thursday and Friday."

Bending down a second finger, Minnie continued. "The people who live along Basin Street also hate the festival. Their windows get broken, garbage gets thrown in their front yards, and the noise is awful. Mike Young is the head of that group."

"Vince's friend from high school?"

"Yes. At the time we worried when your brother stuck by him, but Mike seems to have straightened up quite a bit since his teenage years."

"Oh, yeah. I remember now. He went to prison for a while for dealing drugs."

"Seems okay now. He owns the local photography shop."

"Nice to hear someone made good." Skye closed her eyes briefly and visualized what her life had been like last year at this time. Living in New Orleans had been a dream come true. Everything was exotic and slightly forbidden. She loved nosing out the mysteries of the city. That is, until one of the secrets turned on her and caused her to be fired . . . and jilted. She shook her head. She had vowed not to think of her ex-fiancé and the pain he had caused her.

"Skye, sweetheart, come give me a kiss."

Skye looked up from her reflections into the faded green eyes of her grandmother, Antonia Leofanti. "Grandma!"

The two women hugged fiercely. Skye noticed how frail her grandmother had become in the eight months since she had last seen her. Antonia's pink scalp peeked through her white hair, and her head barely made it to Skye's chest. It felt as if she was embracing a skeleton.

Antonia backed away first and looked confused for a moment. "Oh, Skye . . . ah, Minnie." Her gaze cleared as she turned toward her daughter. "I almost forgot. They've got a problem at the Altar and Rosary Society's craft tent. Someone switched all the price tags around. Iona Clapp's handmade quilt is now marked twenty-five cents, and little Iris's potholder is going for four hundred dollars."

Minnie gave a shriek and took off at a trot.

Antonia spoke over her shoulder to Skye as she slowly followed Minnie. "Now that you're back in town, you make sure you come visit me. It's time I told someone the family history, and I think you're the best one to hear it."

Skye hurried toward the Port-A-Pots. One of the other judges had finally showed up to take over watching the jellies, and Skye was free for half an hour. When she arrived at the toilets she swore under her breath. The line snaked back past both the Lions' lemonade stand and the Knights of Columbus fishpond grab bag game. As she took her place at the end, she heard a high saccharine voice attempting to tell a children's story while a small child screamed in the background.

By standing with her back to the line, Skye was able to observe the performance currently unfolding on the festival's center stage. A tiny old lady, dressed in a loose white dress over a red-and-white-striped long-sleeved turtleneck and matching tights, was trying to ignore two little boys who were fighting over a stuffed animal. After one particularly loud screech, the woman finally stopped her storytelling and crouched next to the unhappy children. Her dress was so long and she was so tiny, the only thing that showed in this position was the rolled-up tips of her pointy-toed shoes.

The old lady's amplified voice could be heard throughout the food and games area. "Sweetie pies, could you do Mrs. Gumtree a big, big favor? If you stop fighting over that itty-bitty teddy bear, Mrs. Gumtree will get each of you one of her dolls when she finishes the story."

The children were quiet for less than a heartbeat, then a reedy young voice piped up, "Boys don't play with dolls."

Skye watched as the two kids, now united against the enemy, an adult, stood and raced off the stage. It was hard to tell from such a distance, but it looked to Skye as if a fleeting expression of irritation crossed Mrs. Gumtree's features before she turned back and pasted a smile on her face.

As Skye used the facilities, smelly as they were, she shook her head over the way Mrs. Gumtree had handled the children. If she ever ran into the woman, maybe she'd give her a few tips on behavior management.

She still had some time before she was due back to judge the chokeberry jellies, so she decided to walk to the pasture where Cow Chip Bingo was being held.

To play Cow Chip Bingo, a flat piece of ground was divided into square-yard plats that were sold for twenty dollars each. On the specified day, plat-holders were provided with a barbecue dinner, which they consumed picnic-style on their section of grass. One well-fed cow was allowed to wander the field. The winner was the holder of the plat in which the cow dropped its chips.

Skye heard screams and laughter as she approached the playing area. Hurrying forward, she saw people running in every direction. She was just in time to watch a father, holding his daughter over his head, step in a cow pie and go down as if he were sliding into home base.

Skye asked a man leaning against the gate, "What's going on here?"

He half turned to her, but kept an eye on the field. "Somebody must've slipped something into the cow's feed. It's dropping a load every few feet. They called for the vet." The man tsked. "Worse part is, no winner can be declared, and all the money has to be refunded. This is really going to hurt the 4-H club."

As he was talking, a middle-aged woman in a go-to-meeting dress and high-heeled pumps ran directly into a large pile of cow chips and went down. When she yelled, "Shit!" the crowd roared and agreed that was what she had stepped in.

Skye watched for a moment longer before turning back to her duties. With all the pranks being played, she didn't want to leave the jellies unguarded.

The crowd inside the corrugated-metal building where all the domestic goods were to be judged was buzzing when Skye returned.

Her fellow jelly judge was bursting with news. "Did you hear what happened at the go-cart races?"

"No." Skye felt her stomach tighten. She had always been afraid someone would kill themselves on the go-kart track. "What happened?"

"Someone poured water in all the gas tanks. All the

karts are ruined." The woman's face was so red from the excitement, Skye was afraid she was going to have a stroke.

"How awful. I just came from Cow Chip Bingo and it was spoiled, too."

After Skye gave her the details, the woman excused herself. "It's only quarter to. I'll be back by three and we can get the judging going. I've got to find my sister and tell her the latest."